A KIND OF MAGIC
A SHIELD NOVEL

DONNA GRANT

A Kind Of Magic

Excerpt from *A Dark Seduction* copyright © 2012 by Donna Grant

Cover artist: Croco Designs

Cover design: Syd Gill

ISBN: 0988208423
ISBN-13: 978-0-9882084-2-1

Praise for
DONNA GRANT

5! Top Pick! "An absolutely must read! From beginning to end, it's an incredible ride."—*Night Owl Romance*

5 Hearts! "I definitely recommend *Dangerous Highlander*, even to skeptics of paranormal romance – you just may fall in love with the MacLeods."—*The Romance Reader*

5 Tombstones! "Another fantastic series that melds the paranormal with the historical life of the Scottish highlander in this arousing and exciting adventure. The men of MacLeod castle are a delicious combination of devoted brother, loyal highlander Lord and demonic God that ooze sex appeal and inspire some very erotic daydreams as they face their faults and accept their fate."—*Bitten By Books*

4 Stars! "Grant creates a vivid picture of Britain centuries after the Celts and Druids tried to expel the Romans, deftly merging magic and history. The result is a wonderfully dark, delightfully well-written tale. Readers will eagerly await the next Dark Sword book." —*Romantic Times BOOKreviews*

"Donna Grant spins a searing and intense tale [that] will keep readers spellbound." —*Romance Reviews Today*

"Highly enjoyable and super sexy."—*The Book Lush*

"Donna Grant's Dark Sword series is slowly climbing to my top three. LOVE IT!" —*Good Choice Reading*

DONNA GRANT

Titles by DONNA GRANT

THE DARK SWORD SERIES
Dangerous Highlander
Forbidden Highlander
Wicked Highlander
Untamed Highlander
Shadow Highlander
Darkest Highlander

THE DARK WARRIOR SERIES
Midnight's Master
Midnight's Lover
Midnight's Seduction
Midnight's Warrior

THE DARK KINGS SERIES
Dark Craving
Night's Awakening
Dawn's Desire

SISTERS OF MAGIC SERIES
Shadow Magic
Echoes of Magic
Dangerous Magic

THE SHIELD SERIES
A Dark Guardian
A Kind of Magic
A Dark Seduction
A Forbidden Temptation
A Warrior's Heart

THE WICKED TREASURE SERIES
Seized by Passion
Enticed by Ecstasy
Captured by Desire

DONNA GRANT

DRUIDS GLEN SERIES
Highland Mist
Highland Nights
Highland Dawn
Highland Fires
Highland Magic
Dragonfyre

STAND ALONE BOOKS
Savage Moon
Mutual Desire
Forever Mine

ANTHOLOGIES
The Pleasure of His Bed
The Mammoth Book of Scottish Romance

Chapter One

Present Day
Houston, Texas

"Sex. It's the answer for everyone. Most especially you."

Elle Blanchard choked on the peanut sliding down her throat. She looked at her best friend since sixth grade to see if she was serious.

Jennifer was definitely serious.

While Elle's eyes hastily scanned the crowded, noisy bar to see if anyone had overheard Jennifer, she drank some of her pinot grigio to help the peanut down. She slowly placed her wine glass on the bar and stared at her friend.

"I don't need sex," she whispered.

Jennifer laughed and nodded her head as she sipped her Chocolate Martini. "Oh, but you do, sweetie. How long has it been?"

Elle hated when Jennifer turned their conversation to her love life, or lack thereof. "Can't we talk about something else?"

"Not tonight. I've let you change the subject for the last time." Jennifer grabbed her arm and grew serious. "You need more than the ancient artifacts in the museum, hon. You need a man that will spend time with you, care for you. Love you."

Elle laughed. "Look at me," she said and pointed to herself. "Men don't look at women like me. They look at women like you and them," she said and pointed to two women at the end of the bar.

She stared at the gorgeous women while three guys stood around them talking. Elle might be many things, but a fool she wasn't. She turned back to Jennifer and shrugged.

"No amount of expensive clothes, make-overs, or attitude is going to change what I am. Plain. I have always faded into the background."

"Elle, hon," Jennifer said, her Texan drawl coming out. "That bastard put too much into your head. If I ever find him...."

She trailed off, but Elle knew exactly what Jennifer would do – castrate him. Literally. She loved Jennifer more for it too. Friends like Jennifer didn't come along often.

"I'd rather not talk about him. Instead, I'm going to enjoy this expensive pinot grigio and then head back home."

As soon as the words left her mouth, Elle regretted them.

"There's another problem. How do you expect to find a man when you live in the Montrose area? Honey, that's gay central. It's hard enough finding a guy in today's world without living in an area where men have no interest in women."

Elle chuckled and shrugged. "Exactly. I feel safe there. When I see a man, I'm not worried about them raping me."

"No, it's the women you've got to worry about."

Leave it to Jennifer to tell it like it was.

"Excuse me," a deep voice said from behind Elle.

She turned, her heart thumping at such a voice. But when she looked at him, his eyes were on Jennifer. She wasn't surprised. Jennifer was pretty. She might be of average height, but her athletic build and outgoing attitude turned many a head.

"May I buy you a drink?"

Jennifer looked the man up and down, her dark brown eyes critical. "I'm fine, but my friend needs a drink."

Elle could have cheerfully rammed her foot up Jennifer's ass. She didn't look at the guy, because she knew what was coming.

"Ah...," the guy mumbled and looked over his shoulder. "My friends are calling me. I'll be back."

"Sure you will," Elle said after him. She looked at Jennifer. "I really wish you wouldn't do that. It's embarrassing."

"I'm sorry," Jennifer said, her lips turned down in a frown. "I just thought..."

"I know."

Elle envied Jennifer more than she liked to admit. Jennifer always got the guys in school that Elle had a crush on. Those guys never even looked twice at her. And now, Jennifer had a guy most women would kill for. Not only was he as wealthy as Prince Charles, he could be a pin up guy for Calvin Klein underwear. To top it off, Alex was a nice guy. It would only be a matter of time before he proposed to Jennifer.

And then where would that leave her?

Alone.

As usual.

"Have you decided what you want to do this weekend?" Jennifer asked.

Elle was grateful for the change of subject. "Nothing."

Jennifer rolled her dark brown eyes and shoved her long brunette hair over her shoulder. "Puh-leeze, darlin'. I know you better than that. Birthdays mean a lot to you, and this one is going to be better than ever. Trust me."

Elle couldn't help but smile. Ever since their sixth grade year when Jennifer found out Elle lived with her aunt and uncle and four cousins, Jennifer had done something special for her birthday. This year would be no different.

Elle swirled her wine around in the glass, the goldish liquid catching the dim lights of the bar. There was only one thing she really wanted, and Jennifer couldn't get it for her.

"How about we spend part of the weekend at the beach? We haven't been to Galveston in a couple of years."

The idea had merit, Elle conceded. "All right. That sounds good."

"We can shop, people watch, and soak up some rays. And one of the guys I work with at Events just bought a beach house he's renting out. It'll be perfect."

Elle looked at her when Jennifer glanced at her watch and squealed.

"Ohmigod. I'm going to be late for my dinner with Alex," she said and slid off the stool, the pinstriped dark gray Donna Karan pantsuit fitting her frame perfectly. "I'll call you tomorrow to work out the details. Oh, and I'm paying for the beach house," she said and kissed Elle on the cheek.

Elle smiled and waved her off. Once the door clicked behind Jennifer, she sighed. A weekend. At the beach. She wasn't fooled. Jennifer was looking for a guy for her.

Too bad the search would be in vain.

Chapter Two

This must be what Hell felt like, Roderick thought as he wiped the sweat from his face. Again. He wished for snow as he looked around him. His gaze found one of the many limbless trees that stood in a row and had wires connecting them. It took him a moment to recall what exactly they were – utility poles Aimery had called them.

"Admit it," Val said though his eyes followed two women with nearly every inch of their skin exposed. "You like it here."

"Nay. This heat is draining my brain," Roderick grumbled.

Val shook his head and returned a smile one of the women gave him.

Roderick glared at his friend and fellow Shield. Val, or Valentinus, if you really wanted to raise his ire, loved adventure of any kind, and the more dangerous the undertaking the better. Women seemed to sense and flocked to him, despite the scar that marred the right side of his face.

Not that Roderick had a problem getting women when he wanted. He could hold his own against Val. The Roman would argue differently though.

Despite their bickering, they had become very close while

fighting the ancient creatures for the Fae. And though Roderick was an immortal from another realm, he and the Roman had a lot in common.

"When I heard of this place, I knew it would be the best location to find the woman," Val said, interrupting Roderick's thoughts.

Roderick glanced at a female walking by him with a thin piece of bright yellow fabric that barely covered her woman's area and disappeared between the cheeks of her buttocks. The top wasn't much better. Her breasts were about to spill out of the little top, and Roderick was sure he saw part of a nipple.

"If she's here, there's a good chance we'll find the mark. These women aren't afraid of showing themselves off."

Val laughed. "I love it. We Romans were never afraid either."

"What if she isn't here?" Roderick didn't want to reflect on his apprehension the first night they arrived in the place called Galveston. The city was huge, with more people than on his entire planet. It boggled his mind every time he thought on it.

Val turned from his ogling and shrugged. "I don't know. It was the only thing I could think of. We're running out of time."

"I know."

Roderick's eyes were drawn to the dark waters. He heard someone call it the Gulf, but he had no idea what that meant. It looked like the ocean to him, but the waters were much darker than the oceans on his planet, though his people were often found at the water's edge just like the ones in this time period.

"You two might want to think of blending in a bit more."

Roderick and Val turned as one to the voice behind them.

"Aimery," Roderick growled. "Don't sneak up on me like that."

The Fae's unusual swirling blue eyes sparkled with laughter for a moment. "I've supplied you both with a place to live, the currency to purchase whatever you need, and information about the current times. I would have thought you would have shed the leather jerkins, pants, and boots."

"And wear what?" Val asked. He pointed to a man behind him. "I'm not wearing that."

Roderick looked to what Val pointed out and nearly laughed out loud. The man wore pants so large they hung on his hips – barely.

Aimery shook his head. "At least you don't attract too much attention."

"Trust me," Roderick said as he pushed away from the bare tree, "there are many others that attract attention much more than we ever could."

"True," Aimery agreed. "What brought you two to this place other than for Val to look at the women? I thought you were supposed to be in Houston."

This time Roderick did laugh.

"Watch it, Faerie." Val put as much sarcasm as he could on the word "faerie".

Roderick quickly explained. "Val thought this might be a good place to find the girl since everyone seems to go without too much clothing."

"Good idea, Roman," Aimery said and crossed his arms over his chest. "Have you found anything?"

"Nothing, but not for lack of trying."

Val grunted and watched a petite redhead wave at him. Roderick looked at Aimery and studied the Fae. Something was bothering him.

"Is there anything else you can tell us about this girl? How old she is? Where she is exactly?"

"I would have given that information to you if I had it," Aimery muttered.

Val raked his hand through his shoulder length brown hair. "So much for the all knowing Fae. Aimery, we need more information."

"I had no idea this city would be so massive," Aimery said defensively. "I send you where the creatures are. I don't get to pick the location or the time period."

"We know," Roderick said. "Val and I are just discouraged. We've never been this far into the future with so little information."

Aimery ran his hands down his face, his unusual blue eyes troubled. It was a good thing the people around them couldn't see Aimery, or he could have caused quite a commotion with his nearly white blonde hair and tall, lean form. His strange white clothes didn't help either.

Roderick decided to change the subject for a moment. "How are Hugh and the other Shields?"

Aimery's lips flattened even more. "They are all doing fine."

"Did they get the creature?" Val asked over his shoulder.

"Aye," Aimery answered. "Happiness has once again found Stone Crest."

Happiness. Roderick had nearly forgotten what that was it had been so long since he had felt that particular emotion. He had a feeling the creatures would have overrun his realm before he ever conquered them on Earth.

"Call to me if you find anything," Aimery said just before he disappeared.

Val cursed. "I'll never get used to that."

"There's nothing here," Roderick said as he stepped beside Val and looked around him. "Let's walk down on the beach."

Without a word Val began to cross the busy street. Roderick hurried to catch up. He didn't like all the horseless carriages he saw, not to mention they didn't stop for people. He hated this time and longed to return to…anywhere but here.

They finally crossed the wide street and stopped to look at the beach below. The boardwalk is what Val had been told it was. With a nod to him, Val turned to the left and began to make his way to the stairs that would lead them down to the water's edge.

When their boots hit the sand, they stopped for a moment and glanced around them. People were everywhere.

"Reminds me of home," Val mumbled.

"Was Rome this big?"

Val nodded. "Nearly. Come, Thalean. 'Tis time we really start our search."

For a moment Roderick didn't move. It had been many years since anyone had called him Thalean. Thales was his realm, a place so beautiful and peaceful that it was hard to believe it actually existed.

Roderick let Val walk a little ahead of him. It was something about this time and city that caused him to think of his own realm and family, a family he hadn't seen in nearly ten years.

He raised his face to the cloudless blue sky, the sun's rays beating against him fiercely. This was his punishment for his brother's death, he realized.

"Roderick."

He jerked his head toward Val. "What is it?"

"I think I saw something."

The intensity of the Roman's pale green eyes alerted Roderick that this was serious. "Lead the way."

They lengthened their strides and shuffled through the thick sand until they came to more stairs and returned to the boardwalk. Roderick's eyes were always glancing around them, but he noticed Val was intent on something.

Val brought them to a café that had people sitting outside at tables drinking. Loud music came from little black boxes attached to the ceiling and blared deafeningly as he followed Val inside the café.

Roderick rubbed his ears, sure that he had gone deaf. He stopped beside Val and surveyed the room.

"There," Val said and pointed to a table in the far corner where two women sat.

Roderick stared at them a moment. "Did you see it?"

"I think so. I need a better look."

"Then let's get closer."

"It isn't quite that easy."

Roderick sighed. "Where is the mark?"

"On the inside of her right thigh."

"Of course," he grumbled and scratched the back of his head. "Is nothing ever easy?"

"I could find out," Val said with a twinkle in his eye.

"Fine," Roderick said. "We'll follow her and let you make your move."

Elle looked over her shoulder sure someone had been staring at her, but all she saw was a dark corner in the little ice cream parlor.

"I knew this was what you needed," Jennifer said as she put a spoonful of chocolate chunk in her mouth.

Elle crinkled her nose at the chocolate. She was one of those strange people that just didn't like chocolate. "Yep. You were right."

The hot July heat had gotten to her quicker than she realized, but Jennifer had seen her red face and ushered her into the small pallor. What little air conditioning reached her before it went out the open windows and doors along with the fans on full blast managed to cool her down some. Not to mention the pistachio ice cream.

The weekend had started out nice until it was all too clear that Jennifer had one goal in mind – finding Elle a man. Even if it was only for a night. Elle quickly put her foot down.

She was different. She wanted someone she could lean on, someone she could spend her life with, someone she could spend her passionate nights with, grow old with and have children with. She wanted romance and love, but she feared she would never find it since it was slowly fading from sight in the modern world where divorce was more prominent than anything else.

Elle finished off her ice cream to see Jennifer looking around the shop. "Oh, no you don't," she said and jumped to her feet. "I'm headed back to the beach house."

Jennifer quickly caught up with her. "What's wrong with

you? I just want to help."

"This weekend was enough. Let's just enjoy our time together."

Jennifer laughed and hugged her. "Whatever you say, birthday girl."

"That isn't until tomorrow," Elle pointed out.

They hadn't taken two steps out of the ice cream parlor when Alex stepped in front of them.

Jennifer squealed and launched herself into his arms. For all the years Elle had known her, she had never heard Jennifer squeal about anything.

Elle sat back and watched as Jennifer and Alex hugged and kissed and whispered into each other's ears. When they finally separated, she wondered if Jennifer had forgotten her.

"Do you mind if I steal Jen away for a few hours?" Alex asked.

"Sure, go ahead." *Bastard. This is our weekend.* Elle put a wide smile on her face in hopes that he couldn't read her mind.

Jennifer took her hand. "Are you sure?"

"I'm sure. I'm heading back to the beach house to take a shower and get some of this sea salt off me."

They all laughed as Jennifer tossed her the car keys, but the smile died on Elle's lips as soon as they walked away. She turned toward the sidewalk and began the long trek back to Jennifer's car.

While she walked, she chided herself for being so mean to Alex, even if it was internally. The guy was sweet, and he treated Jennifer like a queen. What else could a friend ask for? No, she was just being selfish and bitchy.

By the time she arrived at Jennifer's convertible Mustang, she felt lower than a snake. She vowed to make it up to him when he brought Jennifer back to the beach house.

Elle pulled into the heavy traffic and made her way to the west side of the island. She admired the beautiful homes being built along the beach and wondered if she would ever live in a house as grand.

By the time she pulled into the driveway of the beach house, she was tired and looking forward to their night of snack food and movies – more importantly Viggo Mortensen in Lord of the Rings.

Ah, to find a man like Aragorn, rugged, handsome, skilled with a sword and who spoke Elvish. Not that he existed, but it was nice to dream.

Elle unlocked the door and let herself in. As she pushed the door closed behind her, she flicked on the light switch and walked to the radio to turn it on. The rock station she and Jennifer had found last night came to life and one of her favorite songs was on. Aerosmith blasted through the house, and Elle stripped off her sweat soaked bikini and headed for the shower to dream some more of Aragorn.

Chapter Three

Roderick shut off the motorcycle and glared at Val who pulled up beside him. "You just had to get one of these."

Val grinned. "I thought it was better than the other option."

Roderick hated when he was right. If it hadn't been for Aimery, he doubted he would ever have learned to drive the motorcycle, and even after nearly a month of riding it, he wasn't comfortable. He much preferred a horse.

"Are you sure this is where she went?"

Val nodded and stuck his helmet on the seat of the motorcycle. "Come on."

After he unbuckled his helmet and placed it on the seat, Roderick followed Val. They found the woman's car easily enough. He wondered at her status in society since her car didn't have a top on it like most.

Then he looked up.

"We have a problem."

Val elbowed him in the ribs as he took the stairs to the front deck of the house.

"Val," Roderick whispered, but the Roman was already knocking on the door.

Roderick stood beside the woman's car and looked up

through the cracks in the wood just as the door opened.

"Excuse me," Val said and took a step away from the door.

"Can I help you?"

Her voice was soft and smooth. Roderick wanted a good look at her, but the planks didn't afford him the luxury.

"I was wondering if I could use your phone to call a friend. My motorcycle ran out of gas."

She hesitated a moment. "You don't have a cell phone?"

Val chuckled and shrugged. "I'm from the old ways."

"Hang on a moment," the woman said before she shut the door. It was just a moment later that she opened the door and handed Val something black.

Roderick clenched his hands impatiently. Obviously Val was taking to this modern world much easier than he was. For a moment he had forgotten what a phone was.

"Thank you. I'll just be a moment."

Roderick couldn't wait to see what Val did next. Neither of them knew how to use a phone, much less had anyone that they would need to call. He watched as Val pretended to punch some numbers and speak softly into the phone asking for some gas. Roderick was still shaking his head when Val turned back to the woman and returned her phone.

"Thank you, Miss..."

"Elle."

"What a beautiful name. I'm Val."

"As is Kilmer?"

Roderick chuckled when he found Val at a loss for words.

"Val Kilmer," Elle said. "The actor."

"Right," Val said.

"It isn't a name I hear very often."

Val gave her his most charming smile. "I didn't expect to find someone as beautiful as you to come to my rescue. I don't suppose I could return the favor."

"Thanks, but no thanks," she said, her voice now cold. "If you don't mind, could you wait below? I would hate to have to call the police."

Roderick had never doubted Val's capabilities with women, but this was a first.

"What happened?" he whispered when Val came downstairs.

"Damned if I know."

With the desolate landscape not offering much in the way of hiding, they knew they had to get some place where they could keep an eye on the woman.

Elle.

It was a pretty name.

Elle couldn't wait to tell Jennifer of Val. She still couldn't believe someone like him had come onto her, but for all her surprise and his good looks, there was something missing. She knew Jennifer was going to have a cow when she realized Elle had let him go.

The clock turned from three to four, and Elle found it hard to wait to eat. She was starving and decided to go ahead and eat without Jennifer. As she ate her boneless buffalo wings, chips, and chili con queso, Elle popped in her favorite movie, Lord of the Rings. It had been their idea to watch all three extended versions tonight, and Elle decided to get started on them early.

Almost five hours later as she was ejecting the second disc to the first move she heard someone walking up the stairs. Jennifer breezed through the door, a bright smile on her face.

"Do you like my new outfit?" she asked as she twirled around.

Elle eyed the slinky red dress that graced Jennifer's build perfectly. "It suits you."

"Alex demanded we go to dinner, and I had nothing to wear."

"Uh, huh," Elle murmured as she picked up the remnants of her dinner and carried them into the kitchen.

"I'm glad you ate without me."

"Yeah." Elle turned on the water to begin washing.

Jennifer folded her arms on top of the bar and laid her chin on her hands. "Are you that mad at me?"

Elle put down the dish she was washing. "A phone call would have been nice."

"Well, I hope this makes up for it," Jennifer said as she put a small box on the counter.

Elle rinsed and wiped her hands before she reached for the box. She untied the pink ribbon and opened the box to reveal a necklace with a smooth blue stone about the size a small egg nestled in intricately worked silver and gold to form a Celtic design. The chain itself was made of silver and gold cords that intertwined.

"Oh…my…gosh."

Jennifer smiled. "Does that mean you like it?"

"I love it. I don't own anything near this beautiful. Thank you," Elle said and came around the bar to hug her friend.

"Don't thank me," Jennifer said as she pulled out of the hug. "Thank Alex. He found it the other weekend and thought it would be perfect for you. That's why he came today."

"Oh." Elle felt lower than dirt now. "That was very thoughtful of him."

"He is pretty wonderful, huh?"

Elle nodded and moved her hair aside to put the necklace on.

"Let me get out of this dress and into my pj's, and then we'll watch the second and third LOTR."

Elle could only nod as she looked at her reflection in the mirror. She had a feeling she would wear the necklace often. Never had she worn anything that made her feel so special and…sexy.

Roderick shifted his feet and stared at the house across the small road. Elle's house. He had hoped that he would have been able to contact Aimery tonight and let him know they had found the woman.

"I still can't believe she said nay," Val grumbled. "It's not normal."

Roderick hid his smile. "Buck up, Roman. Not all women will fall at your feet."

He grunted in response. "I hope the owners of this house don't return tonight."

"Me as well. It's the last thing we need."

"We'll have to find a better place if this is where the woman lives."

Roderick watched as the other woman returned to the house. He eyed the man with the other woman and how they touched each other. It had been the same way when he had seen them outside the café.

His realm was openly affectionate, but not that affectionate. Besides, he had gotten used to the times of Earth and how in some time periods couples could hardly touch each other in public.

"I need a woman."

Roderick rolled his eyes, though Val couldn't see him. "You always need a woman."

"Absolutely."

"You Romans were too free with your sex."

Val laughed. "Not true. In fact, there was much more I could have done. It's you who needs to loosen up."

He decided not to answer and get into another discussion on the amount of sex a man needs in his life. He'd had too many of those discussions before. Instead, Roderick took first watch of the house.

Tomorrow would give them another chance to get a look at the woman's leg and the mark that would let them know if she was the one they had been searching for.

Chapter Four

"Was it memorable?"

Elle shot Jennifer a bright smile as she unlocked the door to her beloved house on Michigan Street. "Of course. You out-do yourself every year."

"As long as you have a good time." Jennifer skipped down the steps and got into her car. "Gotta run. I have a date with Alex tonight."

Elle loved Jennifer dearly, but she was glad to be home. She couldn't shake the feeling that she had interrupted a weekend that Jennifer would have preferred to spend with Alex.

With a sigh, she pushed open her door, the bell on the doorknob jingling. Elle dropped her bags at her feet and secured the deadbolt and two other latches on the door before she grabbed her bags and walked to her bedroom.

Her house wasn't large. It had two bedrooms, two baths, a great foyer, and a formal living room. She had just finished upgrading the kitchen and her bathroom, and she had a nice den in the back where she watched TV, which is why there was a bell on the front door knob. With her mainly being in the back, she'd never hear anyone come in without it.

First things first, she quickly made a run to the fridge and grabbed a Diet Dr. Pepper. She opened one of the little bottles and drained half of it.

"Now that's good," she said.

Just as she turned to head to the bathroom and a hot shower, her phone rang.

❦

"Why do they build their dwellings so close," Roderick said with a grimace as he tried to get comfortable against the tall wooden fence and Elle's house, which only had about a foot of distance between them.

Val chuckled. "You should have seen Rome."

"Nay. I think not."

"At least we know this is where she really lives. Makes it easier to watch her here."

Roderick had his doubts about that. Who would have guessed she had been in the same city he had been searching in for a month?

As they sat and watched her talk on the phone, he wondered who she was talking to and about what. The conversation lasted a terribly long time. When she finally did get off the phone, she went to her front door and retrieved some papers out of a little metal box.

He watched her throw most of the papers in a tall black barrel and open others. Some were special he supposed since she placed them aside.

"It's getting late," Val said as he walked to Roderick.

"Where have you been?"

"I went looking around the house. This window looking into the kitchen is a good one. If you want to look into her bed chamber, there is a window on the back that will give you a good view of the entire room and bathing chamber."

"Me?"

Val nodded. "She turned me down, which means it's up to you to learn her habits and likes and dislikes since you'll be the one that gets close to her."

"Fine. Where will you be exactly?"

"First, I'm going to get us some food. After that, I thought I would search out the city to see if I can figure out which creature has been summoned."

Roderick leaned his head back against the fence. "I don't think they are here yet, my friend. News travels fast in this city, and if anything out of the ordinary were here, it would be on that big black box that has pictures in it."

"A TV. Remember? Aimery told us what it was."

Roderick slapped at tiny bugs that buzzed around him and left the most wicked of bites. "This city is awful."

"A most pleasant place for a creature to wreck havoc, aye?"

He watched Val saunter off. It was but moments after that the rev of Val's motorcycle could be heard. Roderick grimaced when he realized he should have told Val to stay away from the food place named McDonald's. He was sure the Highlanders he had met from the clan MacDonald wouldn't have been happy to see their name put on such a place.

He caught a glimpse of Elle as she walked from the kitchen. He waited a moment to see if she would return, and then moved to the back of the house to the window Val told him about. The window was fairly large and with the fading light outside, he would be able to get right next to it, and she wouldn't be able to spot him.

He sat on her porch and watched as she turned on some music and unpacked her bags. It wasn't until she began to strip out of her clothes that he took real interest. He had seen many women naked but never tired of looking.

A smile tugged at his lips when she turned up the music and began to dance around the room. The smile turned into a groan when he saw the slinky little light pink underthings she wore. He had glimpsed her breasts while they were at the beach, but it was nothing compared to what he saw now.

They were large on her small frame, but not too large. He could just make out her dark nipple against the pink lace holding her breasts.

Then she turned around.

Roderick nearly fell off the porch. He had seen quite a few things since his time in Houston, but the tiny pink lace that disappeared between her lovely firm buttocks had him clenching his jaw together.

To his dismay, he felt himself grow hard. It was unthinkable. He had seen that much flesh from the women on the beach, but it was something about that pale pink lace that did him in. He closed his eyes and tried to get himself back under control. About that time, Val came around the corner with a white bag in his hands with a big yellow M on it.

"Oh. My. Gods," Val murmured as he came to a dead stop beside Roderick.

It gave Roderick a small amount of pleasure that Elle hadn't wanted Val. He had never seen a woman turn Val down. Until her.

Roderick snatched the bag of food from Val's hands. "Don't stare."

"I can't help it," he said as he sank onto the porch next to Roderick.

"Well, try." Roderick had no idea why he was so testy. Maybe it was because he had wanted to keep this image of Elle to himself.

Val whistled softly. "I should have tried harder."

"You lost your turn, Roman. It's mine now."

Val's pale green eyes jerked to him. "All right, Thalean. Let's see what you can do." With that, Val rose and walked away.

Roderick sighed and turned his attention back to Elle, his food forgotten. It was a good thing he hadn't taken a bite of the food, for he was sure he would have choked on it. Elle had unhooked the thing holding her breasts while her back was to him, but it wasn't until she began to pull off the tiny lace that he wished she would turn to face him.

She never did, and it left him wondering just what she

looked like completely naked. Just the thought of seeing her nude had his cock throbbing with need. She walked into the bathroom and turned on the water. Roderick didn't pay much attention to her as he thought about how he liked the readily available hot water and the showers this time gave him. It was one thing he would miss when he left.

He reached into the white bag and began to lift out the food Val had brought him when he glanced up and spotted Elle. His fingers loosened, and his food crashed into the bag as his eyes stayed riveted on the woman.

The view of her through the distorted glass as the heat from the water rose around her sent his body aching for release. He didn't move, barely breathed, as she lifted a leg to wash. With short, round strokes she moved from her ankle up her shapely thigh and then repeated it on the other leg.

Roderick's mouth had gone dry. Then, she moved her hands to wash her breasts but turned away at the last moment, giving him a view of her back. Her silhouette gave him just enough to entice him as her pale pink underthings had.

And left him yearning for more.

When she exited the shower with a towel wrapped around her, Roderick was in a painful state, and he knew the only thing that could relieve him was a woman. Try as he might to focus, he couldn't. Then he remembered what he was supposed to be doing – looking for the mark.

Roderick cursed and ran a hand through his hair. He had missed his chance, but hopefully he would gain another one.

"Maybe Val's right," he muttered. "Maybe I do need a woman for a night."

It was well past midnight when Val returned. They exchanged few words as Roderick left Val to keep watch as he returned to their home for some rest. But rest didn't come. Every time Roderick closed his eyes he saw Elle in her lacy pink underthings or her silhouette in the shower. It was enough to drive him daft.

When the sun began to peek over the horizon, Roderick rolled out of bed and faced the expanse of windows that overlooked Houston and the buildings that nearly reached the sky.

He walked naked into the bathing quarters and eagerly jumped into the massive shower. As the hot water cascaded around him, he decided today would be the day he introduced himself to Elle. They couldn't afford to wait any longer.

After the shower, he stood in front of the mirror and raked his hands through his blonde hair that stopped just short of his shoulders. It had a tendency to curl at the ends, something he had inherited from his mother.

Since there wasn't much he could do with his hair, he gave up. Instead, he turned to the chamber that held his clothes. Aimery, it seemed, had taken it upon himself to fill it with more modern clothes to help them fit in.

Roderick looked over the clothes and admitted that at least Aimery had stayed with darker colors that Roderick preferred. Too bad he wouldn't be here to see Val's expression when he saw his clothes.

The pants were the first thing he came too, and he grabbed one of the many black pair and wasn't surprised to find they fit perfectly. He picked up the first shirt he found, a short sleeve gray shirt that hugged his chest and abdomen like a second skin.

He looked at himself in the full-length mirror once he had pulled on the black boots laid out for him. His reflection staring back at him didn't look too bad. The only thing he didn't like was the absence of his weapons, but he had learned early on in Houston that he couldn't walk around with his sword and flail without causing mass hysteria.

Roderick was just walking to the door when it opened, and Val stepped inside.

"Why are you here?"

"I followed her to the place she works, and since you didn't know where we were, I decided to come and get you." It was then Val noticed him. He looked Roderick up and down several times before he shook his head.

"I'm sure you have a chamber full of clothes just like I do," Roderick said as he grabbed the keys to his motorcycle. How he missed his horse.

Val growled. "I hope Aimery left me with at least the same kind of clothes as you."

Roderick didn't waste time talking about the many jests Aimery had played upon Val. "Where did you leave Elle?"

Val turned and narrowed his pale green eyes at him. "The woman works in a museum."

"Museum?" He had no idea what that was.

"A place where people go to look at paintings and such. They even have dinosaur bones."

Roderick wasn't about to ask what a dinosaur was. Instead, he got the direction to the museum and prayed he didn't get lost.

He heard Val cursing from his bedchamber as Roderick walked from their home into the hallway and the box that he rode down to the place where his motorcycle was parked. Luckily, he remembered the direction to the museum without difficulty, and finding a place to park the motorcycle was easy since it was so small.

"I miss my damn horse," he muttered as he put the stand down that kept the motorcycle from falling over.

He unbuckled his helmet and swung his leg over the back of the bike as he stood up. His eyes roamed over the large building that stood in front of him. It was then he realized he hadn't asked Val where she was located in the structure.

Roderick had a feeling he was going to spend most of the day looking for Elle. He paid his way to enter the museum and found himself in a quandary. Which way to go? Where could Elle be? What he should do is ask someone, but he didn't know her last name, nor did he want her to know he was looking for her.

Nay, he would have to search her out himself.

He didn't know how long he had wandered the museum. He found it hard to realize he was here looking for Elle instead of gazing at the interesting pictures and other things that were in the building.

As much as he hated to admit it, he found himself taking the most time in the dinosaur chamber. He never realized creatures such as those roamed this planet. He saved his favorite chamber for last.

Ancient weaponry.

The various displays of weapons throughout the times amazed him. Many of the weapons he had used at one time or another and some he was sorely tempted to try out. He turned from one amazing display of halberds to see someone coming down a flight of stairs. Out of the corner of his eye he saw long auburn hair. Instantly, his eyes turned to the woman.

Elle.

Her hair hung thick and straight to the middle of her shoulders, and she constantly tucked some of the auburn tresses behind her ears. Little gold earrings dangled delicately from her ears and matched the necklace around her throat.

He let his eyes roam over her body and the dark green skirt that hugged her curves and ended at her calves. The cream shirt she wore buttoned up the front and was plain other than the low dip just before her cleavage started.

Nothing dramatic, but on her, it was elegant.

Roderick had to think quickly. It had to appear an accident or she would never believe him. He noted how distracted she looked as she hurried over to a sword displayed in the center of the room.

He watched as she carefully examined the paper in front of her, then the sword. She was talking to herself, but he couldn't make out the words, though it was obvious she was not happy.

She took a step back, and Roderick knew his time had come. He lined himself up behind her and turned his back to her as though he were looking at a sixteenth century shield. And then it happened.

She backed into him.

Roderick was quick to turn and catch her in his arms before she fell. It wasn't until he looked into her clear blue eyes that he realized just how stunning she truly was.

Chapter Five

Elle's breath caught in her throat as she gazed up at the man who held her in his arms. She found herself staring into eyes of dark blue, like the churning waters of the Atlantic.

"I'm sorry," she mumbled incoherently.

One side of his mouth lifted in a smile as he stood her up and on her feet.

"Nothing to apologize for."

She couldn't stop staring at him. He looked like he just stepped off the cover of GQ with a body she was sure he spent half a day in the gym to get, and a face that made her knees weak. Literally.

When she managed to look away from his fascinating eyes, she found a strong jaw line, wide, thin lips, and a high forehead. Dark blonde hair hung to his shoulders, adding more appeal to him. A regular rugged looking man, if you liked that type.

Which she did.

She cringed inwardly and tried to swallow as she looked away from his face. Wrong move, since she found herself now gazing at his amazing chest and arms. She had never really cared for the body building type, but on this guy all those muscles just added to his good looks.

Her eyes went to his wide shoulders and the steel gray shirt that molded to his body. She knelt down to pick up her clipboard and let her gaze wander down his long legs incased in black denim. He wore jeans like only male models could. Perfectly.

She was dying for him to turn around so she could get a view of his butt.

What is wrong with me, she thought to herself.

You want him.

So she did. Men like him didn't pay her a bit of attention. To her surprise, he bent down next to her and helped her pick up her papers.

"Do you work here?" he asked.

This time she noticed his peculiar accent. "Yes. You're not from around here, are you?"

He shook his head. "First time in Houston."

"What do you do?"

"Do?" he asked, his brows bunched together in confusion.

Elle finished gathering her papers and stood. "Job. What kind of job do you have?"

"I don't."

Great. Here I thought I had found someone good, only to find he's a bum. A good-looking bum, but still a bum.

"Oh. Where do you live?" Elle didn't know why she asked that, just being nice she supposed.

"The Huntington in River Oaks."

Her mouth nearly dropped open. That was one of the nicest condominiums a person could live in Houston. He wasn't a bum, he was rich.

"Ah," she managed. "I hear that's a nice place."

He shrugged his thick shoulder. "Why don't you come by sometime and take a look?"

Had he just asked her out? No, couldn't be. He said 'sometime', which translated into 'I'm just being nice'.

"Maybe," she said and turned back to the Viking sword.

"How about tonight?"

Her pencil dropped from her fingers as she faced him. He bent down to retrieve it, giving her time to regroup. She stared at his large hand as he handed her the pencil.

"Interested? I would love to take you to dinner, but I don't really know the town."

Despite the fact that she had lived alone long enough to know not to go to a strange man's house, much less let him know where she lived, she felt a strange sense of trust with this man that she had never felt with anyone before.

"Tonight?"

His face fell. "You must already have plans."

"Actually…I don't."

The smile returned. "So, you'll come?"

"What floor?"

"The top."

She thought it over for a moment. "All right, but for one drink only."

"Perfect. My name is Roderick Thales," he said smoothly.

"Elle," she said and extended her hand. "Elle Blanchard."

He took the hand she offered and brought it to his lips. "A lovely name."

His eyes bored into her as his lips lightly grazed her knuckles. Her breath rushed past her lips that had parted slightly, and she knew at that moment, had he taken her, she would have let him.

"Until tonight," he said and released her hand.

As he walked out of the weaponry exhibit, she finally got her view of his butt.

Perfect. Just like the rest of him.

"Out, Roman." Roderick was afraid he would have to bring out his flail to make Val leave. They had been arguing for the last hour as Roderick readied for the evening.

"She won't remember me."

"You don't know that."

"Fine," Val said as he reached for the doorknob. "Do what you have to but find out for sure."

When the door closed behind Val, Roderick ran to his bedchamber to change. He didn't know what to wear. He hurriedly stripped out of his clothes and tossed them into the bathing quarters on his way to the clothing chamber.

His eyes roamed over the many clothes, unsure of what to pick. Finally, he decided on a shirt that he liked, a black long sleeve that buttoned up the front and black pants that matched.

He didn't like having so many options to choose from. Even on Thales, as a prince, he hadn't owned this many clothes. He had just finished buttoning his pants when the door chimed. With one last glance at his clothes, he walked to the front door and opened it.

"Hello," he said when his eyes fell on her. She looked nervous, unsure of herself, and he found it charming. "Come in," he said and moved aside.

After a brief hesitation, she stepped into his home. He stood back and watched her look the place over. It was evident by her wide eyes and gaping mouth that she thought the place very fine indeed.

"Is it what you thought it would be?" he finally asked.

"More than I had imagined actually."

Roderick smiled in spite of himself. He hadn't thought much of the place, but he was glad Aimery had made it their home if she was impressed.

"Oh, the view," she gasped as she hurried to the window behind the dining room table. "I bet you look out here a lot," she said and glanced over her shoulder.

He didn't, but he wasn't about to tell her that. Instead, he shrugged. She moved away from the window to turn toward him and that's when he saw it.

The blue stone nestled against her chest just inches away from her cleavage.

For a moment, Roderick couldn't speak. Never had he

imagined he would find the stone so soon and before he and Val found the creatures.

"Peculiar necklace," he said and took a step toward her.

Elle looked down and fingered the stone. "Odd isn't it? My best friend gave it to me just yesterday for my birthday."

Roderick was so relieved to hear it was a gift that he almost didn't respond to her. "I hope you had a great day."

"It was all right. Jennifer wanted to take me down to Galveston for the weekend."

So that explained why she was there as well as who the other woman was. He would have to get Val to find out all he could on this Jennifer and just how she came to have possession of the stone.

"Do you mind?" Elle asked and pointed to the array of liquor bottles on the cart next to the window.

Roderick mentally shook himself. "Please. Help yourself."

"Would you like for me to fix you a drink?"

"I'm fine, thank you."

She walked to the cart, her shoes soundless against the white marble flooring. He eyed her clothing again. She had changed before coming over. A long, full skirt that fell just past her knees in a nice shade of mixed blues. She wore another long sleeve white shirt that buttoned up the front, but this time she only buttoned one button right under her breasts. The shirt fell open to reveal another shirt underneath of blue.

Her feet sported the shoes he had seen nearly everywhere. Val had compared them to the shoes he'd worn in Rome, and Roderick had to admit they looked comfortable if one could get used to something being between the toes.

"You like my flip-flops?" she asked.

Roderick jerked his head up. "I don't think I've seen any like that."

She took a drink and smiled. "I sewed the sequins on myself a couple of months ago when I got the skirt. Now you can find flip-flops with sequins everywhere."

Roderick wasn't about to ask what a sequin was, but he

supposed they were the shiny things on her...flip-flops. He looked at the shoes again. Well, they did make a flip-flop noise when one walked.

He moved his eyes away from the shoes and found himself staring at the necklace again. "Anything odd happen since you received that necklace?"

"Odd?" she repeated. "The only thing odd to happen is bumping into you. The museum isn't normally a place I meet men."

Roderick motioned to the sofa in the next room. "Why don't we sit?"

Her eyes darted into the room before she walked ahead of him. She settled herself on one end of the sofa next to the fireplace and faced him.

"So tell me about yourself. Where do you come from?"

He'd dreaded this question. "Some place very far away."

"That would explain the accent," she said and took another drink of the merlot. "I loved geography in school. What country did you grow up in?"

"Thales," he answered, though it wasn't a country, it was his realm.

Her brow furrowed. "I don't think I've ever heard of that country."

"No one ever does. Where do you hail from?"

She laughed, the sound filling the large place with warmth and energy. "About two hours east of here in a very small town. When I graduated, I packed my bags the next day and moved here. It was about two years later that Jennifer moved as well."

"You and this Jennifer have been friends a long time."

"Since sixth grade," she said, a small smile on her face as if she were remembering the day. "We were inseparable during junior high and high school."

Since Roderick didn't know about sixth grade, junior high or high school, he just nodded. "It's nice to have a friend for so long."

Suddenly, soft music filled the air, startling Elle. Roderick barely moved even though he knew Aimery had something to do with it. He found it hard to imagine the Fae commander had no idea Elle wore the necklace, and with so many creatures being released, there wasn't time for any of them to become involved with anyone.

"Oh," Elle said and sighed. "You must have it on a timer."

"That's right," Roderick answered and rose to get himself a drink. He needed something strong.

"I love Mozart."

He stopped just before he began to pour the drink and looked over his shoulder at her.

"The man who wrote this music."

"I know," he murmured the lie and finished pouring the amber liquid into the glass. Scotch.

"Where are you from really?"

Roderick spun around to find Elle just behind him. "Thales."

"Where is that? Europe?"

He nodded and lifted his glass to drain the contents. He needed to distract her to get the necklace off her and destroyed. It would be nice if Val were here. Val was going to be saying 'I told you so' for a month once he discovered Elle had the stone.

Chapter Six

Elle knew something was wrong the moment he refused to answer her. "I shouldn't have come," she said as she sat down her wine glass and began to back up.

"I need you to listen a moment, Elle. You could be in danger."

"Yes. From you." She tried to run around him, but he caught her and held her back against his chest, his arm under her breasts.

If it weren't for the fact that she was scared witless she would have been turned on by the way he held her. It had been so long since a man had touched her that she wished he was normal. "Please let me go."

"Not until you agree to listen to me," he whispered in her ear, his hot breath fanning her skin, causing it to tingle.

What choice did she have? At least if she listened or pretended to, she might get a chance to escape. "All right."

As soon as the words were out of her mouth he released her. She pushed aside the fact that she missed his arms around her and concentrated instead on slowly making her way toward the door.

"Can you take off your necklace?"

"What?"

"I need to destroy the stone."

She backed away from him and shook her head. He was nuts. "What kind of drugs are you on? This is just a stone. A harmless, meaningless stone."

"'Tis far more than that."

She had to give him credit, he stayed where he was, his arms calmly to his sides, and his voice low and soothing as if he were speaking to a wild animal.

But something he said caught her attention. "Who says ''tis' anymore anyway?"

"What?"

She opened her mouth to repeat her question when she spotted something on his balcony behind him. She closed her eyes and took a deep breath before she opened them again. Yet, they were still there.

Her lips tried to form the words, instead all she could do was mumble incoherently and point. Roderick looked over his shoulder and swore.

"Get down," he shouted as he dove at her.

His strong arms came around her and pulled her to the ground with him. Just when she thought she would get the breath knocked out of her when he landed atop her, he deftly rolled, and she found herself on top of his chest.

"Stay down," he said as he moved her to the side and got to his feet.

She watched as he disappeared into a hallway. She was about to get up and follow him when she heard scratching at the window. Slowly, Elle got on her knees and looked over the back of the couch at the three women, no birds...things...trying to get in.

There was no mistaking what they were. Her mind was just having a hard time adjusting to the fact that Harpies were at Roderick's window. Harpies. The kind of creatures she had read about in countless ancient Greek and Roman tales. They were mythological and not supposed to exist.

"I told you to get down," a voice growled in her ear.

She let Roderick pull her back down behind the couch. "Either that drink went to my head much too fast or there are Harpies at your window."

"They are Harpies all right, though I have never encountered them before."

What?

She turned her stunned gaze to him to find him shirtless and carrying a sword and flail. She wished she could gawk at his wonderful pecs but danger lurked just a few feet away.

"Do you often carry a sword and flail?"

He shot her a glance that screamed 'of course' and began to rise.

There was no way she was staying here by herself. "Where are you going?"

He knelt beside her and took her chin in his hand. "I've got to kill them before they kill more people."

"You can't do it alone."

"I have to try. It's what I do."

Somehow, she believed him. But that wasn't what scared her the most. What terrified her was that he might be killed, leaving her to the mercy of the Harpies. "Isn't there someone that can help you?"

"They are too far away," he said absently as he started to make his way around the couch. He stopped and turned to look at her. "They are here for you, so no matter what, don't let them catch you."

"What?" she cried the same time something hit the windows and glass flew around the room.

She heard Roderick curse again as he lunged back at her. Her eyes were glued to a long piece of glass that protruded from his left bicep.

"Elle," he bellowed.

She pulled her eyes away from the glass to his face.

"We have to get you out of here. Are you hurt?"

She shook her head, unsure. "I don't think so."

The high-pitched screams of the Harpies rang around them. While Elle covered her ears, Roderick reached over and pulled the glass from his arm. Blood sprayed her clothes, but it was the last thing on Elle's mind. All she wanted was to get away from the Harpies and certain death.

"Run," Roderick said and pointed to the hallway.

Elle didn't hesitate. She jumped to her feet and ran as fast as she could, the sound of Roderick's boots right behind her. He took hold of her arm and pulled her into a room she was about to pass.

She stood, shaking, as he hurriedly shoved aside an armoire to reveal a hidden room.

"Inside. Quickly," he urged her.

Elle entered the dark room and waited for Roderick as he followed her and pulled the door closed behind him.

"That won't fool them for long," he said. "The stone will guide them to you."

She was about to ask what he was talking about when one of his arms came around her and brought her hard and close to his chest. Breath left her lungs at the feel of his hard body against hers.

"Hold on."

No sooner had the words left his mouth than Elle felt herself falling. She gripped his muscled bare arms as if he were life itself. A scream lodged in her throat as they fell, and she knew, had there been light, her life would have flashed before her eyes. His arm tightened around her just seconds before she felt her feet hit the floor.

Light filtered in from a source behind her, and she saw him holding a thick rope with his right hand.

She pulled out of his arms and felt something sticky on her hand and looked down to see it covered in blood. Roderick's blood.

"Oh, my gosh." She jerked off her favorite Abercrombie and Fitch shirt and reached for his arm.

"What are you doing?" he scolded. "We have to get

moving."

"Not with you bleeding all over the place. Now be still," she said and wrapped her shirt around his arm.

When she finished she stepped back to look at the finished product. She wouldn't win a nurse award, but it would do until she could get him to a hospital.

"Thank you."

The words were softly spoken. She raised her eyes to his face and found him staring at her strangely. "Why do I get the feeling you don't trust me?"

"Come," he said in answer and took her hand as he pulled her along winding staircases and long hallways until they came to the garage.

She wondered what kind of car he drove as they ran passed Porches, a Ferrari, Mercedes, and her favorite, Jaguars.

When he finally stopped in front of a motorcycle, Elle nearly laughed. When he handed her the helmet and straddled the bike, she let out a strangled cry.

"Get on."

"I hate these things. They're dangerous."

"It's either this or the Harpies."

At that moment, she heard the Harpies scream, and she hastily jumped on the back of the bike.

"Don't kill me on this thing or I'll come back and haunt you."

She was sure she heard him chuckle, but she didn't get to think long on it since he gunned the bike and they flew through the garage, narrowly missing other cars.

Elle finally gave up and squeezed her eyes closed, refusing to open them. She had no idea how long they traveled, but she was too scared to do anything other than hang on and pray.

"Where do you live?" she heard him ask over the howl of the wind as they sped down the street.

"In the Montrose area."

She opened one eye to find them on Westheimer only blocks from her home. She quickly gave him directions to her house, thankful that he had to slow because of an intersection.

By the time he pulled into her driveway, her entire body shook. She hopped off the bike and found her legs barely supported her. Instantly, strong hands grabbed hold of her.

"Are you all right?"

She looked up into his clear blue eyes and shook her head. "No. I'm not. I've been chased by Harpies, dropped to what I thought was my death, and then rode on one of the things I swore I would never get on. I just want to curl up in my bed with a glass of wine and forget about all of it."

"Give me your keys."

Without hesitation, Elle pulled her keys out of her hidden pocket in her skirt, a skirt splattered with blood, and handed them to Roderick. She went along when he put his hand on her back and guided her up the steps to her house, and then inside once he had unlocked the door.

She left him at the door and walked to her room. A nice hot shower was just what she needed. She stripped her clothes off as she walked into the bathroom and turned on the shower. As soon as her clothes were off, she stepped into the spray of the scalding water.

Steam rose around her, shielding her from the horrors outside and the questions running amuck in her mind.

Roderick watched Elle walk to the back of the house. He wasn't afraid of where she would go since the place was only about a third in size of his home. He flexed his left hand and felt a small sting from the vicious wound on his upper arm from the glass. It would heal quickly enough. He walked into the bedchamber and unbelted his sword and flail from his waist and laid them on the bed. He wanted them within reach at all times.

With a sigh, he sank onto the bed and thought of the creatures. Harpies. He needed to contact Aimery and Val quickly.

The sound of the shower running drew his attention. He turned his head and saw the steam rolling from the shower. His body cried out to join Elle, but his mind had a firm control for the moment and kept him from making a fool of himself by joining her.

It was the tinkling sound from the front of the house that had him up and reaching for his sword. He grasped the pommel and raised the sword toward the ceiling as he stepped from Elle's bedchamber into the hallway.

With his eyes closed, his listened as the footsteps slowly and quietly drew near. When the person was about to turn the corner, Roderick whirled around and swung his sword. At the last moment, he jerked his downward swing to a stop as he spotted Val.

"I could have killed you," he growled.

Val raised an eyebrow and glanced down.

Roderick followed his gaze and saw the dagger near his gut. He lowered his sword and swore. "You could have told me you were in the house."

"I didn't know if you were here," Val argued. "I saw your bike, but she could have taken it."

Roderick raked a hand through his hair. "Have you been by our home?"

Val's eyes narrowed as he crossed his arms over his chest. "Nay. What happened?"

"There is no need for you to roam the city trying to determine what creature is here. They attacked tonight."

"They?" Val repeated. "What 'they'?"

"Harpies."

For a long moment, Val didn't move. "If the myths were true, we're going to have a Hell of a time killing them."

"That's not all," Roderick said when Val turned to walk to the kitchen.

"There's more?" the Roman asked as he braced his shoulder against the door jam.

"I know who has the blue stone."

Val jerked away from the door jam. "Elle."

"She received it yesterday from a friend. There is no way she could have been controlling the Harpies all this time."

"Have you destroyed it yet?"

Roderick shook his head. "I was a little more concerned with getting our arses out of there alive. They wanted her. Badly."

At that moment, the shower cut off. Roderick pointed to the kitchen and turned to retrace his steps to Elle's bedchamber. He walked in just as she wrapped a towel around her glistening wet body.

He salivated at the glimpse of exposed skin. Her wet hair hung around her shoulders dripping droplets of water down her arms and shoulders.

Damn, but he wanted her.

Chapter Seven

Elle ignored the water dripping onto her bath mat and floor as she stared at Roderick. She couldn't take her eyes off his luscious body, and she was quite certain she had never called any man luscious before. His muscles bunched and moved as he lowered his sword on the bed.

Sword!

"Just who are you?" she asked, her near nakedness forgotten.

"Get dressed and come into the kitchen. I'll explain everything."

He turned and walked from her bedroom, and all she could do was think how yummy he looked. She caught a glimpse of her shirt tied around his arm and hurried to dress so she could see to the wound. It would be just her luck that he passed out in the kitchen from loss of blood.

She yanked open a drawer in her lingerie armoire and grabbed a set of apricot colored bra and panties. Then, she tugged on a pair of yoga pants and another tank before she quickly combed through her wet hair and made sure all her mascara was off her face.

And that's when she spotted the necklace. She hadn't even realized she had showered with it on. It wasn't like her to leave any jewelry on in the shower, but then again, she had never been chased by Harpies before.

She unclasped the necklace and tucked it away in the jewelry armoire. She had a feeling Roderick wanted that necklace, and she wasn't about to part from it. It was a gift from Jennifer, and she planned to treasure it always. After she put away her jewelry, she walked into the kitchen and came to a dead stop.

All thoughts of Roderick's injury fled from her mind as she stared at the man next to him – a man she'd previously met.

"I have to admit I feel as though I have a need for a stun gun."

"Stun gun?" Roderick asked as he looked at her.

"It isn't a coincidence that…Val, is it…came to our beach house?"

She had to give Roderick credit. He didn't look at all happy at the situation. Val, on the other hand, simply stared at her.

"We were looking for you," Val answered.

Whatever hope she had that Roderick really might like her vanished like smoke. She should have known that men like him didn't notice women like her, but it still stung, more than she liked to admit.

"Me? Why?"

"Elle," Roderick said as he slid off the bar stool and came to stand beside her. "This is all going to sound very strange."

She rolled her eyes. "You mean like the Harpies that attacked us at your penthouse?"

Roderick sighed. "You might need to sit down for this."

By the looks on both of their faces and the sword and flail on her bed, Elle didn't think she had much of a choice. She'd had such a good vibe about Roderick. Who would have known he was a serial killer.

"Just kill me now."

"What?" the men asked in unison.

"I saw the weapons, Roderick. You both admitted to looking for me. Obviously, you both have escaped some psycho ward or prison."

Val snorted. "If we wanted to kill you, you would have been dead on the beach."

Roderick said something to Val in a language that sounded suspiciously like Latin and then turned to her. "Please," he said and motioned to the sofa in the living room.

She decided to comply, simply out of curiosity. She doubted there was anything that they could tell her that would be stranger than what she had seen at Roderick's penthouse. Besides, her legs still vibrated from the awful motorcycle ride.

Elle sank onto the couch while Val took the chair to her left and Roderick sat on the stool in front of her. She watched Roderick as he seemed to search for a way to start.

After several minutes, it was apparent he was having a hard time.

Val mumbled under his breath. "Elle, we're looking for a woman with a mark on her."

"Mark? What kind of mark?" she asked.

"An unusual mark that looks similar to the Celtic symbols that you know."

Elle felt the breath rush from her body. "Why?"

"Do you have the mark?" Roderick asked, his eyes on the floor.

"Why?" she asked again.

He raised his dark blue eyes. "Please. Do you have the mark?"

She slowly nodded her head.

"We need to see it," Val said.

Elle bent over and lifted the hem of her pants, thankful that they were cotton and lycra and stretched. She pulled up the pants until she reached the mark that looked similar to a Celtic eternity knot circled by a thick, solid line on the inside of her right thigh.

"We found her," Val said, relief shining in his green eyes.

Elle released her pants and looked at Roderick. "What is that mark?"

"Twas placed on you before you were sent here."

"From where? And there is the "'twas" again. Who speaks like that?"

"From where we come from it's normal," Val said.

A chill ran down Elle's back at his words. "And where do you come from?"

"I'm from Rome."

From the expectant look on their faces, she realized they anticipated for that to bother her. "So."

"79 BC."

It was a good thing Elle was sitting for her entire body began to shake. She moved her eyes to Roderick. "And you?"

He took a deep breath. "I am not from this realm."

Elle looked from one to the other and began to laugh. It was either that or cry. Surely these two men were delusional. There was no way they could be telling her the truth.

"I am not lying," Roderick said softly.

She stopped laughing and wiped her eyes. "How can I believe you?"

He licked his lips, then untied her shirt from around his arm. Where there should have been a huge gnash, there was nothing.

Elle gasped and vaulted from the couch to kneel beside him. She reached out to touch him but stopped at the last moment. Her eyes lifted to his face. "How did that happen?"

"I'm immortal."

She sat back on her heels and tried to take it all in. "I thought that only happened in movies."

Roderick shook his head. "I can only be killed one way."

"By chopping off your head?" she asked, thinking of the movie Highlander.

"A special weapon that isn't in this realm."

"So far," Val added.

Roderick threw him a look before he turned back to Elle.

"You don't feel as though you belong here, do you?"

"What has that got to do with anything?"

"You aren't from this realm either."

That actually made a lot of sense to her, but she wasn't about to tell them that. She was beginning to think she was as nuts as they were. "And what realm am I from?"

"Ronnoc. It was destroyed by the same evil that has descended on Earth."

Elle rose to her feet and began to pace her tiny living room. "This is like something off of the Sci-Fi channel."

"It's the truth," Roderick said as he stood.

Elle nearly ran into his rock solid bare chest. She raised her face to look him in the eye. "It's too bizarre to be real. I have an aunt and uncle and cousins. I'm part of a family."

"There's more," Val interjected.

She glanced at him, not sure she could take more. "More?"

Val nodded his head.

"What else?" she asked Roderick.

"How do you think we came from ancient Rome and another realm?"

She shook her head. "I don't think I want to know."

"The Fae," he finally said.

"The Fae? As in Faeries?"

"Is that so hard to believe?" a deep voice asked from behind her.

Elle whirled around to see the most striking creature she had ever laid eyes upon. He had long, straight flaxen hair that reached halfway down his back. He was incredibly tall and lithe, but power radiated from him letting all know just how much strength he had.

His face was so perfect even Adonis would cry. But it was his eyes that drew her attention. They were blue, but a mystical blue. They shimmered and swirled as if they had a life of their own.

"Who are you?" she asked.

"Aimery," he said, a soft smile pulling at his perfect lips. "I am commander of the Fae army and messenger to the Shields from the king and queen of the Fae."

"Shields?" This was just getting weirder and weirder.

"A group of hand picked men from all times and realms that battle the creatures that have been called up to destroy the Earth."

"Why don't you fight them?"

He lowered his eyes. "We cannot, dear Elle. It's my greatest desire to do just that, but we are bound to stay in our realm."

"Why?"

"Because we once roamed Earth and are still attached to it. If the realm of Earth ever ceases to exist, so do we, which is why the Shields were created. We found the most skilled warriors throughout time and realms and brought them together. Roderick and Val are two of the Shields. They were sent here to find you and kill the creature."

She laughed then. "The Harpies? Are you kidding?"

Aimery jerked his gaze to the men, his smile gone, replaced by pinched lips. "Harpies?"

Roderick nodded. "They attacked us at my home."

"I must tell Queen Rufina and King Theron."

"Wait," Val yelled. "We also found the stone."

Aimery's eyes narrowed. "So we know who is controlling the Harpies?"

Val looked away, causing Aimery to turn to Roderick.

"Elle has the stone," Roderick answered.

Aimery closed his eyes as if pained. "Destroy the stone."

Elle blinked, and he was gone. "Where did he go?" she asked as she looked around her living room.

"Back to the realm of the Fae," Val answered. "We don't have a lot of time before the Harpies find her again, Roderick. Destroy the stone, and we can return home."

Elle waited until Val walked from the room before she turned to Roderick. "Why do you want to destroy my necklace?"

She let him pull her down onto the couch. "The stones are what called the creatures from their ancient Hell. If the stones are destroyed, then so are the creatures."

"It's just a stone. Are you sure it's the same one?"

"Positive. There is no mistaking the stone."

"I can't let you obliterate my necklace. It was a gift from Jennifer."

He raked a hand through his hair. "You would let the people of your city die?"

"Have you been here long?" she asked. "People are murdered right and left. Children are abused, abandoned, kidnapped, and sold daily. This isn't exactly a place I would want to save."

"And the innocents? Like the children? You would condemn them to death?"

She closed her eyes as tears threatened. "No."

"Then help me."

"What do you want me to do?" she asked as she opened her eyes.

"To kill the Harpies we must destroy your necklace."

Elle had no idea how she was going to explain this to Jennifer, and she had no idea why she believed every word that came out of Roderick's mouth. "How do I know you aren't lying?" she asked.

"You don't."

"If the stone was given to me as a present, then who called the Harpies?"

Roderick sighed. "I don't know. My mission was to find you, kill the creatures, and destroy the stone. I can do all of that now and return to the other Shields."

"Why did you need to find me?"

"Your people sent twelve babes to Earth just before your realm was destroyed. There are only five of you left. You are the second one we have found."

Elle sat back and let his words soak in. "And we all bear this mark?"

"Aye, in different places. Mina's is on the back of her neck."

"Mina?"

"She is in England, in the time of 1123."

Elle's mouth dropped open. "So we are scattered through time?"

"We don't know."

"You don't know a whole lot, do you?" she said and rose to her feet.

"I know you can save this city."

She looked down at him. "Whoever has the stone controls the Harpies, right?"

He slowly nodded.

"Since you're here with me, you know I'm not controlling them. Right?"

Again he nodded.

"I need time to think about this."

"We'll need an answer soon, Elle."

"You'll have one by tomorrow," she promised.

Chapter Eight

Roderick heard the cry rent the stillness of the night and leapt to his feet. He had been sleeping in Elle's front room and hurried to her chamber. He spotted her thrashing around on her bed and knew she was in the grips of a nightmare. He straddled her and took a wrist in each hand.

"Elle," he said. When she didn't respond, he called out a little louder.

"No," she screamed and tried to kick him off of her.

"It's me," he said as he struggled to wake her.

Of a sudden, her thrashing stopped, and he looked to find her eyes open and staring at him.

"Elle?"

He immediately noticed how close their faces were and the fact his body straddled hers. Her breasts pressed against his chest, and his cock, hard and throbbing, rested against her stomach. All he had to do was lean down and take her mouth in his.

"It was just a dream," he said as he released her hands and moved off her.

She curled on her side but didn't say anything. Roderick could only imagine what was going through her mind. So far, she had handled things relatively well, and it would depend on how strong she was mentally if she could believe them.

He was about to walk away when her hand reached out and took his. He looked at their joined hands, then her face.

"Thank you for saving me."

He knew she was referring to the Harpies. "They won't kill you. You control them, but they are thirsty for blood and want more."

The moonlight streamed in from windows on either side of her bed, illuminating her face and light blue eyes. "Don't let them take me."

"I give you my word I will protect you with my life." He bent down and gently tugged his hand free. "Sleep, Elle," he commanded as he moved the covers over her shoulders.

He checked to make sure her eyes were closed before he rose and walked from her chamber.

"Is she all right?" Val asked as he stood in the hallway.

Roderick nodded. "I don't know if she believes us."

"We may have to take the stone from her."

Roderick looked at the woman sleeping so soundly. "We might."

"She's got until tomorrow. I wish to return to Hugh and the others."

Roderick nodded and thought of Hugh. He was their leader, and the best of them. Roderick missed them all, Hugh, Darrick, Gabriel, and Cole. They were his brothers in arms.

He returned to his place on the sofa and stared into the darkness. What he should do was go in Elle's chamber, find the necklace, and destroy it, but he had promised to wait for morning. And wait he would.

"Morning, Elle," a female voice called from the front of the house.

Roderick and Val glanced at each other. Elle still slept, so Roderick walked into the front room to find Elle's friend,

Jennifer.

"Well, hello," she said and looked him up and down. "I didn't realize Elle had company."

"I'm just a friend."

"Ah," she said and nodded. "And needed a place to crash." She walked past him toward Elle's bedchamber. "I'm Jennifer."

"Roderick," he said as he followed her.

"I'm just going to borrow a shirt Elle said I could use," Jennifer said when she reached Elle's door.

Roderick had no choice but to let her go in. He waited with Val in the front room, but as each second ticked by, Roderick felt the urge to drag Jennifer out of the chamber.

"Well, hello," Jennifer said again as she walked out of Elle's bedchamber.

Val immediately perked up at finding a woman interested in him. "Hello to you, as well."

"It's too bad I'm already taken, or I'd be very tempted," Jennifer said as she walked by Val, her finger trailing across his chest. "I just love the accent."

Roderick was hard pressed not to roll his eyes.

"Tell Elle I'll return this later," Jennifer said as she held up a shirt just before she walked from the house.

"Fairly decent in looks, aye?" Val asked him.

Roderick shook his head and returned to the kitchen. "Could you keep your mind on other things than bedding a woman?"

"Then what would the world come to?"

Roderick couldn't help but chuckle. "One day, Val, you will find a woman that will knock your feet out from underneath you, and I pray I'm there to see it."

Val put his hands over his heart and let his head fall back. "Ah, never say such words."

"It'll happen. That I promise you."

Val sat up and studied him. "Has it happened to you?"

Roderick shook his head. "Hasn't yet, and I hope it doesn't.

At least not until I've vanquished the evil here and can help my own realm. If it still exists."

"It does."

Roderick clenched his jaw and gripped the counter top, the rooming spinning at Val's words. "What?"

"You might not want to ask Aimery for fear of discovering bad news, not to mention you have a hard time dealing with why you left, so I asked for you."

"Well," he prompted the Roman, his patience fast running out.

"Thales still stands. It is being ravaged, but not as severely as Earth."

Roderick breathed a sigh of relief. He had desperately wanted to know how his realm was doing but couldn't work up the courage to ask.

"Why did you leave?" Val asked.

Roderick had told no one the reason for his departure of Thales, but Aimery knew. Thankfully, the Fae never said a word, and the other Shields hadn't asked since each of them carried their own secrets and demons.

"You've never asked me that before."

Val shrugged. "It's always been an unspoken rule that we leave the past behind."

"So why ask now?"

"I'm curious. I saw the pain on your face when I mentioned Thales. You are a prince there, Roderick. What could have made you leave?"

Roderick bowed his head and took a deep breath. There was no way he could tell his friend and fellow Shield just what he had done. "Something so awful I'm trying to redeem myself in my family's eyes."

Val said no more, and for that Roderick would be eternally grateful. Talking of his home and his parents brought him so much pain that he rarely did it. One day soon, however, he would return to them and hopefully be forgiven for the most unforgivable of sins.

Elle woke slowly, the sun shining brightly in her room. She glanced at the clock, saw she would be terribly late for work, but didn't care. Her hand snaked out of the sheets and reached for the phone. A quick call letting them know she was sick—which wasn't a lie, she was sick in the head for believing Roderick – and she could face the day and the horrors that waited.

She sat up and stretched her arms over her head as she heard mumblings from the kitchen. It was easy to determine which one was Val and which was Roderick as they talked. Val's voice was deeper, rougher, while Roderick's held a refinement that she would almost compare to royalty.

Try as she might, she couldn't make out their conversation without getting out of bed, and since she wasn't an eavesdropper, she decided to make a quick trip to the bathroom to take care of business before heading into the kitchen. As she walked past her mirror she saw her silky chemise she wore to bed and hastily tugged on a robe.

When she walked into the kitchen, neither man was speaking. Val spared her a glance and a nod as she walked past him.

"Morning," she mumbled.

She wasn't what was considered a morning person. It took her a bit to wake up and start functioning properly to go out into the real world, which is why she hated having company.

"Did you sleep well?" Roderick asked from beside her.

Elle covered her mouth as she began to yawn. "Not really," she answered and reached into the fridge for a Diet Dr. Pepper. All she needed was a little caffeine in the mornings, and she was fine. She didn't even need the whole bottle, just a few swallows and she was set.

"You?" she asked as she replaced the can and shut the fridge door.

"Well enough."

As Elle leaned against the fridge, she couldn't get the image of the Harpies out of her mind. They had plagued her all night. "Will the Harpies attack during the day?"

Both Roderick and Val shrugged.

"Some creatures sleep during the day," Val answered, "and some don't. Not sure about the Harpies, but something is telling me they won't."

"Great," she mumbled as she pushed off the fridge. "You would think something like women with lower bodies of birds flying around the skies of Houston would have been reported."

"I would have thought so, too, so my only guess is they haven't been seen," Roderick said.

"Wonderful. This just keeps getting better and better."

"Have you decided anything?" Val asked.

Normally, Elle was a quiet, rarely riled type of person, but for some reason, she was finding a side of herself she had never seen, and she quite liked it. "I've been asleep. I didn't get much thinking done."

Val growled something under his breath in another language.

"Val," Roderick warned before he turned to Elle. "This isn't a jest we are playing on you. This is people's lives on this realm and others. It's very important that the necklace and creatures be destroyed."

Elle still couldn't believe she actually believed him. Had she been asked a week ago if she believed in Harpies and immortals she would have laughed in their faces. "I don't have a choice."

"Not if you want to do the right thing," Val said.

She looked first at Val and then at Roderick. "What do I need to do?"

Roderick took a step toward her. "Get dressed, get the necklace, and we'll go destroy it."

"Go?"

"The stone shatters," Val told her. "We need to do it some place away from everything."

"That only leaves the woods, which will be a good hour or more away from here, or the top of a building."

Val and Roderick looked at each other. "The house," they said in unison.

Elle assumed they meant the apartment. "I'll get dressed."

She shuffled into her room and ignored the bed that she usually made faithfully every morning. Instead, she went to her closet and grabbed a pair of shorts and a shirt. A quick dusting of bronzing powder, eyeliner, and mascara was all she chanced before tackling her hair. She ran a brush through the long length, grasped her hair in one hand, and twisted. Once she had it where she wanted, she reached for her large clippie and secured it.

Her fingers ran through her bangs that fell over her right eye as she surveyed her image. She would never be a model, but she was passing fair. At least men didn't turn away in disgust. They didn't look twice at her, if they looked at all, but that was much better than them turning away.

She grabbed her red sequined flip-flops to match her shirt and wiggled her feet in as she opened her jewelry armoire. No matter how hard she searched, she couldn't find the necklace. Panic began to set in as she searched one drawer after another.

"I forgot to tell you that your friend came by this morning," Roderick said from the doorway.

"Jennifer?" she asked, still digging in the armoire.

"Aye. She said she was borrowing a shirt."

Elle stopped and closed her eyes. She knew which shirt Jennifer wanted to wear. Her blue silk shirt she had gotten from the Ralph Lauren store and that also explained the missing necklace.

"Oh my goodness," she murmured as she closed the drawer.

"What is it?" Roderick asked.

Elle slowly stood up and faced the man before her. "She took it."

"Your shirt? I know."

She shook her head. "No, Roderick. She also took the necklace. It matched perfect, and it's just like her."

For the first time since she had met him, she saw the anger lighting his dark blue eyes. "Without asking?"

"I'm afraid so."

"Where is she? We must get it back."

Elle ran to the phone and dialed Jennifer's home number. "No answer," she said as she hung up and dialed the store. "Jennifer, please," she told the girl on the other line.

As soon as she asked for Jennifer, she realized it was her day off. "Never mind," she told the girl and hung up.

Next, she dialed Jennifer's cell phone. "Jennifer always answers her cell phone," she told Roderick, praying that she was right.

But she wasn't. Jennifer didn't answer.

Chapter Nine

"Where is Jennifer?" Roderick asked.

"I don't know." Elle felt sick to her stomach at knowing the necklace was out of her hands. "I think she and Alex were doing something."

"Where?"

"I can't remember if she told me."

A sound from the doorway got her attention, and she turned to find Val leaning against the door with his arms crossed.

"It's gone?"

She tried to swallow, gave up, and nodded instead.

"Let's go," Val said.

"Where are we going?" Elle asked as Roderick took her arm and raised her to her feet.

"We must get ready for battle," Roderick replied.

Battle, Elle mouthed as they left her house.

She locked her door and turned to find both Val and Roderick on their motorcycles. The last thing she wanted was to get back on the movable death trap, but it was obvious she didn't have a choice since her car was still at the Huntington.

The only good news was that Roderick was still shirtless, and, as ridiculous as it was, it was all she had to hold onto at the moment.

After a quick prayer for her safety, she walked to Roderick's bike and climbed on. He handed her the helmet, and, once she had it on, she reached around and clasped her hands together on his deliciously rippled abs of steel.

Yummy.

Even though he didn't want her, she wasn't about to pass up the opportunity to touch a body like she had only seen in ads or the TV.

Out of the corner of her eye, she saw Val pull beside them as they turned off Michigan Street on to Dunlavy. She spotted Roderick's sword and flail attached to one side of the bike, and as Val sped ahead of them she saw his sword.

She had never been so thankful to live next to the wealthiest part of the city. River Oaks was nestled next to her Montrose area, and the Huntington was the only high-rise apartments in River Oaks.

They pulled onto Kirby, and as usual, there was constant construction, but somehow Val and Roderick bypassed the traffic and arrived at their apartment within minutes. No high speeds this time, but then again the Harpies weren't after them.

Still, by the time Roderick had pulled into his parking space and shut off the bike, Elle's legs where trembling. Gingerly, she got off the bike and returned his helmet to him.

"I think next time we'll take my car."

He looked over at her dark green Civic and then back at her. "Not if you need to outrun the Harpies."

She hated that he was right. Houston traffic could be a bitch. With her knees still knocking together, she followed the two hunks onto the elevator. She didn't know if it was on accident or by design, but they stood on either side of her.

And for the few minutes on the ride up to the penthouse, Elle let herself daydream. It was delicious, too. In her daydream, she was a woman that Roderick wanted for his own, a woman he had gone to great lengths to procure. She would give herself fully to him and find a man that knew how to treat her like a lady, give her excitement and love like no one ever had before. And since it was her fantasy, the sex would be the most explosive she had ever experienced. The passion would consume them, and the need for each other would grow each time they shared their bodies.

She had to admit it was better than a romance novel, if she did say so herself.

The elevator chimed their arrival, jerking Elle out of her musing. She took a deep breath as the doors opened. Just as she was about to step out, Val put a hand out to stop her.

She watched as he went ahead, and Roderick kept the elevator doors open. When Val had made sure no one lurked in the hallway, Roderick took her arm and led her out of the elevator. There was tension about them that let her know absolute quiet was necessary for survival.

"Stay behind me," Roderick whispered as he raised his flail.

Elle glanced at the two wicked looking spiked balls about cantaloupe sized hanging from chains attached to a thick wooden bar with grooves for his fingers. On the handle were the most beautiful Celtic knotwork she had ever seen. There was something different about it, magical almost. Her eyes went to the spikes and noticed they were varied sizes, some as long as three inches.

She would hate to encounter that weapon if it came at her, and by the way Roderick handled it, he was a master at it. Her feet took her a step back to put more distance between her and the ferocious weapon.

Val walked into the apartment first, his boots soundless on the marble. Elle peeked around Roderick's wide shoulders and saw Val motion for them to enter. Elle wasn't one of those people that liked danger. When she visited the Six Flags theme park, she didn't even ride anything. She liked her adrenaline to stay just the way it was. And yet, here she was walking behind two warriors from another time and realm to see if any evil lurked in wait for them.

A shiver raced down her spine, as though to warn her that her life was about to change.

Glass littered the floor, and furniture was overturned. Elle couldn't believe the damage to everything as she glanced around the apartment.

"What a mess," she mumbled as she picked up one of the glasses she and Roderick had drank from just the evening before.

Val disappeared into the hallway while she and Roderick stayed in the front rooms. Roderick went onto the south balcony and looked around. The wonderful part of having the penthouse was the balconies on each of the corners of the building.

Elle, not knowing what else to do, stood in the center of the living room and watched Roderick walk from the south balcony to the east balcony. Her eyes followed the flow of his muscles as they bunched, stretched, and flexed. It should be against the law for a man to look that good, she thought to herself.

"Nothing and no one is here," Val said as he returned from the hallway. "They found the hidden doorway."

Roderick closed the balcony door behind him and nodded. "I assumed they would. They followed the stone."

And suddenly it hit Elle. "If they came after me because of the stone, wouldn't they go after Jennifer?"

Roderick's eyes stared hard at her. "Aye."

Elle sank onto the sofa, her head in her hands. Jennifer wouldn't survive. Alex might be good sized, but he was no Roderick. Her best friend was going to die.

"This can't be happening. Jennifer won't know the necklace controls them."

"The Harpies will tell her," Val said as he came to stand at the end of the sofa.

She looked up into his pale green eyes, his long, light brown hair pulled away from his face in a ponytail. He didn't try to hide the condemnation in his gaze. "What are you saying?" she asked him as she rose to her feet.

Roderick walked until he stood beside Val. "Have you ever thought that she might have something to do with them?"

Elle laughed and shook her head. "Why would she? Jennifer only thinks about her career and Alex. Trust me, I've known her for nearly fifteen years."

"The stone does odd things to people," Val said. "It can turn a good person bad."

"You've got it wrong," she told the warriors. "Alex, her boyfriend, found that necklace and picked it out as a birthday present for me. They bought it in Galveston."

Roderick took a step toward her. "Where?"

"I have no idea. You don't ask someone that when you receive a gift."

"Val," Roderick said.

"I'm going," Val replied and ran for the door.

Elle was becoming more confused by the minute. "Where is he going?"

"To see if that necklace was indeed purchased in Galveston."

"He'll be searching for days."

"Nay. He'll return in a few hours with an answer."

"And until then?" she asked. "Do we wait around here?"

He turned his dark blue eyes on her. "There is no place I would rather be. Our weapons are here, which means this is our best defense."

"All right," she agreed. "But I can't just sit around. I need something to do."

For the first time that morning, she saw a hint of a smile on his wide lips. "How good are you at research?"

"The best. It's what I do at the museum."

"Great," he said and took her hand as he led her into another room.

Elle tried to ignore the ripple of pleasure he caused by holding her hand. She kept telling herself it meant nothing, but she couldn't help but wish that it did as her eyes soaked up his naked torso.

"We will be able to find information in here on the Harpies," Roderick said as they entered the library.

Elle stared in shock at the fourteen-foot ceilings that were lined from floor to ceiling with rows upon rows of books. "Good grief," she mumbled and ran her hand along the spines of the books.

"It's impressive," he admitted. "Aimery thought it best we have this library to help us locate anything we might need."

"There are a lot of books here, but there's no guarantee they'll be the right ones."

"It's a start though."

Elle turned to him and smiled. "Aye, 'tis."

She thought he might have chuckled, but she was too far away to tell. "Let me know if you need anything," he said as he headed toward the door.

"Where are you going?"

"To gather our weapons and change. I'll just be down the hall."

After he closed the door behind him, Elle let out a loud sigh. Light shown from two windows on the wall where the books only went up halfway, the other half was all windows. She could get used to living like this.

As she scanned the books, she noticed most of them pertained to ancient monsters or creatures that were told of in myths and legends. She decided her first place to start was looking up Harpies in a text dedicated to the monsters in Greek myths. By the time Roderick returned two hours later, Elle had discovered quite a lot about the Harpies.

"I see you have found some information."

She nodded as she glanced up and saw him in black leather pants, but not the shiny leather she was used to. These were soft, almost like suede, and what looked like a dark padded jerkin for a shirt. A quick look down showed her boots that she had only seen from Medieval times.

"I took a Greek/Roman mythology class in college, but

there is stuff in here they never covered."

"Such as?" he asked as he sat opposite her in the large leather chairs in the middle of the room.

"Mythology calls them daughters of Electra and Thaumas. They were most often sent by the gods to punish people."

"I don't suppose you found anything on how to kill them?"

She shook her head. "Not so far. From what I've read their wings are made of metal, but I don't recall hearing that sound when they attacked."

"It was hard to hear anything over their screams."

She shifted books around until she found what she was looking for. "This book says their screams are semi-human and gives warning to their victims only at the last moment," she read and then handed the book to him.

Once he had read the passage and the notes she had made, he sat back and locked his fingers behind his head. "The Harpies are near impossible to kill when all three are together. If we can separate them, we might have a chance."

"There are three of us."

He shook his head. "You couldn't hold them longer than a heartbeat. What we need are more Shields."

"Can't your Fae friend bring more?"

"I wish it were that easy, but there are only a handful of us left, and we are needed elsewhere. Only Val and I could be spared to come here."

"Then I'll have to do the best I can."

Roderick had the almost uncontrollable urge to reach over and pull Elle into his lap to ravage her lips. She had no idea what she was talking about facing, but she was willing to face it to kill the Harpies.

"Thank you for being so brave," he said as he scooted to the end of the chair, "but you will be needed once all of you are found."

"For what purpose?"

"It's been said that you hold a key to the entity distributing the stones. You and the others are the means to ending the evil."

Chapter Ten

"But I don't know anything."

Roderick could feel her fear and uncertainty. "Together you all will. Until then, it is imperative that you stay alive. Originally, there were twelve infants sent to Earth, six boys and six girls. All the boys and one of the girls are dead. Only five of you remain, and we are unsure with only five of you that we will discover the answers we need."

"And if we don't know the answers?"

He rose to his feet and turned his back to her. "Let us think about the Harpies for now." He had no wish to think what it would mean to his realm if Elle and the others didn't have the answers. They had to have the answers. He had lived with his sin for too long, and his people had suffered for too long for there not to be a solution.

"Roderick?"

He jerked at his name and turned toward her. "I know this is hard for you, but I need you to trust me and Val. We will keep you alive."

Before she could respond, he heard the door to their home open and close. A moment later the door to the library opened, and Val and Aimery stepped inside.

"What did you find?" Elle asked as she came to stand beside him.

"No one in Galveston ever sold the necklace," Val said.

"You must not have checked every store."

"We did," Aimery said softly.

Roderick glanced at Elle to see her face crumble.

"No," she cried, unconvinced. "Jennifer told me Alex found it in a shop in Galveston, and they went to buy it."

"She could have lied," Roderick said.

Elle turned her pale blue eyes on him, and the anger and confusion tore at his gut. He remembered seeing the same look in his sister's eyes, a look he had hoped to never see again.

"Jennifer wouldn't lie to me."

Aimery stepped forward. "Tell me, Elle, has Jennifer never lied to you before?"

Roderick wanted to punch Aimery for crushing Elle like he had just done. Her face fell as her eyes shown with tears, but she held them back. She was much braver than he gave her credit for.

"With the stone now missing, I think I should take Elle with me to keep her safe," Aimery said to Roderick and Val.

Roderick knew it was a wise decision, and it would be one less distraction for him and Val, but he felt responsible for Elle now.

"I won't go," Elle said loudly. "I lost the necklace, and I will get it back."

Aimery's brow furrowed. "Haven't you listened to anything Roderick has told you? There are only five of you left. We need you to survive."

"Roderick will keep me alive."

It surprised him how her words pleased him, and the fact she had such faith in his abilities. It had been a long time since anyone had put that much devotion and trust in me.

Aimery shook his head. "Roderick needs to concentrate on finding a way to kill the Harpies, not worry about keeping you alive."

"I'm not going," Elle declared.

Roderick watched her walk from the library, leaving him with Aimery and Val. He returned Aimery's stare, knowing the Fae commander was about to give him a piece of his mind.

"Is there something going on between you two?" Aimery asked.

Roderick crossed his arms over his chest. "Why ask me when you can dig through my thoughts and discover for yourself."

"I already have. I want you to answer me."

His words stunned Roderick. If Aimery had already seen the answer to his question, why then did he ask? "Nay."

For several heartbeats Aimery didn't move. Finally, he gave a small nod of his head. "I will leave her, but only because I cannot shift her through time without her agreement. Convince her to come with me, Roderick."

And with that, Aimery vanished.

"Nice mess we've found ourselves in," Val grumbled.

"It always is."

Elle stared out over the city she had called home for seven years. It wasn't because she loved the city, in fact, she preferred a nice quiet small town, but she had needed to escape after high school, and Houston had been the closest place.

She couldn't complain. She had gotten a decent job to work her way through college at the University of Houston and had managed to land a job at the museum, which she loved. The job supplied her with a nice income, which allowed her to buy her house. It wasn't much, but it was better than an apartment.

And despite her home and her job, she could easily leave this town and not look back. It was crowded, noisy, and could be downright dream crushing on occasions, much like any large city.

"Elle?"

She jerked slightly at hearing Roderick's soft timbre. She

hadn't even heard him enter the living room.

"Don't try to convince me to go with Aimery," she said before he had a chance to open his mouth. "I need to fix this."

She felt more than saw him stand beside her. "I understand," he said.

"You do?" she asked as she turned to look at him.

He nodded. "There are times in a person's life when they need to take a stand and mend a wrong. I suppose now is your time."

"And if I die?" She didn't want to think about it, but she was curious as to why he had given in so easily. "You and Aimery keep telling me it's imperative that I stay alive since there are only five of my kind alive."

"True," he said and looked out the large two story windows. "I cannot promise you'll live, but I'll do everything I can to make sure you do."

She studied his profile a moment. "That's all I can ask."

"Aimery isn't going to like this," Val said from the hallway.

Elle turned to him. "I need to do this, Val. Will you help us?"

He smiled, a smile she was sure had melted many hearts. "Of course. I just had to say the obvious. There's no way I'd allow Roderick to do this alone. We are brothers, warriors." Val looked from Elle to Roderick. "'Tis time to go ahunting."

Elle glanced over in time to see Roderick grin, a wicked gleam in his eye. "I suppose this is something y'all like to do?"

"Y'all?" Roderick repeated.

"Yeah. Its kind of like your ''tis'. It's a Texan thing."

"If you say so," he said and walked to his room.

Elle followed him and stopped in her tracks when she entered his domain. The front of the apartment was made to look as though he and Val were men of the twenty-first century, but his bedroom was another matter entirely.

Hanging from the ceiling in various lengths and thicknesses were sheer panels of the darkest burgundy and gold. On the floor were pillows of all sizes in matching colors. There was no bed but what looked like a mattress with a black fur blanket thrown over the top of it.

No lamps, ceiling fan, radio or TV was in the room. Instead, candles where everywhere, hanging from the ceiling like a chandelier, beside the bed on a candelabra, and en masse throughout the room.

The room took her to another time and place, one that she liked. As soon as she stepped into the room, she was instantly at peace, as if she had come home. And she could well imagine the romantic ambiance this room invoked when he brought a woman inside. That thought irritated her, so she turned her mind to wishing she were in his room because he was attracted to her, not because they were trying to save the world.

This room was straight out of one of her fantasies and so was Roderick.

"Incredible," she breathed as she fingered one of the sheers beside the bed.

Roderick turned to her and glanced around the room. "It's very similar to the chamber on my realm. The only difference is the color."

"What colors did you have?"

"White and silver."

"Pretty colors," she said, thinking how soothing that could be.

"It's very nice together, but when I became a Shield, I found a love of darker colors that I never knew." He shrugged and waved a hand around the room. "These are my colors now."

"I love it."

Their eyes met and held, and for an instant she could almost imagine that they had shared a connection. She glanced away and licked her lips.

When she raised her gaze, Roderick had walked a few paces from her and opened a door she hadn't seen. Inside was an array of weapons like only a collector could dream of owning.

"Goodness gracious," she said as she hurried to stand beside Roderick and gawk at the weapons. "In all my years working in the museum, never once did we encounter anything like this."

"As a Shield, the Fae equip us with any weapon they think will aid us. We also have a shield that has our personal emblem on it, though Val and I agreed to keep them hidden here."

She heard the note of pride in his voice. "Incredible," she breathed. "I would hide them."

"Why?" he asked as he looked down at her, his brows furrowed.

"I'd be afraid that I would damage or lose something."

"The Fae replace it if I do," he said and reached out to grab a small dagger. He handed it to her along with its sheath. "Do you know how to use this?"

"No," she answered honestly as she reached for it. "But, I can figure it out."

A faint smile touched his lips. "I will always be beside you, as will Val, but if something should happen, I want you to have a weapon."

"Are you sure one is enough?" she asked as she looked longingly at a jewel encrusted sword.

Roderick chuckled as he closed the doors. "Maybe another time. For now, the dagger is enough."

Elle wasn't so sure, but she didn't argue with him. She bent down and tied the sheath to her thigh. Once it was secure, she placed the dagger inside and straightened. She watched as he belted on his sword at his waist, a long dagger at his thigh, and slid another into his boot. He then reached over and grasped his two-headed flail.

"Where do we start our hunt?" she asked.

Val walked into the room, his sword buckled to his waist, and holding a halberd of the like she had never seen. She gasped and walked to him.

She saw him look over her head at Roderick.

"She likes weapons," Roderick explained.

Elle examined the seven foot tall halberd as if it were a Faberge` egg. The base looked like wood, but as she ran her hand over it, she knew instantly that it wasn't like any wood she knew.

"It was made from a magical oak tree that only grows in the Fae realm," Val said as he watched her.

She nodded and noted the intricate scrollwork that had been etched on the metal that came to a point as if a spear. Attached to the spear on one side was a thick blade like one would see on a war axe and the other side came to a startling needle sharp point.

Her hand lightly traced the surface of the blade and saw a design that resembled the Celtic knotwork on Roderick's flail.

"It's our mark," Roderick said.

She looked over her shoulder at him. "Mark?"

"The Shields," Val said. "That mark is on all our weapons and anything else given to use by the Fae."

Elle looked again at Roderick's flail and spotted the design on the handle as well as on each of the spiked balls. "Incredible work," she said as she stepped away from Val.

"I've seen some fine halberds and flails before, but nothing like what y'all have."

"Enough about the weapons. I'm eager for a hunt," Val said, one side of his mouth pulled in a smile.

Chapter Eleven

Elle was once again seated behind Roderick on his motorcycle. She had tried in vain to get them to use her car, but he and Val had adamantly refused.

"And if someone spots us carrying those weapons?" she had asked.

"They won't," was all Val would say.

"Where do we start?" she asked as she finished buckling the helmet in place.

"We follow the stench," Val said just before he started his bike.

She waited until he had ridden off before she asked Roderick, "What does he mean?"

"We can smell evil, Elle. The truly nasty evil like the Harpies, and the people that have the blue stones."

She shuddered and held on as he started the bike and raced after Val. Maybe she had made a mistake in not going with Aimery.

∞

Roderick hated Houston. The air hung with smells of

73

rotting garbage and other things he couldn't name that poured out of huge cylinders that Elle called refineries. He didn't care what they were, they were killing the air.

He pulled off the side of the rode they had been traveling on for the better part of two hours and waited for Val. Most of the day had been spent traveling down roads Elle had pointed out to them, but they had found nothing.

An entire day's search, and they hadn't found one clue.

"Smell anything?" he asked when Val shut off his bike.

Val grimaced and shook his head. "I can hardly smell anything over the nastiness that hangs in the air." He looked at Elle. "How can you stand to live here?"

She shrugged. "It's all I've ever known. The refineries have started to get clean, though only because the government is making them. They've polluted our waters and air for many, many years."

"I know," Val grumbled.

"We've looked nearly all day," Roderick said and glanced at the sky and sun that was beginning her descent.

"Since Elle doesn't have the necklace, we can't bait the Harpies," Val said.

Roderick turned and looked at Elle over his shoulder. "Jennifer still hasn't called?"

"No, and it's not like her. I can't help but feel she's in trouble."

"Would her man harm her?"

She shrugged. "I don't know Alex all that well, but I don't think so."

Roderick pushed his hair out of his face and looked around. They had driven aimlessly, trying to pick up the scent of the Harpies, but had found nothing.

"We're wasting time," Val said. "Let's return home and look for them in the sky. They will attack somewhere tonight."

"Good idea," Roderick said and started his motorcycle. He led the way back to the Huntington with Elle shouting directions in his ear.

At first he hadn't felt comfortable with her on the back of his bike, but the more she was there, the more he found he liked it. Her arms held snuggly against him, but they didn't dig into him, and the feel of her full breasts against his back made him hot and hard.

When he had turned onto Kirby and realized where he was, he felt her lay her head on his back. It had been a long time since a woman had been this close to him and, the protective feelings Elle stirred in him could only get him in trouble. He knew that, but he couldn't help it. All he could do was not act on his feelings.

He turned into the garage and parked the bike. Just before he turned it off, he felt her squeeze him slightly before she lifted her head. She got off the bike first and stood beside him. There was a look in her light blue eyes, a longing he couldn't quite identify.

"Are you all right?" he asked.

She inhaled deeply and nodded. "I just want this over with. I should have listened to you last night and destroyed it then. I'm sorry."

"Don't apologize," he said and swung his leg over the bike. "We didn't expect for you to believe everything we told you, especially after finding out so much in one night."

He took the helmet she offered him and watched her comb her fingers through her long hair. As he sat the helmet on the bike's seat, all he could think about was running his fingers through her hair as he plunged inside of her. Instead, he followed her and Val into the little box that raised them to their home.

He normally hated the ride, but this time as he stood behind and to the right of Elle, he watched her and her easy manner.

She was petite in height, with a body that held all the right curves, curves he wanted to run his hands over. He remembered her lacy pink underthings and wondered what she had on beneath her clothing now. He yearned to know so badly he nearly yanked her clothes off.

The bell chimed as they reached the top floor. As they entered, he heard Elle gasp and knew it was because the place was now clean and everything mended. No more broken glass or destroyed furniture.

"The Fae?" she asked after a moment.

"Aye," Roderick answered as he shut the door behind him.

"They're rather handy to have around," she said with a bright smile as she walked to the kitchen. "I don't know about you, boys, but I'm hungry."

"Can you cook?" Val asked.

She looked over her shoulder at him. "I'm decent, but nothing to write home about."

"What?" Val asked.

"It means I'm all right but not the best," she answered.

"As long as there is food, I'll eat it," Val said as he went to the balcony.

Roderick watched Elle rummage around in the tall box that kept things cold. What had Aimery told him it was? Ah, yes, a refrigerator. It was a great concept, and he wished he could take it back with him when they left this time. He seated himself on the stool as Elle pulled out a package of meat.

"Chicken," he heard her mumble.

"You don't like chicken?"

She shrugged. "Chicken is chicken. I like it fine. Do you have any other meat?"

"I'm not sure what is in there."

"Great," she said as she opened the refrigerator again.

When she didn't find anything else, she shut the door and turned to the package of chicken. Roderick had really liked the idea of not having to skin an animal. The meat was already skinned and cut for him. Another great idea.

Apparently, Elle didn't share his opinions.

He had to cover his mouth with his hand to keep from laughing as she picked up a piece of the chicken between her thumb and forefinger, then dropped it like it scalded her. She then proceeded to take a knife and try to cut it, but every time she had to touch it, her body would shiver. Finally, she gave up and turned towards him.

"I hate the feel of raw meat in my hands. Chicken is some of the worst," she said and shivered again.

Roderick kept his laughter inside as he rose and went to stand beside her. "I'll cut it. Just tell me how you want it."

After she showed him what to do, Roderick set about cutting up the chicken as she rummaged around in a small closet that held more food. When he was finished with the chicken, she gave him another knife and an onion.

"Since you're so talented at cutting things up," she said with a bright smile.

Roderick took the knife and onion and chopped it up. He glanced over as she cooked and found he liked helping her, something he had never considered before. He heard her humming a tune under her breath, almost absently, as she worked. She took the chopped onion and put it in the pot and poured some wine over them.

"Want to do something else?" she asked him.

And to his surprise he answered, "Aye."

"Will you butter the bread?"

And like a servant in his household on Thales, Roderick picked up the brush and began to butter the loaf of bread she had given him.

He wasn't finished with it when Val walked in and Elle asked him to set the table. Without blinking, Val grabbed the plates and sat them on the table. Roderick had expected Val to refuse or complain, but he was seeing a side of his friend he had never known. A short time later, all three stood in the kitchen as Elle cooked.

"What are you cooking?" Val asked.

"A specialty of mine. Usually I cook it without meat, but I figured you boys might want meat."

"Of course we want meat," Val said. "How can you eat a meal without meat?"

Roderick had been about to ask the same thing.

She laughed. "There are some people that are vegetarians."

"What?" he and Val asked in unison.

"People that don't eat any kind of meat or fish," she said as she dumped some long thin things in boiling water. "They won't even eat eggs because it comes from a chicken."

"And I thought Rome had problems," Val said to Roderick.

It wasn't long after that they were sitting down to eat. Roderick couldn't remember the last time they had sat at a table with a cooked meal. It had been so long ago it was a distant memory.

Worse, the easy charm of Elle brought back long buried memories of meals with his family on Thales. It was so poignant that, for a moment, Roderick couldn't breathe.

"Are you all right?"

He looked down at Elle's small hand on his arm, then raised his eyes to see the concern reflected in her gaze. "I'm fine."

"Are you sure? If you don't want this, I can cook something else," she offered.

"Nay," he stopped her as she started to rise. "The food looks and smells delicious."

She stared at him a moment before reaching for the fork and dishing out the food to first Val and then him. As he accepted his plate, he caught Val's gaze. The Roman observed him quietly, as though he knew what troubled him.

Roderick watched in amusement as Val lifted the food on his fork and smelled it.

"What is it?" Val asked Elle.

"Its one of my favorites dishes that I make," she said. "It's chopped chicken in a lemon butter sauce with angel hair pasta."

Roderick took a bite and loved the light taste of the noodles. "It's very good."

Elle lowered her eyes, and he could almost swear she blushed. He glared at Val, daring the Roman to say anything bad about the food.

He took a bite, then another before the turned to Elle and said, "It is good. I didn't think I would like it."

Roderick was nearly done with his food when Elle placed a large bowl on the table.

"I forgot the Caesar salad."

Val's eyes lit up. "Ah. Something Roman."

"Not exactly," Elle said as she dished some onto each of their plates.

Roderick moved the green stuff with whitish liquid around on his plate. "It looks like leaves."

She laughed again, the sound magical to his ears. Even her eyes sparkled. "Its Romaine lettuce. Just try it."

Roderick took a deep breath, speared the leaf, and put it into his mouth. He was more than surprised to find he liked it. He gave her a nod and motioned for Val to try it.

Reluctantly, Val put a piece of the lettuce in his mouth. "It isn't Roman."

Once the meal was finished, Roderick found that he didn't wish to leave Elle. He helped pick up the table and turned to find Val doing the same. The Roman constantly surprised him, even after all the years they had known each other.

When the table was clear, Val picked up his halberd. "I'm going to make a round."

Elle rinsed one of the dishes she had been washing and saw Val leave. "Where is he going?"

"To take a look on the roof."

She had been pleasantly surprised to find Roderick willing to help her cook and clean. Since he was such a warrior, she figured him to be the barbarian type and not touch anything to do with the kitchen.

With Roderick's help, the kitchen was cleaned in record time. She wiped her hands dry on a towel and watched him gaze out the windows.

"How long do we have?"

He shrugged without looking at her. "I honestly don't know. From what we can tell, the Harpies haven't done any major damage or killings, but that doesn't mean they won't start now."

"Part of me wishes they would," she said as she walked to stand beside him. "At least then we would know where to find them."

"Me, as well," he admitted.

"You're worried, aren't you?"

He nodded and turned to her. "We've fought many creatures, but only one at a time. Never have there been more than one."

"Do you think the Harpies were called up separately?"

"I don't know." He sighed and glanced out the window. "My gut tells me nay, that it was one summoning, but I cannot know that for sure."

"And the Fae? Can they not help?"

"Their sight into who is doing this is limited."

"I don't understand that. I thought they were all seeing," she said as she leaned against the window and crossed her arms over her chest.

"Since the Fae once roamed Earth, they are connected in a way a mother and child are. If the connection is severed, they both will die. As soon as the first creature was summoned, the realm of the Fae felt the reverberations from Earth."

"That's when they put the Shields together?"

He shook his head. "Nay. They went looking for what had occurred and found the creature. Despite their attempts to kill it, they couldn't. They cannot interfere."

"That doesn't make sense to me."

"It didn't to me either at first," he admitted. "For whatever reason, the Fae aren't telling us why they cannot fight, they just can't."

"What happens if they do?"

He looked away from her and took a deep breath. "I asked that same question.

No one answered me, but from what I could tell, when they first attacked, the retribution was horrendous."

"Doesn't seem quite fair, does it?"

"Nay, but then again, whoever is sending the blue stones out knows what they are doing."

"How so?" she asked.

He turned his midnight blue eyes to her. "My thought is that they want to destroy the Fae realm. What better way to do that than to destroy them through Earth, a people that the Fae have guarded and helped since the dawn of time."

She blew out a breath. "I feel like I'm in a bad dream. If what you say is correct, then why not just attack the Fae realm."

"They are too powerful. The Fae have more powers than you could imagine."

"Ah," she said and nodded.

"What I don't understand is why destroy other realms," he muttered.

"Whose realm was destroyed?"

"Cole's. There is nothing left for him to return to. Yours. There are others that are either already destroyed or on the verge."

Elle bit her lip. She couldn't imagine her world gone, but then again, her real world, the realm she was born in was gone. Because of the creatures.

It must have been something in Roderick's eyes, but she had a feeling his realm had either been destroyed or was about to be. Since he didn't wish to talk about it, neither did she.

The door opened and slammed shut behind Val as he stalked toward them.

"Do you smell it?" he asked through gritted teeth.

Elle turned to see Roderick lift his head and close his eyes as he inhaled deeply. Of a sudden, his eyes flew open.

"They're here," he said as he grabbed his weapons.

Chapter Twelve

Adrenaline pumped through Elle as she raced after Roderick as they took the stairs to the roof of the Huntington. As the two men, weapons in each hand, looked around, Elle held onto the doorframe as if it were her anchor to life.

The sky above them churned with dark clouds that rolled in ominously. At least she didn't think it had something to do with the Harpies since a hurricane was stirring up the waters in the Gulf of Mexico.

Still, she couldn't dismiss the unease growing in her stomach, a feeling like her life was about to be forever changed...or ended.

"Do you see it?" Val yelled at Roderick.

"Nay," he shouted as he walked around the roof as if they weren't thirty stories up.

She fingered the dagger on her thigh and took a deep breath. No more hiding in the corner for her. She was responsible for the necklace leaving her care, and she would get it back.

"There," Roderick bellowed.

She turned her head and saw the three large figures flying through the air, almost obscured by the dark clouds and night closing in. Even their semi-human cries wouldn't be heard over the constant din of honking cars and loud music below. It was no wonder they hadn't shown up in the news. No one looked up anymore.

Elle moved away from the door towards Roderick. "Oh, my God. They're heading towards the CenterPoint Energy Building."

"What building?" Val asked.

"It's a huge black building downtown. Very recognizable with its six story cap on top with a hole cut into it."

Roderick turned and headed toward the stairway. "Then that's where we need to be."

"Wait," Elle called as she ran after him. "You can't just walk into the building and take the elevator up to the top. There's security in that building. Not to mention, it's after hours. No one will be there."

Roderick's dark blue eyes burned into hers. "Trust me."

And despite the warnings in Elle's head, she did.

Roderick's heart hammered as they drove their motorcycles toward the tall black glass building. The need for a battle, to redeem himself in his family's eyes, pounded in his veins.

He followed Elle's instructions as she shouted in his ear and fearfully clutched his abdomen.

"We can't do this," she whispered as she stared up at the building as he shut off the bike in the deserted parking lot.

"Trust me," he told her again. He rose from the bike and looked around him. "We cannot climb it."

Elle laughed shakily. "No, we can't."

"We'll have to go in," Val said. "Elle, you know this time. Can you get us in?"

Roderick watched as panic took hold of her.

"I'm not a good liar, and I'm a terrible actress."

He took hold of her arms and turned her until she looked into his eyes. "Will you at least try?"

She swallowed, then nodded. She moved out of his arms and paced in front of them. Suddenly, she stopped and turned to smile at them. "I have a plan."

Elle took a deep breath and walked up the steps to the front doors of CenterPoint Energy. Just as she thought, they were locked. She cupped her hands and placed them on either side of her face as she peered inside.

A security guard approached and unlocked the door. She gave him a smile as he opened it.

"Can I help you?"

"Am I too late?" she asked.

The balding, pot bellied security guard crossed his arms over his chest. "For what? Everyone has gone home."

"Oh, no," Elle cried. "My aunt told me to meet her here. I came earlier to meet her for lunch and when I tried to leave, my bike wouldn't start," she said and pointed to Roderick's motorcycle they had moved into view of the doors.

"She told me to come back and she would give me a ride home."

"Sorry, miss. Everyone is gone."

"Are you sure everyone is gone?" she asked, giving him her most innocent look. "My parents are going to kill me when they find out. Can't I at least come inside and try to call her?"

The security guard looked unconvinced, and Elle felt her panic growing.

"No cell phone?" he asked.

"No," she said and rolled her eyes. "My parents took it away when I dropped out of college last month. I came here to my aunt's office to try and find a job." She couldn't believe this imbecile was buying what she told him.

After a moment, the security guard sighed and motioned her inside. "I'll give you five minutes. After that, you've got to leave."

She rushed inside after the security guard. When he handed

her the phone, she dialed her home phone and kept an eye on the door. When she saw Roderick and Val sneak inside, she cursed under her breath.

"Dialed the wrong number," she told the guard. "I'm still getting used to Houston."

He smiled. "No problem."

She turned so that the guard turned with her, putting his back fully to the doors. As she dialed slowly, she saw Val and Roderick slip up behind the guard.

When Roderick lifted the hilt of his sword, Elle put down the phone and looked at the guard. "I'm really sorry."

"For what?" he asked, just as Roderick brought the hilt down on his skull. The security guard crumpled to the ground.

"There will be more," she said as she pushed them toward the elevators. "We haven't got long before someone comes in and finds him."

As the elevator took them to the top of the building, Elle could hear the unearthly screams of the Harpies. "They sound so close."

"Because they are."

She shivered at Val's words. Her gaze sought Roderick's. "What are we going to do when we reach the top?"

"I want you to stay hidden," he told her. "Val and I have done this plenty of times, but with three of them, I cannot watch you as well."

"You're outnumbered."

"We'll be fine."

But she knew they wouldn't. The thought of either man hurt or killed left her with an aching void she didn't want to confront. In a short time, she had come to trust these men with her life, and the least she could do was watch their backs.

When the elevator doors opened to the top floor, Val and Roderick crept out. Elle slowly followed them, keeping an eye out behind her in case someone walked from one of the closed offices.

"There," she whispered and pointed to the doorway that

was sure to lead them to the top of the building.

Just as she expected, the door was locked. In awe, she watched as Roderick took a step back, then kicked the metal door in.

"Wow," she mouthed silently and followed him inside as Val closed the door behind them.

"Vile stench," Val said as they reached the door that would open onto the roof.

She glanced at him. "I don't smell anything."

"It's the evil he speaks of," Roderick said. "Remember," he said as he looked at her. "Stay hidden, Elle. This realm is counting on you."

Great. Nothing like pressure.

He didn't move until she nodded, and then he pushed the door open and he and Val rushed outside. Elle moved slower. She peered around the door to see Roderick and Val, weapons in hand, as they looked around.

She stepped onto the roof and closed the door behind her. She leaned against it and waited, heart pounding wildly.

Then she heard the scream. She recognized the voice.

The only thought running through her head was to save Jennifer. It never dawned on Elle to think twice. She took off toward the sound of her friend's scream "Jennifer," she yelled, only to be jerked back against a wall of solid muscle.

"Nay, Elle," Roderick whispered harshly in her ear.

She watched powerlessly as one of the Harpies held Jennifer over the side of the building.

"Someone help me," her best friend screamed. "Alex! I don't want to die."

Elle felt Roderick stiffen as Alex walked toward Jennifer. "You would live if you had listened to me," Alex said.

"Don't let her die," Elle beseeched Roderick. She looked up and over her shoulder at him. "I'll give you anything you want, just don't let her die."

"I'll try and save her," he promised and ran his finger along her jaw before he gently pushed her away from him. "Stay hidden."

Tears poured from Elle's eyes as she watched her friend dangled from the building. She knew it was going to take a miracle to save Jennifer, but if anyone could do it, Roderick and Val could.

She heard the scrape of something against the roof the same time the smell assaulted her. Elle knew without turning around that one of the Harpies was behind her.

Slowly, she turned and faced the creature.

To her amazement, the top half of the Harpy was a woman so ethereally beautiful as to only be seen on a magazine cover, but the bottom half that was bird was more hideous than any monster Hollywood could create.

"What have we here," the Harpy said as she moved closer. Long, flame red hair spilled over the creature's shoulder as she bent towards Elle.

Elle was short, but the Harpy stood at least seven foot tall, if not taller. Elle's tongue stuck to the roof of her mouth, preventing her from calling out to Roderick.

The harpy closed her eyes as she took a deep breath. Her eyes flew open and narrowed on Elle. "I know your scent. You're the one that eluded us."

Elle didn't know what to say. Her hands slid along the warm metal of the door as she tried to think how she would escape the harpy. She thought to run, but with the harpies metal wings there was no way she could outrun it.

With more courage than she felt, Elle moved to the left and hoped her feet kept up with her heart as she raced away from the creature. She hadn't taken three steps before hands took hold of her.

"Going somewhere?"

Chapter Thirteen

Roderick didn't stop to think. He launched himself at the harpy that had a hold of Elle. A smile formed as his feet landed square on the harpy's back, causing her to tumble forward and release Elle.

"Run," he yelled at Elle as he rolled to his feet, weapons in hand.

Thankfully, Elle did as he asked. But the harpy didn't fight him as he wanted. Instead, she raced after Elle.

He lunged with his sword and slashed at the harpy's arm. A thin line of blood appeared, but she continued after Elle, unthwarted.

"Fight me," he bellowed to the retreating harpy.

"I'll fight you."

Roderick inhaled deeply before he spun around to confront the third harpy. "I wondered where you had been hiding."

She smiled, her beautiful face clashing with the horror of her body. "My sisters were having fun. I was content to sit and watch. Until you came along. 'Tis been awhile since a warrior has been worthy enough to challenge us."

Roderick swung his flail around him. "Never let it be said I kept you waiting."

She laughed just before she extended her wings and lunged at him. Luckily, Roderick anticipated her move and rolled to the right to avoid her. He came up on his feet and swung the flail at her. It bounced against her iron wings, clanging loudly.

He heard a scream behind him, thankful it wasn't Elle, but her friend. His mind focused on the battle as the harpy turned to him.

"Very good." She eyed him thoroughly. "Mortal you are not."

He smiled, ready for the fight. "I am not."

"Ah, but even immortals can be killed."

A cold chill raced down his spine. "Everything can be killed. Including you."

She laughed, her black hair blowing in the wind. "Aye, even I can be killed. But do you know how?"

"Don't mock me, creature."

"I have a name," she screeched. "'Tis Kaleno."

Elle heard the flap of wings behind her and knew Roderick hadn't gotten the harpy's attention. She raced along the rooftop as fast as her legs would carry her, but it wasn't fast enough.

A jerk on her hair brought her to a sudden, and painful, halt.

"Why run when you know you will die?" the harpy asked.

Elle turned and glared at the offensive creature. "Why stay when you know the Shields will kill you?"

The harpy laughed. "Too bad you are mortal. You would make an excellent harpy."

Out of the corner of her eye, Elle saw the dark-headed harpy and Roderick circling each other as they talked. She couldn't imagine what they could be discussing, but she had problems of her own.

She had to somehow get away from this harpy without help from Roderick or Val, who was trying to get the other harpy to release Jennifer.

"Enough," a voice boomed around them.

Ellen watched as Alex walked onto the roof, the necklace in hand.

"Alex, help me," Jennifer pleaded.

But Elle knew he would offer Jennifer no aid. Elle briefly closed her eyes and silently screamed for not realizing just what Alex had been. He'd been too good to be true, which should have sent warning bells off in her head. Instead, she'd been too jealous of Jennifer's happiness to notice.

When Elle opened her eyes, she saw the harpy holding Jennifer also had a hold of Val. The second harpy with Roderick still circled him.

"Ah, Elle," Alex said as he moved toward her. "What are you doing with the Shields?"

"You know of them?"

He laughed, his once handsome face now ugly to her. "I know much more than you realize. Now answer me. What are you doing with them?"

Nothing on this earth could make her tell him just who she was. She continued to glare at him. "I'm a woman who is here to help a friend."

Alex moved around her, and it was everything Elle could do to keep still. When he stood in front of her again, the third harpy at his back, he leaned close to Elle. "You're the one, aren't you?"

"I don't know what you're talking about."

"You know, if Jennifer hadn't taken the necklace from me, none of this would have happened. But, she saw it hidden in my drawer and thought to give it to you without asking me."

Apprehension shivered down Elle's body. She looked at Jennifer to see her friend's face streaked with tears as she clawed at the hand that grasped her throat.

"It was quite by accident that Jennifer discovered just what the necklace was by eavesdropping on a conversation," Alex continued. "I suppose this is when she thought to steal it from you."

"Now that you have it back, there's no need to kill her."

Alex laughed and reached out to touch her face, but Elle jerked away from him. "The harpies will kill everything in this city," he said with a sneer.

"Then why haven't they?"

"I haven't told them to."

"What's keeping you?" She didn't know what was wrong with her. It wasn't like her to play devil's advocate.

Alex moved closer to her and ran his hand down her arm. "Where is it?"

"What?" she asked. "You have the necklace."

"Where's the mark?" he asked, his voice growing louder.

Elle's blood went cold. Every fiber of her being wanted to turn towards Roderick, but she knew to do that would give away just what she was.

"I don't have a mark." She prayed he didn't hear the break in her voice.

For several minutes he simply stared at Elle before he turned his back on her. "Kill them."

In a mere heartbeat, the harpies turned into vicious killing machines. Elle saw the fist coming at her face, but try as she might, she couldn't duck it. The blow sent her flying backwards. She scrambled to her feet and raced away from the harpy.

"Elle!"

She turned in time to see the harpy release Jennifer, and her friend fall to her death.

"No," Elle cried as she rushed to the side of the building to see Jennifer already at the bottom. Dead.

"'Tis just you and me, little one," the harpy said.

Elle turned to face her executioner, rage simmering just below the surface. "You might kill us, but more Shields will come for you."

"We're counting on it," she said as her arms snaked out and took hold of her.

Elle fought, but it was useless. The harpies had the strength of Hercules, and she was just a mere mortal. Her eyes found Val who fought valiantly with his halberd. Roderick and the other harpy were locked in battle perilously close to the edge of the roof.

How she wanted to help them, and she realized the only way for that to happen was not to cry out and divert their attention.

She looked into the black eyes of the harpy. "You'll be defeated."

Roderick saw Elle in the same position her friend had been in moments before, and he knew he had precious seconds to rescue her.

He kicked out his legs and connected with Kaleno's, sending her to the ground with a hard thud. Without a second glance at the harpy, he rushed toward Elle.

Just as he reached Elle, the harpy opened her wings, which knocked him in the face. He stumbled backwards from the blow but was determined to get to Elle. As he started towards the harpy again, he heard something behind him. He turned to find Kaleno flying towards him and the only thing he could do was brace himself.

Her claws caught him in the chest and threw him over the side of the building.

"Roderick," Elle screamed as he fell. Tears blinded her as she kicked and punched the harpy that held her.

Through her tears, she saw the harpy that had thrown Roderick over the side of the building advance on Val and the harpy he battled.

"Look out, Val," she screamed in a last ditch effort to save him. To her relief, Val turned and saw the second harpy in time.

"Time to die, little one," the harpy said just before she released Elle.

The scream died in Elle's throat as she began to fall.

Chapter Fourteen

Roderick saw Elle falling towards him and reached out in time to grab hold of her arm. She came to a halt, jerking his already dislocated shoulder painfully.

"I've got you," he said as she looked up at him.

"Don't let go."

She was hysterical, not that he could blame her. He'd had a moment of panic himself as he went over the side of the building, but training and instinct had taken over, which is how he had managed to grab hold of the ledge.

"Elle, listen close. I need you to climb up me and get a hold of the ledge."

He knew she wanted to say nay, but she nodded through her tears after looking above them. She took hold of his leg with her other hand. Just as he was about to release the arm he held so she could continue her climb, he heard it. The harpy's scream.

He raised his gaze and saw the harpy coming at them.

"Hang on," he warned just before the harpy slashed at Elle with her talons.

Elle screamed through the pain but managed to keep her grip on him despite the tugging the harpy had done.

"Climb," Roderick yelled as she watched the harpy circle back around.

"Roderick," Val hollered.

He looked up in time to see Val and Alex wrestling, the necklace about to fall from Alex's hand. With one massive punch, Val knocked Alex's head back, knocking the vile man unconscious. Despite Val trying to reach the necklace, it fell from Alex's hand to land about twenty feet above Roderick.

Roderick realized too late that if Val and Alex were fighting, that meant all three harpies were....

Elle's hand was torn from his grasp as the harpies pulled at her, jerking her from his grasp. He looked down to see her mouth open on a silent scream as she fell. Knowing he had only one chance to save her, he let go and fell after her. As she flailed through the air, he lengthened himself and caught up with her.

"Think Stone Crest, England 1123," he yelled in her ear as he wrapped his arms around her. "Hurry, Elle. Say it with me."

Elle could barely think much less hear Roderick, but somehow his words got through. "Stone Crest, England 1123. Stone Crest, England 1123," she repeated time and again.

Suddenly, the fading light of Houston was replaced by pitch black as the air began to swirl around her. Though they still fell, Roderick held onto her and she him. A sound similar to a vacuum surrounded her just before she was jerked backward, and no matter how she tried to hold onto Roderick, he slipped out of her arms.

She screamed out his name, praying he might somehow hear her. Her eyes strained to find some glimpse of him through the blackness when light suddenly surrounded her. It was so blinding, Elle had no other choice but to close her eyes or go blind.

Abruptly the vacuum sound was gone, yet Elle still fell for a moment before she landed with a bone-jarring thud, her breath rushing from her body. For several minutes she didn't move as she willed her lungs to take in air.

Finally, she was able to take a deep breath. Her head pounded fiercely, and her entire body felt as if she had been trampled. She opened her eyes only to find that not only couldn't she see anything, but she was freezing.

It was then she knew. She was in Hell.

She thought she had lived a decent life. No, she didn't attend church every Sunday, but she did go. She abided by the Ten Commandments and was a very giving person.

Slowly she sat up and felt the rocks and snow beneath her. She used her hands to feel around her before she got up the nerve to try to stand. Her ears strained for any sounds of people or animals, but only silence filled the void.

When she got to her feet, she discovered her shoes gone and her feet becoming numb in the snow. It wasn't until she tried to walk that she discovered she had sprained her ankle.

"I'm in a Hell that is freezing instead of hot, blind with a sprained ankle," she mumbled to herself as her head continued to thump with an atrocious headache that put migraines to shame.

Roderick came awake to the sounds of his name being shouted.

"Over here," he croaked out. He tried to lift his arm only to remember too late that it was the same shoulder he had dislocated. He cursed and rolled onto his side, the snow crunching beneath footsteps that hurried toward him.

"Roderick," Val said as he kneeled beside him. "Are you hurt?"

"My shoulder."

"Gabriel can mend you," he said as he helped Roderick to his feet.

"Where is Elle?" Roderick asked as he looked around the field, then to his friend.

"I don't know. I found you first and just assumed she would be with you."

"I tried to hold onto her, but she was jerked out of my arms. We need to find her."

Val nodded, and they set off in search of her. But the longer it took them to locate her, the more anxious Roderick became.

"Maybe I should return to the castle and get the Shields."

Roderick shook his head. "We don't know how much time has elapsed, Val. For all we know, Hugh and the others are already gone."

Val nodded and pointed to something moving in the shadows of the woods. "We might want to take a look there."

Roderick followed him as they ran towards the trees. He nearly walked past her. He wasn't sure what stopped him and made him look to his left, but there Elle sat huddled against a tree with her head resting on her arms.

"Elle?"

She raised her head and blinked her eyes several times. "Roderick? Is that you?"

He knelt beside her and brushed the hair from her face. It was then he saw the nasty bruise on her face. "Are you all right?"

She shook her head. "I hurt all over, and my ankle is sprained. I thought I had gone blind, but I'm beginning to see a few things now."

"It was the light. I didn't have time to warn you to close your eyes."

"At least I'm not dead," she mumbled.

"I'll go see who is at the castle," Val said as he hurried away.

"Castle?" Elle repeated, her voice holding a note of panic.

Roderick took a deep breath as he sat beside her and pulled her into his arms to warm her, careful of her wound on her side from the harpies. "Do you remember what I said to you as we fell?"

"Vaguely," she murmured as she settled against him. "Something about Stone Crest."

"I sent us back in time, Elle. To the time I last was, where the other Shields were."

She stilled, and he worried that this might be too much for her to take in. Then she exhaled loudly. "Somehow, this doesn't surprise me."

Despite their dire situation, he smiled.

"Shouldn't we call Aimery?"

"Not unless we really need him. If Val discovers the Shields have already left Stone Crest, then aye, we will call him."

"Like to do things yourself, huh?" she asked, her teeth chattering.

He sat beside her and pulled her into his arms to try and warm her. No matter how hard he tried, he couldn't ignore the way her body fit so snugly against him, or how much he enjoyed having her in his arms. "You could say that."

They rested as they waited for Val to return. Roderick leaned his head against the tall pine and tried his best to keep Elle warm. He didn't want to think about how eagerly she had melted against him when his arm had gone around her. He needed to think of only killing creatures and destroying blue stones so he could save Thales. Maybe then his family could allow him back home. But he couldn't help but feel her soft breast press against his arm, nor could he ignore the blood now pooling in his cock.

A sound similar to a falcon's call sounded from the trees ahead of him, and Roderick raised his hand to let Val know all was fine. Val rose from the bushes and hurried to them.

"Hugh is bringing horses."

Relief poured through Roderick. He had hoped Hugh and the others would still be here. "What creature do they hunt?"

"Look around you," Val said. "Does it look like it did when we first arrived here?"

Roderick looked around him. "It does look a little different. Why?"

"If you ask me, the creature is gone."

"Then why is Hugh still here?"

"Maybe he wanted to stay," Elle said as she straightened from Roderick's chest.

Roderick and Val exchanged glances as the sound of horses approaching reached them. There wasn't time for them to discuss it further as Hugh rode up with two horses.

Roderick carefully sat Elle aside as he rose to greet Hugh.

Hugh vaulted from his horse and embraced first Val then Roderick. "I never thought to see either of you again," he said, his smile wide. "It's good to have you back."

Roderick could tell Hugh wasn't the same. Gone was the reserved man who had led them for more years then he could count, and in his place was a man that had found his place in the world. Finally.

"It is good to see you as well," Roderick said and glanced down at Elle. "We need to get Elle inside."

Hugh's gaze followed Roderick's. "I didn't realize you brought someone along."

If he noticed Elle's clothing, he didn't mention it as he pulled off his cloak and handed it to Roderick.

"She's going to need that," Hugh said as he reached for one of the horses.

Roderick took one of Elle's arms and pulled her to her feet to wrap the cloak around her. "How is your sight?"

"Getting better every minute," she said through teeth that chattered from the cold.

Hugh tsked as he mounted his horse. "You didn't tell her to keep her eyes closed?"

"There wasn't time," Val said as he too mounted.

Roderick carried Elle to the horse since her feet were bare and lifted her onto the saddle before he climbed up behind her. The ache in his arm had lessened, but he knew it would intensify again once the joint was put back in place.

Roderick didn't wait for Hugh or Val but spurred horse toward Stone Crest so he never saw Val and Hugh share a look.

Elle's eyesight was slowly returning, but not fast enough for her. She had been terrified at the thought of going blind, and when she had heard Roderick's voice, she had wanted to cry from relief.

"Almost there," Roderick said in her ear.

She snuggled against his chest and further into the warm cloak that had been given to her. She had never felt cold like this before. Her feet were already numb, and she feared frostbite. In Houston, it rarely got below freezing, but now she was sure it was well below zero, and she worried she might never thaw out again.

"Where are we going?"

"Stone Crest Castle."

A real castle? Elle had only seen them in pictures and movies, and if she wasn't so cold and scared she might have been excited about seeing her first castle.

"Open your eyes," Roderick said.

The horse slowed, and Elle dared to open her eyes to find that her vision had all but returned. "I can see," she said with a smile as she looked up at Roderick.

It was a mistake as soon as she did it. He was too near her, his body surrounding hers. She looked into his midnight blue eyes and wanted nothing more than to lean up and kiss him. His lips, full and straight, were so close to her she could feel his warm breath. Desire spread through her as she felt her breasts grow heavy and her sex clench with need.

And as they stared at each other, Elle couldn't help but wonder what might happen if she were prettier instead of the plain mouse that she was.

"Thank you," she whispered.

"For what?"

"Saving my life again."

For a moment, she could have sworn his head moved toward hers, but then Val and the other man rode up on either side of them, and Roderick raised his gaze from her. Elle's heart fluttered. She had read of moments like these in books and seen them in movies, but to experience one herself, even if Roderick didn't feel it too, would stay with her forever. She wasn't a fool. She knew Roderick didn't desire her, but there was no doubt about her desire for him that grew with each moment they were together.

"Stone Crest," Roderick said.

Elle turned her head and gasped. Before her stood a mighty stone structure with round turrets, battlements, a gatehouse, and a massive wooden gate that two sword wielding men stood on either side of as they approached.

"It's a real castle."

Roderick's chest rumbled as he chuckled. "That it is. I didn't realize how much I had missed the ancient times until I was thrust into your world."

"I would miss it to," she said as she looked around at the absence of utility poles, roads, and cars. Even the air smelled cleaner without the many pollutants filling the air and water.

"Much different, aye?" Val asked.

"Very," she answered. They drew toward the gatehouse, and Elle raised her head to see the huge stones that were used to build the gatehouse and the surrounding wall. "Wow."

"And Stone Crest is one of the smaller castles," the man on the other side of Roderick said.

Since her back was to him, she couldn't look at him, nor could she imagine a castle bigger than Stone Crest. It was very large in size. But her gaze shifted from the castle to the bailey. People teemed about as children ran and played, knights trained and guarded, and people worked. Medieval studies had been part of her curriculum in college, and she had loved it so much she had even taken two extra courses on it.

The horses stopped before a set of steps that led up to a large door that could only be the entrance to the castle. A woman with strawberry blond hair stood waiting for them with a warm smile on her face.

"Mina," Roderick called as he slid from his horse. "It's

good to see you in one piece."

She laughed and embraced Roderick. "It was close, but we survived."

"We'll have the entire story later," Val said as he approached her and also received a hug.

Elle watched it all atop the horse. Both Roderick and Val seemed more at home here than they had in the twenty-first century.

"We weren't introduced properly," Roderick's friend said as he approached her. "I'm Hugh, Lord of Stone Crest."

He was tall, probably an inch or two taller than Roderick with long dark brown hair that hung freely about his shoulders and sherry brown eyes. He was handsome and had an air about him that people would notice as a leader. His clothes were dark like Roderick's and Val's, and she soon noticed the sword at his hip and the wicked looking crossbow he held in his hand, each displaying the mark of the Shields.

"I'm Elle Blanchard."

"Nice to meet you," he said with a friendly smile as he looked her over.

"Hugh? I thought Hugh was leader of the Shields?"

"I was," he said. "Since neither Roderick nor Val have heard the story, I'll wait and tell all of you later this evening when we eat. Now, come. Let's get you inside to warm yourself."

Elle was about to slide into Hugh's arms when Roderick stepped beside him.

"I will see to her."

She was surprised at Roderick's gruff tone but was too happy to be in his arms again to care. She slid off the horse into his strong arms as he cradled her against his chest and strode into the castle.

Elle drank in the sight of the great hall with its painted wall behind the table on the raised platform, a dais if she remembered correctly. Candles were placed throughout the hall to help shed light in the dark hours. She found herself eager to explore more of the castle to see if her history classes had gotten it right.

"I hope you like it here," Roderick said. "I fear you'll be here awhile."

Chapter Fifteen

Roderick followed Mina as she brought him to a chamber for Elle. Mina stood at the door as he walked inside the chamber and released Elle's legs so she could stand on the rug placed before the hearth.

"I never imagined anything like this," Elle said in awe.

"This chamber has always been one of my favorites," Mina said as she approached Elle. "My name is Mina."

"Lady of Stone Crest?" Elle asked.

Mina smiled and glanced at Roderick. "Aye. I've ordered a hot bath to help you warm up."

"Sounds wonderful."

Roderick turned to Mina. "Is there any way you can find a gown for her to borrow?"

"She needs a gown?" Mina asked.

In response, Elle opened Hugh's cloak to reveal her shorts, shirt, and bare feet.

"Oh, my," Mina said as she drew closer to Elle. "I never knew such clothes existed." After a few moments, she turned to Roderick and nodded. "I'll gather the necessities immediately," she said before she walked from the chamber.

Roderick turned to Elle. "Are you all right?" He imagined

she was in shock and hadn't had the full force of what all had occurred hit her.

She gathered the cloak around her as her eyes filled with tears. "Jennifer is dead."

"Aye." He hated when women cried. Never did he feel so helpless than when the tears started, but Elle had every right to weep after what she had witnessed.

"I've lost my best friend," she said as the tears coursed down her face.

In two steps Roderick was before her. He gave the only comfort he could think of as he opened his arms. She came easily into his arms and held onto him tightly as her tears soaked the front of his jerkin. They stood in the middle of the chamber as the sobs wracked her body.

Her tears began to dry, but he knew Elle was far from finished with her mourning. He reached down and gathered her in his arms to carry her to the bed. Her hands reached around his neck as her head buried against him. He stood beside the bed as he held her. He knew he needed to go below and speak with Hugh, but he longed to stay with Elle. As much as he hated to admit it, what he felt for her was going beyond mere responsibility.

She had a soul-stirring vulnerability about her that tugged at Roderick. He couldn't deny it any more than he could deny the breath that entered his lungs. He turned his face toward her as Elle lifted her head. Her red-rimmed eyes and tear spiked lashes broke his heart. He regretted not doing more to save Jennifer. His sole concentration had been Elle and keeping her alive.

As if she read his thoughts, her hand reached up and cupped his check. "This wasn't your fault, Roderick. Nothing any of us could have done would have saved Jennifer."

It suddenly became hard to breathe. Roderick had never known just how much he needed forgiveness until that moment. His eyes lowered to her dusky pink lips. He knew he shouldn't want her, knew just what could happen if he became involved, but he couldn't stop. He needed to taste her, to sample the innocence and woman that was Elle's alone.

Her lips parted, and he was lost. His head lowered until their mouths barely touched. He heard her slight intake of breath as he moved his mouth against hers, his tongue sliding out to lick her full lips.

One taste wasn't enough. He needed more, yearned for more. This time when his lips touched hers, he was more forceful. Her head turned to the side granting him better access to her sweet mouth.

He brought his raging body under control as his tongue slid into her hot mouth giving him a small taste of paradise, but when she gave a small whimper, it was his undoing.

She opened her mouth wider and leaned into him, her hands threading into his hair. Her tongue touched his, sending sparks of raging desire to run rampant through him. He wanted nothing more than to lower her to the bed and push himself inside her, to feel the weight of her breasts in his hands, to see her head thrown back as her release wracked her body.

But he allowed himself this one kiss instead.

With his control rapidly running out, he lifted his head and looked into her eyes. Her breathing was as ragged as his own, and the longing he saw reflected in her blue eyes nearly made him come undone. She laid her head on his shoulder and for long moments Roderick was content to hold her. When her breathing evened into sleep, he gently lowered her to the bed.

He covered her with the thick blankets and smoothed her auburn locks from her face. "I'll keep you safe," he vowed before he straightened and turned from the bed.

When Roderick returned to the great hall, Val and Hugh sat at the dais talking.

"We wondered what happened to you," Hugh said with a smile.

Val, on the other hand, knew. "Is she grieving?"

Roderick nodded and sat with a sigh as Val poured him a goblet of wine. "She's strong. She will get through this."

"I've no doubt," Hugh said. "Do you want to tell me what happened?"

Roderick looked around the great hall, noticing the other Shields were absent. "Where are Darrick, Cole, and Gabriel?"

"Cole and Gabriel left to fight more creatures."

"And Darrick?" Val asked.

Hugh sighed and looked down at the table. "I'll take you to him." He rose and walked from the castle.

"What happened?" Roderick asked as he stared down at the marker of Darrick's grave.

"He died protecting Mina. The gargoyle went to kill her, and he stepped between them."

"Darrick died a warrior's death," Val said softly, his voice laced with sorrow at losing a brother.

Roderick turned away from the grave and looked at the land around him. It was a beautiful place and Stone Crest a good home. "I take it you killed the gargoyle?"

"We did. We also found the blue stone and destroyed it. The rest of the story will have to wait. I promised Elle she would hear it with the two of you."

Roderick didn't care. He still grieved over the loss of Darrick. Darrick had been a welcome addition to their group. Where most of them had come to be in the Shields for reasons they kept hidden, Darrick came because he wanted to be a part of something great. Where as most of them rarely smiled and had nothing to laugh about due to their pasts, Darrick would always manage to lighten the mood and even get a few laughs from them.

Without him they were a somber group to be sure.

"I'll miss you, my friend," Roderick said into the wind.

"Aye," Val agreed as he came to stand beside him. "We'll be joining you soon, Darrick."

⟋⟍⟍

Elle woke to find Mina sitting beside her. She jerked upright and touched her lips. Memories of her kiss with Roderick swirled through her mind. She had never had such an erotic kiss before. Even her body still pulsed with need.

"Is everything all right?" Mina asked.

Elle dropped her hand and looked at Mina. "Yes, I'm sorry. I was just thinking of something. Did I sleep long?"

"Nay. It's barely been half an hour since Roderick came downstairs. Are you ready for your bath?"

Elle nodded and climbed out of the warm cocoon of the bed. "Where is Roderick?"

Mina pressed her lips together as she turned away. "He and Val have gone to see Darrick's grave."

"Was he a Shield?"

"Aye. He gave his life for mine."

"An incredible sacrifice," Elle said as she walked to the tub where steam rose to the surface.

"I'll return shortly," Mina said as she walked to the door. "I have found some clothes for you and put them on the bench at the foot of the bed."

"Thank you."

Mina stopped just short of leaving and turned back to Elle. "Do you need any assistance?"

"No, thank you. I'll be fine," Elle replied and returned the smile Mina sent her.

When the door closed behind her, Elle quickly shed her clothes and climbed into the hot water. It wasn't as hot as she normally liked, nor was the soap her usual Bath and Body, but it did wonders to revive and warm her.

She didn't wash her hair, though she was tempted. Instead, she quickly washed and rinsed her body before the water chilled and rose from the tub. After drying off before the fire, she turned to the bench that held her clothes.

It took some doing, but she managed to get everything on like it was supposed to be, though she was sure Mina had laid things out in the order to help her. Elle wished she had a mirror to see herself. The gown was a decent fit, if not a tad too long. The shoes were going to take some getting used to, but all in all, she felt much more comfortable than in her shorts since she was in Medieval England. She had just finished combing her hair with her fingers when Mina returned.

"That was quick."

Elle laughed nervously. "I was cold."

"Do you come from somewhere warm?"

"Blistering hot is more like it," Elle said.

Mina's brows drew together. "I cannot imagine."

"Believe me, it's better than this cold."

Mina laughed and took Elle's hand. "Come. Roderick grows impatient."

Just the sound of his name sent a shiver through her. Elle tried to tell herself the kiss meant nothing, but the fact was, it had rocked her world. Literally. There hadn't been fireworks, but there had definitely been something that had moved deep within her, soul scorching in its intensity.

She followed Mina's graceful form down the stairs to the great hall where all three men sat at the dais. Val and Hugh were deep in conversation, but Roderick, his feet propped up on the table stared off into the distance.

It wasn't until Elle had nearly reached him that he turned his head towards her. Had it been her imagination or had he looked happy to see her? All three men rose to their feet at her and Mina's approach. Mina went to Hugh and sat beside him while Roderick pulled out a chair between him and Val. Elle took the chair and smiled her thanks at him.

"How fare you, Elle?" Hugh asked.

"I'll be fine."

"Good." He took a deep breath. "I will get on with my story first since I know Val and Roderick wish to know the details."

"Here, Elle," Mina said as she handed her a goblet.

Elle took it and looked inside to see what looked like water. Thankfully when she tasted it, that's what it was. She wasn't sure about the Medieval wine, mead, or ale they had. Sticking with water seemed the safest bet.

"As I already told Val and Roderick. We lost a Shield," Hugh continued.

Elle nodded sadly. She glanced at Roderick and Val to see their distressed expressions. "Darrick. Mina told me."

"Cole and Gabriel were sent on another mission as soon as we killed the gargoyle."

Elle froze. A gargoyle? Those things weren't supposed to be real. Only in the comics and cartoons did gargoyles come to life.

Hugh looked at Mina. "I couldn't leave.

"We had fallen in love," Mina finished for Hugh. "Aimery offered Hugh the best of both worlds. He is still a Shield who could be called upon if needed."

"However, I would normally be used to house Shields that needed time to heal or rest," Hugh said.

Elle looked at Val and Roderick, but neither man said anything. She leaned forward and smiled at Mina and Hugh. "That was very nice of Aimery to offer you a solution after years of service."

When Roderick still didn't say anything, she kicked both him and Val under the table.

"Owww," Val yelped.

"What is it?" Mina asked.

Elle glared at Val, daring him to tell Mina what she had done. Apparently, Val thought better of it.

"Just a sore leg," he murmured.

Roderick leaned foreword until his forearms rested on the table. Elle's kick had barely grazed him, and though he knew he should say something, he didn't know what. The truth was, he wasn't happy about losing Hugh.

"We're pleased for you, Hugh," Roderick finally said. "Sad to lose you in the field but happy to see you have found love and a life that suits you."

He felt Elle's eyes on him. Ever since she had come to the hall, he had tried his best not to stare at her, but it was becoming increasingly more difficult. Seeing her garbed in the dress of the time did something to him. No complaints had she uttered, and she looked as if she had been born into those clothes.

Finally, he turned and looked at Elle. She gave him a half smile that brought a surge of emotions he hadn't explored after learning of Darrick's death. He couldn't think of Darrick right now, he needed to focus on what was ahead of them.

"Now," Hugh said after he cleared his throat. "Why don't you tell me what happened to bring you three here?"

Roderick turned his eyes to Hugh. "Harpies."

Chapter Sixteen

"What?" Hugh bellowed.

Roderick nodded. "Three of them."

Hugh ran a hand down his face. "Three? We've never faced more than one at a time."

"At least we've lost them for awhile."

"Don't count on it," Val said.

Roderick look at his friend. "Why? What happened?"

"After they knocked Elle out of your arms and you two fell into the time tunnel, I saw the harpies return for Alex, grab the necklace, and find a tunnel themselves."

Roderick rose to his feet and paced in front of the table. "They would only venture into the tunnel if they knew where we were."

"Exactly," Val agreed. "I expect them to show themselves at any moment."

Roderick glanced at Hugh and Mina and knew he couldn't put them in danger. "We need to leave."

"I'll get my stuff," Elle said as she rose to her feet.

"Nay," Hugh and Mina said in unison as they stood.

"You're better off making a stand against the harpies here," Hugh said.

Roderick shook his head. "I cannot put the two of you in danger."

"This is what I agreed to when I decided to stay," Hugh argued. "Mina and I have been preparing for something like this."

"It's more than just the both of you. There is an entire village full of people that will be put in danger."

Hugh smiled. "After dealing with the gargoyle and the prospect of future occurrences, we had each cottager dig a chamber below them to hide in. There is food and water in each that is changed out each month and will last them a week."

"Trust me, Hugh," Val said. "These harpies are nothing like the gargoyle."

Hugh stared hard at Val. "We will find a way to kill them just as we did the gargoyle and the many other creatures we have faced."

Roderick knew he should take Val and Elle and leave, but making a stand at Stone Crest was a good idea. He turned to Val. "What do you think?"

Val thought about it a moment, then raised his eyes to Roderick. "We stay and prepare for them."

"Elle?" Roderick asked. Since her life was also at stake, it was only right that he ask her opinion as well.

"Personally, I would rather never see them again, but if they're coming for us, then I agree with Val."

Roderick sighed. "All right." He resumed his seat, as did the others.

Hugh was the first to break the silence. "Why did they follow you?" he asked Roderick.

"They want Elle."

All eyes turned to the woman beside him. She shifted uncomfortably in her chair and glanced at him. He wanted to reassure her, but in truth, he couldn't. There weren't reassurances in this battle.

"Why?" Hugh finally asked.

"We not only found the stone and the creature while we were in the twenty-first century, but we also found Elle. She bears the mark Aimery told us about."

"You do?" Mina asked breathlessly to Elle.

Elle slowly nodded her head.

"So do I."

Roderick watched the excitement register on Elle's face. Two of the five women had been found. It was amazing, but he wasn't going to question it. He was just glad that two had been found.

"We'll talk later," Mina said, a huge smile on her face, "once everything has been decided."

Elle nodded and turned to Roderick, her eyes bright with happiness.

"Do you think the stone was sent to Houston because of Elle?" Hugh asked.

"I don't know," Val said. "I hadn't thought of that. How could they know where the women are if the Fae cannot?"

"Now that's a question I would like answered," Roderick said. "It is very plausible that they might know the locations of the women, but to actually become close to them?"

"What do you mean?" Hugh asked.

"I had the necklace in my hand," Elle said quietly, her eyes downcast at her folded hands.

"Necklace? What necklace?"

Roderick took pity on Hugh. "The blue stone was put into a necklace that Elle's friend stole from a man to give to Elle."

"Jennifer didn't know what it was," Elle said in defense of her friend. "She paid for it with her life."

"I'm sorry for your friend," Hugh said gently. He lifted his eyes to Roderick and Val. "Why didn't you two destroy the stone when you had the chance?"

Again Elle spoke. "I wouldn't let them. At the time I still wasn't sure about everything I had been told. I asked for one night to think about it. When I woke up the next morning, Jennifer had come and taken the necklace to give it back to

Alex."

"The man who controlled the harpies," Val supplied for Hugh when Hugh frowned at Alex's name.

"You shouldn't have given her time," Hugh said.

"It was her necklace given to her as a gift by a friend, Hugh," Roderick said in Elle's defense. "We had the stone, we had Elle. I thought one night would be enough time for Elle to come to grips with all she had been told."

Roderick held Hugh's gaze, daring him to say more on the matter.

"Fair enough," Hugh said when Mina touched his arm.

Roderick relaxed against the back of his chair. "The harpies want to kill Elle, and I'm assuming any other women that came from her realm."

"Then we keep her and Mina safe at all costs," Hugh said.

Val nodded. "Roderick lost his weapons when the harpy threw him over the building."

"You know where the armory is," Hugh said. "Take what you need until Aimery supplies you with new weapons."

Roderick nodded. "My thanks."

"What else do you need?"

Val snorted. "A plan."

"What about what we used for the gargoyle?" Mina asked Hugh. She turned to Roderick and Val. "We cut a tree and shaped it into a large spear, then pulled it back amidst trees. When the gargoyle set off the trap, the tree impaled him."

Val shook his head. "The harpy's wings are made of metal."

"And when I cut one, she healed instantly," Roderick added.

Hugh shook his head. "Just as the gargoyle did."

"Then how did you kill it?" Elle asked.

Mina smiled. "We had to wait until he was asleep, and then we pushed him over the side of the old monastery, and he smashed to bits."

"Too bad the harpies don't turn to stone," Elle grumbled.

Roderick thought the same thing. He shifted and grimaced as his arm pulled. He needed the shoulder put in place soon.

"By the gods," Val roared as he jumped to his feet. "You still haven't seen to that?"

"Seen to what?" Elle asked Val, then turned to Roderick. "What haven't you seen to?"

"He's injured," Val answered her. "His shoulder is out of joint."

By Elle's horrified expression, Roderick knew she was thinking of him carrying her. He wanted to explain that it didn't hurt, but he had a feeling she wouldn't believe him.

"I wish Gabriel were here," Val said as he went to Roderick.

Roderick jumped from his seat. "There is nothing Gabriel could do that I cannot do myself. His herbs cannot put the joint back in place."

"Then I will."

There was no way he was letting anyone do it but himself. "Nay, Val. I will see it done."

He walked to one of the stone pillars, closed his eyes, and gritted his teeth from the pain he knew would come. After several deep breaths, he opened his eyes, reared his shoulder back, and slammed it into the pillar.

The first hit put it back into place, but the pain brought him to his knees. Small hands touched his face, and when he opened his eyes it was to see Elle kneeling beside him.

Sweat poured from his face, and his body shook from the exertion it took not to cry out. His breathing was labored, and the pain put a dull haze around him. Now was when he needed one of Gabriel's foul tasting concoctions.

"What do you need?" Elle asked.

You.

He shook his head and leaned half against the pillar and half against her.

"He needs a bed," Hugh said as he and Val walked up.

Roderick wanted to shake them off as they took hold of

him, but his strength was depleted. Hugh took Roderick's good arm and looped it over his shoulder to support his weight. Roderick kept his injured arm against him while Val carefully took hold of him to help Hugh carry Roderick up the stairs.

It wasn't long after Roderick was laid on the bed that something was pressed to his lips. The smell alone nearly made him gag. There was no mistaking one of Gabriel's mixtures.

"Gabriel left me a few things as well as instructions," Hugh said. "Now drink."

Roderick wanted to say nay, but he knew after drinking the awful brew he would be almost back to normal with very little pain. He took the goblet in his good hand and drained the contents. Sleep pulled at him, but he tried to keep his eyes open. Elle walked to him and laid a hand on his arm.

"Sleep, Roderick."

"I'll see her safe," Val said from beside her.

Roderick trusted Val with his life, but he had made a promise to Elle. How could he keep that promise if he was asleep? Despite what he wanted, the medicine didn't give him a choice. He tried once more to stay awake, but the darkness pulled him under.

Elle sighed when Roderick gave in and slept. She had been worried he would continue to fight it. "Will he be all right?"

Val nodded. "He's immortal, Elle. There is only one thing that can kill him. He can get injured, and he might suffer some pain, but he will be fine."

"I know. I just needed you to say it."

Val chuckled and turned to leave the room. She looked at Mina and Hugh. Hugh stared down at Roderick as if deep in thought.

"Thank you."

He raised his eyes to her. "For what?"

"For opening your home to us. I'm a stranger who didn't destroy the stone when I had the chance."

"If Roderick trusts you, then I trust you. We have been

together so long that the men under my command are more like brothers than my soldiers."

"From the way I heard Roderick speak about you, he felt the same way."

Hugh smiled. "Thank you for that. I never thought to see either of them again, especially not this soon. Come," he said. "Let us go below and eat."

"What about Roderick?" Elle was loath to leave him. He might need her.

"When he wakes, he will be virtually as good as before he hurt his arm. Gabriel's mixtures are magical I think. No one knows what the herbs are, or where he gathers them. They have saved each of us on more than one occasion."

Still Elle didn't move.

"You need your strength as well," Mina said. "We have a long night ahead of us planning for the harpies. Let us get some rest before then."

Elle let Mina and Hugh lead her from the room. She took one more look at Roderick sleeping in the large black canopy bed.

"He'll be fine," Mina said again.

But Elle was more worried about herself. She had never known such panic as when she saw Roderick crumple to his knees. He might not have cried out, but she had when she had heard the joint pop back into place.

She didn't fear the Harpies. She feared the loss of her heart.

Chapter Seventeen

During the meal, Elle and Mina talked nonstop. Though Elle had believed Val and Roderick about her coming from another realm, to actually meet someone who also bore the mark was profound.

There was no doubt now.

She and Mina compared lives. Whereas Elle had grown up without a family, living in foster care, then setting out on her own with nothing more than the clothes on her back, Mina had been raised as a lady. She might not have gotten along with her brother and sister, but she had been a part of the people of Stone Crest.

The only thing they had in common was the fact that neither of them had felt a part of a family. Mina had been raised as a lady of Stone Crest, but the family that had taken her in had never included her in that family.

Mina was a link to a past that Elle couldn't remember. Yet, that link connected her to something, and she didn't feel so alone.

"I cannot imagine being a mother and sending my infant off into a world I knew nothing about to never know if they lived or died," Mina said.

Elle nodded. "That's true. It must have been very hard, but when faced with the alternative of certain death, I would gladly see my child given a chance."

"Aye. I as well."

"What I would like to know is what our parents were like," Elle said. She had dreamed of parents when she was a kid, parents that loved her and were there for her. A far cry from the awful foster care she was given.

"For all we know you came from a noble house, and I was a peasant," Mina said with a laugh.

"Why think on something you will never know?" Val asked.

Elle shrugged. "Why not? You knew your world, Val, but we have only known this. It would be the same as if you had never known your parents."

Hugh leaned over and kissed Mina's cheek. "Maybe when the others are found there could be more answers."

"How, if we were all infants?" Elle asked.

It was Val's turn to shrug. "Only the gathering of the other three will answer that."

"I cannot wait for that time," Mina said wistfully.

"Do not wish too hard," Val cautioned. "I have a feeling that once we gather all of you the creatures will attack."

Elle saw Hugh frown. "We need more information," Hugh said.

"First, we need a plan for when the harpies attack," Elle pointed out. "I've no wish to be caught off guard again. They are tall, strong, and very dangerous."

"Then tell us all you know," Val said.

For the next two hours Elle told them everything she had uncovered about the harpies while looking through the books in Roderick's penthouse. By the time she was finished, Val and Hugh look aggravated.

"In other words," Val said, "they cannot be killed."

"Everything can be killed," Elle pointed out. "In my world, they had a show where certain people were immortal, and the only way to kill them was to behead them."

"Show?" Mina asked.

Elle didn't know how to explain, but fortunately Val came to her rescue.

"Pictures that move and make a story."

"Oh," Mina said, her brow furrowed.

Then it dawned on Elle. "We cut off their heads."

"And if they grow another in its place?"

She whirled around to see Roderick standing at the foot of the stairs. He looked fit and hail and hearty as if he had never been injured. She knew she was grinning like a fool, but she was thrilled to see him up and about.

"I somehow don't think they will," she answered. How she remained seated instead of launching herself into his arms, she would never know.

"Either way," he said as he walked towards her, "we plan in case they do."

"How do you foresee us chopping their heads off? If you didn't notice, they are rather tall," Val said dryly. "And quick. It was as if they anticipated my next move."

Elle smiled at him. "I have a plan."

Roderick followed Elle as she walked among the dense forest near Stone Crest. He noticed some trees with claw marks in them that must have come from the gargoyle Hugh, Gabriel, and Cole fought.

"Here," Elle called.

Roderick turned to see her looking upwards. He followed her gaze and found two stout oak trees. "What do you have in mind?"

She turned her head and smiled at him, setting his heart to fluttering. The more he was around her, the more he wanted to be near her to be granted one of her amazing smiles. It was silly for a warrior such as he to crave a smile from a woman, but he did.

"What I have in mind," Elle said as she walked towards him with her hands on her hips and her head cocked to the side, "is to use those two trees," she said as she pointed over her shoulder to the oaks.

"How?" Hugh asked, curiosity shining in his eyes.

She turned to Hugh and Val. "We're going to need very stout rope."

Roderick found himself smiling as he realized her plan. "You're going to have them fly betwixt these trees and run into the rope."

"Causing their head to come off, if they hit it just right," she finished as she turned back to him.

"Good plan," Val murmured as he walked around the oaks. "And you expect all three to fall for this trick?"

"No, actually, I don't," Elle said as she stared at the trees again. After a moment she turned back to the men. "If we're lucky, one of them will be killed."

"She's right," Roderick agreed. "I don't expect all three of them to be killed, but if we can take one down, that's one less we have to fight."

"Better odds," Val said with a glint in his eyes. "I'll get started on the rope."

"I'll go help him," Hugh said and followed Val.

Roderick's eyes never left Elle. He waited until his friends left before he spoke. "I think your idea might work."

Her clear blue eyes sparkled with a mixture of fear and excitement. "I hope you're right. If not, then I'm not sure what we'll do."

"Don't worry. We've battled many creatures and have managed to kill them all."

"But what if this time is different? You all said you had never battled more than one at a time."

Roderick pushed a lock of her thick auburn hair behind her ear. "It's true. We've never battled three at a time before, but we will succeed. The Fae chose us because of our fighting skills."

"I know," she said and ducked her head. "In my time there were plenty of weapons we could have used to destroy the harpies."

"I'm not so sure of that."

She raised her eyes and frowned. "Why not? My time had guns and weapons that could kill an entire country with just one bomb."

Roderick nodded. "I know, but these creatures that are being brought into this realm are different."

"I sure wish the Fae could help."

Roderick did as well, but there was no use thinking about it. "Do you wish to remain here or return to the castle?"

Elle shrugged. In truth, she wanted some time alone, but with the threat of the harpies return, she knew that would only happen at the castle.

"What troubles you, Elle?"

Roderick's deep voice filled with concern nearly did her in. It was all she could do to keep the tears back. As long as her mind was focused on something she forgot about everything she had lost and would never return to, but most especially Jennifer.

"Elle?"

"I'm fine," she lied and turned away so Roderick's dark blue eyes couldn't see the truth. She wanted him to think her strong, not weak. "I think I would like to return to the castle and rest," she said after a few minutes.

"Of course."

When she finally reached her room, Elle shut the door and leaned her head back against it as the tears fell in hot streaks down her face.

"Jennifer," she whispered into the large room. "I miss you so very much."

Weariness and grief took hold of her now that her mind wasn't on a plan to kill the harpies. She stumbled to the bed and fell across it as the tears continued to come.

⟡

Roderick looked at the stairs again. He had lost count of the times he had done so since returning from the forest. Elle hadn't seemed quite right, but she had assured him she was. Yet he didn't believe her.

"Why don't you check on her?" Val grumbled.

Roderick glared at his friend. "I think I will," he said and pushed away from the table. He knew the conversation he, Val, and Hugh were having of another plan would continue once he returned.

He took the stairs three at a time until he reached the floor in which Elle's chamber was. In no time at all he was before her door, and there was no mistaking the sobs from within.

His eyes briefly closed as he wished there was a way to diminish her grief, but only time could do that. Silently, he opened her door to see her lying across her bed as she cried. The knot that twisted in his gut at her obvious pain had him clenching his jaw. He might not be able to take away her pain, but he could offer her comfort.

Without a second thought, he went to the bed and sat beside her. She lifted her tear streaked face, her lashes spiked from the crying. No words were needed as he turned sideways to lean against the head of the bed and moved her until her head was against his chest and her body lying over his lap. Her hand fisted in his jerkin as the tears continued.

The last time he had seen such grief was when he had told his mother of her eldest son's death. Roderick had never wanted to see such pain again, yet, in his arms was one that suffered just as his mother had.

He ran his hand down Elle's arm and then back up again to stroke her face. It was when he looked down at her that he realized his mistake. She was vulnerable, and he craved her as a dying man craves water. He knew he needed to move away, but no matter how hard he tried, his body wouldn't move.

Her hand loosened her hold on his jerkin and crept toward his jaw. A blaze of heat followed in her wake, and Roderick's body cried out for him to take her. Breathing became difficult the more he stared into her beautiful clear blue eyes, and he knew he was lost, lost to the desire that swept over him.

His head lowered until their mouths were breaths apart. He could feel the rapid beat of her heart against his chest and knew he affected her in much the same way she affected him. The taste of their first kiss was still vivid in his mind, the hunger, the passion deep within her. He wanted to be the one to unleash what she kept hidden, and he was sure she didn't even realize the passion she held locked inside. But he would show her.

Starting now.

He captured her lips and heard her breathy moan as her hand crept to his neck and her fingers curled in his hair. As much as he tried to go slow, his body had other ideas. The instant his lips claimed her sweet mouth, he forgot reason, forgot time, forgot everything except the woman in his arms.

The kiss grew in intensity, igniting his blood. He took her mouth again and again, leaving himself just as breathless as she. Her hands clawed at his shoulders and back, and her breasts pressed against his chest, but it wasn't enough.

He wanted her. Now.

Chapter Eighteen

With the slightest of movements, Roderick shifted Elle and her skirts so that she straddled him. Her eyes were glazed with desire, her lips wet and swollen from his kisses and parted for more. His rod was pressed tightly between her legs, and he could feel the heat of her. His mouth went dry as he thought of sinking his finger in her wet sex.

"Roderick," she whispered just before he took her lips in another kiss.

This wasn't the time for talking.

His hand cupped her deliciously firm behind and slowly moved over her waist, lower back, and then up to her shoulders. As he did, he moved his mouth to her cheek, then down to her neck. She responded just as he wanted her to. Her back arched, thrusting her breasts outward.

Blood pooled in his rod, making him grow harder, if that was possible. He moved his hands to her side and cupped each breast then flicked his thumb over her nipples. She gasped, then sighed as he began to fondle her breasts.

The need to see her nude was growing nearly as fast as his need to be inside of her. Though it had been awhile since he had taken a woman, he didn't think that was the reason for his urgent need for Elle, he knew it was Elle herself. There had been something unique about her from the first moment he had seen her.

It took him a moment to realize that it was Elle who pulled at his jerkin. He helped her remove it and watched in wonder as her hands glided over his chest, her normally clear eyes now darkened as she looked at him.

Elle's hands shook as she moved them over Roderick's washboard stomach, bulging biceps, and pecs to die for. His skin was bronzed and warm, and the more she touched, the more she wanted to feel…and taste. She raised her gaze to find him watching her. She almost reached up to pinch herself to make sure this wasn't a dream.

Almost.

Instead, she closed her eyes as his hands moved from her side up to her neck until his hands were on either side of her face. He kissed her forehead, her eyelids, her ears, and even the tip of her nose, and with every kiss, her blood heated until she thought she would melt in his arms. Her sex clenched and liquid pooled in her panties as she ignited.

When she opened her eyes chills raced over her skin at the desire she saw in Roderick's dark blue gaze. It was the kind of look she had read about it books and seen on TV, but never thought to see directed at her.

She leaned forward to kiss him. He let her have control of the kiss, which she greatly enjoyed. His lips were firm yet gentle, and she had never experienced a kiss like his before.

Her tongue slipped between his lips and touched his. In a heartbeat he crushed her to his chest as he took control of the kiss, sending shockwaves of pleasure vibrating through her and a need growing in her core by the second. Sex had never been something she really enjoyed, but this, this was so wonderful she prayed it never ended.

By the time he ended the kiss, Elle was mush. She couldn't have stood had he asked her to. All she wanted was to stay in his arms and receive more of his kisses. And if she was honest with herself, for the first time in her life, she really wanted to make love to someone – Roderick.

His tongue was doing delicious things to her ears. He was sucking on her earlobe, his hot breath gently blowing in her ear, sending chills down her spine. While his tongue worked its magic from her ear to a sensitive place she didn't even know she had towards the back of her neck, his hand had again cupped her breasts.

How he found her nipples through the clothing she didn't know. She nearly came out of his lap when he gently squeezed both of them. The next squeeze was a little harder, and she felt her breasts swell in anticipation of more. The pleasure/pain was unlike anything she could have ever imagined, and, like the kisses, she wanted more, much more.

She felt the moisture between her legs and knew Roderick had caused it. The need was growing, taking over her, ruling her. The need to have him inside of her was foremost in her mind, but she couldn't get close enough to him with her clothes between them. It was as if he read her mind as he began to help her unlace her gown. Just as they were about to pull it over her head someone knocked on the door.

Her eyes locked with Roderick's. In that instant she saw him regain control.

Another knock made her move off Roderick and go to the door. She opened it to find Mina standing before her.

"Are you all right?" Mina asked. "You look flushed."

"I'm still getting used to being here." It wasn't a lie, and Elle couldn't exactly come out and tell Mina that she was in the middle of making love to Roderick.

"I just wanted to check on you. If you need anything, you can ask any of the maids."

Elle gave her a genuine smile. "Thank you, Mina. I will be down for supper."

When Elle closed the door and looked at the bed, Roderick was no longer in it.

She found him staring out one of the narrow windows that

the history books called arrow slits.

He stood rigid with his feet apart and hands fisted at his sides. She wanted to go to him, but something in the way he stood told her to keep her distance. She swallowed hard and licked her swollen lips. Her body still cried out for his touch, but there was no denying that whatever had happened between them would not continue – at least this day.

Suddenly, he spun and faced her. No emotion registered on his face, and her heart crumbled. For the first time in her life she had felt that someone really wanted her. Had she read him so wrong?

Tears came again, but this time wasn't for her loss of her time or Jennifer, it was because she knew Roderick hadn't wanted her.

Roderick wanted to hurl himself from the nearest tower. How could he have been so controlled by his raging body that he had forgotten how vulnerable Elle was? He saw the regret on her face and had never felt so dirty before in his life.

An instant ago, when her kisses had set his blood afire and her hands left burning trails of need on his body, was gone. The hate he felt for himself was nearly as ghastly as it had been when his brother died.

He tried to bring himself to apologize, but the tears swimming in her beautiful clear blue eyes choked him. He looked down, his hands fisted so tightly he shook. It was the first time he had ever shamed the Shields, something he had sworn to Aimery and himself he would never do.

As emotion clogged his throat and gut, he hurried past Elle and out the door. But he didn't stop. He needed to release the rage boiling inside of him for his idiocy.

"Roderick," Hugh called as Roderick crossed the large hall and rushed out the castle door.

He strode into the stables and found a solid white stallion. The horse looked as though he itched for exercise, and his wildness appealed to Roderick. He opened the door and grabbed the bridle on the hook. The stallion stood still, his tail swishing as Roderick finished fastening the bridle. Roderick was leading the prancing stallion out of the stables when Hugh and Val approached.

"You know I don't care if you ride my horses, but I would like to know what is bothering you," Hugh said, his arms crossed over his thick chest.

For the first time since meeting them, Roderick couldn't look them in the eye. "I've done something I swore never to do."

"There is nothing you could do that could be wrong," Val said. "You are an honorable man, Roderick, one of the most honorable I've ever met."

If it were possible for Roderick to feel worse, he did. He shook his head. "You don't understand," he began when Hugh interrupted him.

"Then make us understand."

Roderick sighed and lifted his gaze to his leader. Hugh was the best man he knew. It was near impossible for Roderick to meet his eyes. Finally, he shifted his gaze to Val.

Val narrowed his gaze as he studied him. "Roderick, this isn't like you. Does it have something to do with Elle?"

Roderick winced and turned his back to them. He swung up on the bare back of the stallion and threaded the reins through his fingers. "All I can say is that I'm deeply sorry. I broke my word to the Fae, to myself, but more importantly to the Shields."

"We are brothers," Val said as he walked to the horse. "We will make right whatever is wrong."

"How I wish it were so," Roderick said. He looked once more to Hugh then nudged the horse into a gallop.

Roderick didn't look back as he and the stallion raced through the gates and onto the rolling countryside. Everywhere he looked he saw Elle's beautiful, delicate face and the anguish in her eyes. He caused her that anguish because he had taken advantage of her.

He wanted to ask her for forgiveness, but he didn't deserve

it, just as he didn't deserve to ever return to his realm.

"What was that about?" Hugh asked Val as they watched Roderick race through the gates.

Val rubbed his chin. "I have an idea."

"Well," Hugh prompted. "Are you going to share it?"

Val looked away from Roderick's retreating form to his leader. "There has been a bond between Elle and Roderick that I have never seen before. Between the two of us, she always chooses him, and he is very possessive of her."

"Did something happen between them before they traveled through time?"

Val shook his head. "There wasn't time. Once they arrived here though..."

He didn't finish, didn't need to. Hugh knew exactly what he suggested.

"It's something to think on," Hugh said after a moment. "I, too, have noticed he is especially protective of her, but I thought nothing of it. Even when he was injured and Elle wouldn't leave his side, I assumed she had grown close to both of you."

"Elle might be concerned if I injured myself, but it would be nothing compared to what she exhibited with Roderick."

"What to do then."

"Nothing," Val said as he glanced out the gates. "Whatever happened will have to be mended between the two of them. Our interference will only hinder things."

Hugh nodded. "Truth to tell, I hope never to see Roderick so flustered again. Whatever troubles him, I hope he finds absolution soon."

Elle watched Roderick race across the land. He rode as if the Hounds of Hell were on his trail. Never once did he look back, and she couldn't shake the feeling that, if it were up to him, he wouldn't return. She closed her eyes and recalled the feel of his strong, hard body against hers, the tenderness of his hands as he learned what pleased her, the moan wringing way his lips sent chills across her body.

Briefly, she thought about finding Val and asking him about Roderick's past, but she knew unless Roderick volunteered the information first, Val wouldn't utter a word. She tried to tell herself she had been alone most of her life, that she didn't need anyone. But there was no denying she did indeed need someone – Roderick.

Chapter Nineteen

The sun had nearly set when Roderick returned to Stone Crest. Many times he turned the stallion around to return, but the thought of having to face Elle made him stay away.

"Coward," he mumbled under his breath.

The bailey was virtually deserted as most were at their tables enjoying their suppers. He wondered how Elle had found her first full meal in Medieval England, but he suspected she conquered it just as she did everything else.

"Milord," the stable lad said in greeting as Roderick rode to the entrance of the stables.

"Give him extra oats and a good rubdown. He worked hard this day."

The boy accepted the reins and gave the mighty horse a pat on his shoulder. "Enjoyed yerself, did ye?" the lad spoke to the horse as they entered the stables.

Roderick turned to find Val waiting for him.

"Have a nice ride?" Val asked.

Roderick wasn't fooled by the cool tone. He knew Val too well. "I did, though it wasn't long enough."

"You aren't the kind of man that runs from things."

He snorted. "You don't know me well at all."

"Actually, I know you better than you think," Val responded. "I meant it before. We are brothers, all the Shields."

Roderick sighed and ran a hand down his face, feeling more tired than if he had just battled a hundred men. "I know, and I thank you for that. I just need…to do this on my own."

"You aren't alone. Don't forget that," Val warned.

"I won't fail the Shields."

"We never doubted you would."

They stood silently for a moment as stars began to twinkle overhead. Roderick's mind wasn't on the coming of the harpies but instead was on Elle.

"We had better go inside before Mina sends Hugh out to find us. She was greatly upset at us for allowing you to ride out on your own."

That had Roderick's lips nearly turning into a grin. "I can take care of myself."

"That's what Hugh told her. She in turn gave him a look that would have withered an oak." They turned and started for the castle entrance. "I tell you that woman isn't one I want angry at me."

"I'll keep that in mind."

He let Val enter ahead of him to give himself another moment before having to face Elle. When he stepped into the great hall, he scanned the rows of tables and nodded to a few men. His gaze then found the dais, but Elle was nowhere to be found.

Instantly, Roderick looked around the hall again. Elle wasn't there. With is blood pounding, he strode to the dais and stood in front of Hugh.

"Where is she?"

Hugh raised a brow as he finished chewing his food. "If you mean Elle, she is in her chamber."

Was she ill? Was she dreading looking at him again? "Why?"

Hugh shrugged and took another bite.

It was everything Roderick could do not to reach across the table and jerk Hugh up by his shirt. In all the time they had spent together, Roderick had never felt such anger against any of the Shields. Instead of attacking Hugh, he clenched the edge of the table.

Then a small hand touched his arm. He turned to find Mina. "My lady."

"Roderick, do not be concerned about Elle. She is fine, just adjusting to her life here."

He wanted desperately to believe her, but he knew it wasn't the truth.

"She told me she was a little afraid of eating in front of such a large crowd."

Roderick closed his eyes and clenched his jaw. Nay. What Elle was afraid of doing was facing him, not that he could blame her after he had acted so callously.

Mina's voice reached him again. "You look exhausted. Why don't you sit and eat."

He opened his eyes and looked to Mina. "I think I'll …"

"Elle," Mina suddenly called.

Roderick jerked and slowly turned toward the stairs. Standing at the base was Elle. She didn't look at anyone as she slowly walked to the dais. It wasn't until she reached her chair that she looked up.

"I realize how unkind I sounded earlier," she said to Mina.

"Not at all," Mina assured her. "If the situations were reversed, I don't think I would come down from my chamber either."

Roderick couldn't take his eyes from Elle. He silently begged her to look at him, at the same time he prayed she wouldn't. He couldn't stand to see the scorn in her clear blue eyes anymore than he could look at himself in a mirror.

"Roderick, sit," Hugh ordered.

The only seat left was the one next to Elle. He wasn't sure she wanted him near her, but unless someone moved, he didn't have anywhere else to sit. He walked around the dais and took his seat. As he scooted his chair in, his arm accidentally bumped Elle. She jerked away, and it nearly brought him to his knees.

His parents had raised him to respect everyone, including women, and the thought of having hurt one, especially one he was in charge of keeping alive, left him sick to his stomach.

He knew the food placed in front of him would be delicious, but he couldn't manage to place a bite in his mouth. Instead, he moved the food around on his charger and watched Elle out of the corner of his eye.

She and Val discussed something. She was pale and her eyes red, but she did laugh at something Val said, which should have made him feel better, but didn't. This uncontrollable jealousy was something he had never experienced before, and he didn't like it. Val was his friend, his brother, to be jealous of him or any of the Shields was ridiculous, but absurd as it was, when it came to Elle, he was anything but normal. He had known she was different from the first, but he had no idea she would turn his world upside down.

"The rope is finished," Hugh leaned over and said.

"Good."

"You heard me? I've only said it three times."

Roderick mentally winced. "I apologize."

"No need," Hugh said. "I just wish you would talk to me and let me help you."

"As I said earlier, no one can help me."

Hugh turned to face him, one elbow on the table. "You know that's a lie. You choose not to tell us because you think we won't understand. How do you think I felt when I knew I had fallen in love with Mina and that meant I would have to leave the Shields?"

Roderick shook his head. "I don't know."

"It was the most painful decision I had to make, and I pray none of you will ever be in that situation. The truth is, I couldn't, and cannot, live without Mina. Leaving wasn't an option."

"Did you tell Cole and Gabriel?"

"Not until after I had spoken with Aimery. I knew then that I had been foolish. They would have understood."

"Of course they would have."

"As will Val and I when you tell us."

Roderick stared at the man he had followed for many years. "There are some things too painful, too...," he searched for the right word, "shameful to speak to anyone about."

Hugh sighed deeply. "Roderick, whatever you may think of yourself, whatever you think you might have done, we will still stand by your side."

His words went a long way in helping Roderick, but it wasn't enough to face Elle. Since the conversation was taking a turn that would eventually lead to her, Roderick turned it. "Is the rope already in place?"

"Aye," Hugh answered, though his eyes let Roderick know he wasn't fooled. "Val and I had it put up as soon as we tested it for its strength."

"Good."

"It is, but we still need to come up with another plan."

"We've no time to waste," Roderick agreed.

Hugh nodded his agreement. "Shall we discuss it more once the meal is finished?"

Roderick readily agreed. The sooner he was away from Elle the better. He could think easier without wondering what she was doing or if she needed anything.

"Elle, could you stay as well?" Hugh asked.

Roderick felt as if he had just been punched in his stomach. He looked down at the table and struggled to appear calm.

"Of course," Elle said, her silken voice doing strange things to his mind.

He chanced a glance at her and briefly met her gaze. In that instant, he saw what he had dreaded – indifference. Whereas she used to smile at him and eagerly offer her suggestions, now he knew he would never receive one of those wonderful smiles again.

It was his fault. He had done that to her, turned her inside herself. His hatred grew by leaps and bounds.

All too soon, the meal ended and the tables cleared. Roderick listened as Mina and Hugh told stories of Stone Crest, and Val and Elle continued to talk. He barely heard a word they said as he strained to hear anything that came from Elle's lips. Instead, he heard nothing.

The hall cleared, leaving only them. Roderick could stand it no more and rose to stretch his legs. He heard Hugh talking behind him to Elle, but he no longer cared. The hall had grown smaller the longer he sat beside her.

He grasped a jug of ale just before a servant reached for it. Roderick wasn't one to imbibe too often, but he could have cheerfully drained the entire jug in one gulp. On his way to the jug, he had spotted a clean goblet that he wanted. After all, he couldn't exactly drink from the jug and not embarrass Hugh or Val.

Just as he reached for it, he closed his hand over another softer, smaller hand. He knew without looking it was Elle. His gaze followed her arm up to her face. Their eyes locked, and for a moment, he almost got the words past his lips, the words that might redeem him in her eyes just a little. But nothing came out.

"May I have the goblet?"

Roderick jerked his hand away and nodded. It wasn't until she had walked away that he allowed himself to breathe.

Mina watched Roderick intently. She leaned close to her husband. "Do you think he knows?"

"Knows what?" Hugh asked.

"That he cares for Elle, and that she also cares for him."

Surprise registered on her husband's face. "Do you really think so?"

"It's obvious to anyone who watches. They are drawn to each other."

"That could be the reason he is acting so strangely."

"And the reason Elle chose to stay in her chamber."

"Yet, she came down," Hugh reminded her.

Mina simply smiled. "That's because she wanted a chance to see him."

He sighed. "I'll never understand women."

"And that's the way we like it."

"What shall we do?"

Again Mina smiled. "Nothing. They will come together on their own if it's meant to be."

"Wife, I hope you are right," Hugh said sternly, though his eyes smiled. "I have no desire to see any of my men hurt."

Chapter Twenty

Elle still trembled from Roderick's touch. She had sworn to keep her distance from him, to protect herself from future hurt, but staying away from him was like staying away from the sun.

Her wobbly legs managed to return her to the dais where she slowly sank into the chair. Try as she might, her eyes were drawn to Roderick and the scowl upon his gorgeous face.

"What is it?" Val asked.

He had been the best dinner companion. His conversation had never lulled despite the fact she barely paid attention. Her mind was full of Roderick and the feelings he had drawn from her. She couldn't tuck them away as easily as he, and it bothered her. He didn't even seem happy to see her, but her heart had fluttered and nearly taken flight at finding him in the hall.

"Elle?"

She turned to Val and said, "I'm all right. Just tired."

"If there is ever a time you need me, don't hesitate to ask."

She wondered at his words but gave him a small smile and nodded. "I promise."

He moved his eyes from her face to just over her shoulder,

and she knew Roderick was there. She wanted to run to her room and hide, but Hugh had asked her to stay and she was loath to say no.

She turned in her chair until she faced forward and forced her eyes to look anywhere but Roderick. It didn't help that out of the corner of her eye she could see him just as clearly as if he were standing in front of her.

His arm moved near her face as he handed Val a goblet full of whatever was in the jug he had hurried to get. He didn't offer her the jug, but in her current state, if the beverage was alcoholic, she might be better served without it.

"Shall we begin?" Hugh asked as he filled his goblet.

"Aye," Val said after he drank deeply. "I'm anxious to see everything in place."

"We all are," Mina said.

Elle shuddered as she recalled the harpy speaking to her.

"Is something wrong, Elle? You've gone pale?" Val asked.

Suddenly, four pairs of eyes were on her. She waved away Val's question and shook her head. "The harpies are extremely intelligent. They set a trap for us on top of that building. We might be able to fool them once but not twice. Whatever plan we come up with needs to be carried out in one night."

Hugh stroked his chin. "That hadn't occurred to me, but since I haven't seen the harpies, it's difficult for me to comprehend just what we are facing."

"Elle's suggestion has merit," Val said. "I want them dead soon. I've no wish to continue locking horns with them."

"We could use the monastery," Mina offered.

This piqued Elle's interest. "It's nearby?"

"Not far, and it's abandoned, so setting a trap there could work to our advantage."

"They work as a team, so we might also think of separating them," Hugh said.

"And do what?" Val asked.

"Attack."

Elle shook her head before Hugh finished. "I would dearly

love to, but unless you have weapons that will pierce their metal wings and body, that won't work."

"What we need is a special Fae weapon," Roderick finally spoke.

Without looking at him, Elle said, "I didn't think we could get those."

"If they don't know what it's for, we might be able," Hugh said.

Val laughed. "Aimery knows everything. There is no keeping it from him."

"Unless I ask for it," Elle said. "Since Mina and I are two of five left from our realm, it would seem that it's in the Fae's best interest to keep us alive. To do that, we need to protect ourselves."

Mina smiled. "And if the Shields can have Fae weapons, why can't we?"

"Exactly," Elle said and returned her smile.

"It might work," Hugh said.

Roderick's eyes met Elle's for the brief second before he turned to Hugh. "It'll work."

"So we separate them," Val said. "How?"

Elle watched as Roderick tapped his finger against the bottom of his goblet as he contemplated Val's question.

"If we go in separate ways, they have no choice but to split up," Roderick said.

"This, of course, after we behead the first with the rope."

Val rubbed his hands together, his pale green eyes nearly glowing with anticipation. "And if they know Elle is one from the lost realm, then they will know Mina is also."

"Nay," Hugh thundered and stood. "I will not have my wife mixed into this."

Mina stood and clasped his hand in hers. "Too late, husband. I already am. There is nothing in this realm or another that will keep me from aiding Elle. We are in this together, and you had best realize that."

He ran a hand down his weary face. "Mina, if I lost you…"

Elle lowered her eyes. He didn't finish his sentence, but there wasn't a need. Everyone knew what he meant.

"I know," Mina said and rose up on her tiptoes to kiss him. "I feel the same way, which is why you'll be there to protect me, and Roderick will be with Elle."

Elle wasn't sure Roderick wanted to be with her, but with Mina's words, he couldn't say anything without questions being raised.

"Hugh, take some of your best knights with you," Val said. "Only a handful. I'll stay with Elle and Roderick."

"Aye," Hugh agreed. "You must. She's your assignment, and only you and Roderick can truly protect her."

Elle wasn't sure what Hugh meant but was glad she had an excuse to keep Roderick near her a little longer. She wasn't fool enough to believe she could ever seduce him or turn his eye to her again, but having him near calmed her – as strange as that seemed.

"So," Mina said as she resumed her seat and yanked Hugh down into his. "I suggest we let Elle, Roderick, and Val have the monastery."

"And where will you be?" Roderick asked.

Mina and Hugh exchanged a glance before Hugh answered, "The old Druid ruins."

"I don't like it," Val said. "I recall that place. The stench of evil was very strong there."

Elle watched Roderick's head barely jerk in a nod before he turned his face from her. She studied his profile for a moment, aware that he knew what she did. He was a strong man, both physically and mentally. Whatever he wanted, she was sure he got, and if there was something he didn't want, nothing could make him change his mind.

"Val," Hugh said, breaking into her thoughts. "What better place to kill a creature than from the very place one sprang?"

After a loud sigh, Val shrugged. "You have a point. Just make sure you are protected."

Hugh's eyes burned into Val's. "I'll protect my wife with

my life."

"Let's hope that isn't necessary," Roderick said.

"Since the places are determined," Val said. "How will we then kill them?"

"With the weapons Mina and I will obtain from the Fae," Elle said. "It's the only way unless you come up with a better plan."

"I can't help but think the harpies will outmaneuver us," Val said. "Your weapons will not be any different from ours."

Silently, Elle agreed with him. She had seen first hand what they were capable of, and they knew more about humans than humans did about them. Not a fair advantage. "They want me dead," she said softly. "Which means they'll go out of their way to succeed. We have a good plan in place that has a high percentage of success."

Hugh stood again and waited for Mina to join him. He then turned to look at Elle, Roderick, and Val. "The harpies could attack at any time. We need to be ready. I'm going now to choose my men."

"I wish there were time to take you three to the monastery," Mina said, her lips flattened in regret.

"If you can leave one of your men to tell us if something happens tonight, all should be set," Roderick said.

Elle rose to her feet. "Not quite all. We need our weapons."

Hugh cursed, and Roderick and Val exchanged a quick glance.

Without a word to the men, Mina walked to Elle and took her hand to lead her from the hall.

"Where are we going?" she asked Mina.

"Away from the men," she whispered.

Elle kept silent as she followed Mina to one of the towers. They entered, moonlight spilling into the empty room. She walked to one of the windows and looked down.

"Wow. We're higher up than I expected."

Mina chuckled. "It will hurt if you fall, so don't."

Elle found herself giggling. "How you can joke at a time

like this is beyond me."

She shrugged. "Life is short, and laughter is better than grimacing."

Elle faced her new friend. "Now what?"

"Call Aimery. He'll be more in tuned to you and will hear you better than me."

Elle swallowed. "Do I just say his name?"

Mina nodded and patiently waited.

"Aimery," Elle said and looked around the room. Yet, nothing happened.

"Again," Mina said. "This time close your eyes and think about him."

Elle did as instructed, recalling the first time she had seen the Fae. "Aimery," she barely whispered.

"You called?"

She opened her eyes to find Aimery standing between her and Mina. A smile pulled at her mouth. "It worked."

"Of course it worked," Aimery said and folded his arms over his chest, his silvery blond hair shining in the moonlight. "What is it you need? None of the Shields are hurt."

Elle didn't ask how he knew that, instead, she talked before she changed her mind. "The harpies are out to kill me."

"I know." Aimery shook his head and lowered his eerie blue eyes. "I am still trying to determine how they knew what you were and where to find you."

"Especially when the Fae cannot," Mina pointed out.

"Very true," Aimery conceded.

Elle licked her dry lips and clasped her hands together. "We wondered if the Fae would allow us to borrow weapons to keep safe?"

For several minutes, he stared at her without speaking. Elle feared he would say no, and just as she was about to go into a long speech as to why they needed the weapons, he asked one simple thing.

"Why?"

She glanced at Mina and knew Mina wasn't going to help.

This was her idea, and she needed to see it through. "The Shields have weapons gifted to them by the Fae, weapons that people would think came from this world, but upon closer inspection, the craftsmanship is too superb. Not to mention they pack a Hell of a punch."

Aimery grinned. "There are no weapons like ours."

"Please, Aimery," Elle beseeched him. "Without weapons from the Fae, Mina and I are as good as dead."

"I'll consider your request," he said just before disappearing.

Chapter Twenty-One

Roderick rose to his feet and walked to the stairs.

"Where are you going?" Hugh asked.

He stopped just short of stepping on the first stair and turned to his leader. "To prepare in case the harpies strike tonight."

"A moment please," Hugh beckoned.

Roderick couldn't refuse, though he dearly wished to. He strode back to the table and emptied his goblet.

"We need to discuss what will happen if Mina and Elle do not convince Aimery to give them weapons."

Roderick shrugged. "There isn't much of an option. We use the weapons we have and keep the women alive."

"He's right," Val added. "Our options are few. If we can kill one of the harpies, I'll be happy."

"If we kill one, we'll incite the others," Roderick said. "They're sisters, Val. Blood."

Hugh cleared his throat and rubbed his chin. "We have to make sure we keep them separated. They will still be able to do damage, but not nearly as much as if together."

Roderick turned to Val. "Did you bring your weapons?"

Val nodded. "I tried to reach yours but was unable."

"You don't have your flail?" Hugh asked.

Roderick shook his head. "I dropped it when a harpy threw me over the side of the building. In order to hang on, I had to let go."

"And your sword?"

"It, too, was lost."

Hugh swore, but Roderick wasn't worried. Several times in the past a weapon had been lost for many reasons, and the Fae always replaced them –immediately. Roderick had to worry as to why his hadn't been replaced yet. A talk with Aimery might be in order.

"I'll have my weapons returned," Roderick said and started for the stairs, only to find a woman blocking his way.

"Ev'nin', milord," she said and smiled.

"Good evening," he answered and tried to step around the buxom blonde servant, but she blocked him again. "Can I help you with something?"

She smiled, and he had to admit she was a comely looking woman. Some men might find her very attractive, but he didn't find anything alluring about her.

"Actually, you can. I've admired you all ev'nin'. You've a body women crave to touch," she purred as she stepped toward him and placed her hands on his chest.

With her breasts pressing against him, all Roderick could think about was how different his reaction was when Elle was against him. With Elle he wanted more, with this woman, he just wanted her away from him. "I'm flattered but not interested."

Her smile never waned. "I can get you interested," she said just before she reached up and kissed him.

Elle and Mina returned to the hall to tell the men what had transpired with Aimery when Elle saw Roderick locked in an embrace with one of the serving women.

"Oh, dear," Mina whispered behind her before walking

away.

Elle stood transfixed, unable to move or utter a sound. She had no reason to be jealous if another caught Roderick's attention, but she never expected to hurt so desperately at seeing it. When the woman pulled away, she saw Roderick's lips move as he spoke to her. Then, to make matters worse, the woman threw him a look of promise as she walked away.

She tried to turn away, really she did, but it wasn't in time. Roderick's gaze caught her before she was able to flee. The pain that lanced through her body was unbearable, giving her the push she needed to turn and rush up the stairs.

"Elle," she heard him call after her.

But she didn't stop. She wished she had never kissed him, never felt his hands on her body, and never wished and hoped there might be more.

She reached her room and slammed the door just before he reached it. She turned and stared at the door, then began to back away as she noticed she hadn't locked it. But she wasn't fool enough to try. Lock or no, Roderick would get in the room if he wanted.

"Elle?"

She didn't stop backing away until she hit the wall behind her. She didn't answer him, didn't trust her voice not to betray her.

"Please open the door."

She shook her head, not caring that he couldn't see through the thick wood.

Roderick stared at the door barring his way. He had seen the anguish on Elle's face as the serving woman had walked away. Despite how he felt about himself, he could not allow her to think he was meeting that woman later.

He didn't expect to understand women. Why Elle would be hurt to find him with another when she herself didn't want him didn't matter. All he knew was that he couldn't allow her to think him so womanizing that he would go from one to another in so short a time.

149

With just a kick or a shove he could have the door open, barred or not, but he didn't wish to explain to Hugh why the door needed to be fixed. He reached for the handle and pushed. The door opened easily, and he found Elle across the chamber against the wall.

"Elle," he began.

She shook her head. "I don't want to hear anything."

All his life he had thought what women wanted was simple, but Elle had changed all that in a short time. Now, he no longer trusted what he thought he knew of women. "Why are you upset?"

She laughed hysterically and crossed her arms over her chest.

"What is humorous? I am here to protect you, same as Val. If you are upset, we need to know."

"I was just shocked to see you with that woman," she said, refusing to meet his eyes.

"Why?"

Her head jerked around, her eyes wide with disbelief. "Why?"

"Aye, why?" he asked again and advanced toward her.

He had told himself to stay away because he had known his body would react to hers in a way that left him panting and so passion filled that he couldn't see straight, yet what did he do? He walked into her chamber. Alone.

The hurt in her clear blue eyes made him feel disgusting. Elle was a good person, she didn't deserve to be hurt. She deserved to be cherished, loved until she was sated and lying naked across his body. That image had his blood rushing toward his rod. He knew just how passionate a woman Elle was, and it was too much of a temptation not to experience it again.

"It's my fault," she said.

Her words halted him just before he reached her. "What do you mean?"

"I've been alone for so long, and the few men I have dated

weren't very nice."

Anger bubbled up from nowhere at her words. He wanted to find those men and pummel them into the ground, right after he kissed her.

"Gorgeous men like you don't pay attention to women like me," she whispered, her head bowed. "When you...kissed me, I...thought...never mind," she finished and tried to turn away.

But Roderick brought his hands up and braced them against her shoulders to keep her still. Her eyes rose to him, questioning and a little fearful. "By the gods, you have no idea, do you?"

"What?" she asked.

Could he have been wrong? What he thought was regret in her eyes at the passion they shared earlier might have been something else. Regardless, being this close to her and touching or kissing her was driving him wild with a need so intense he wondered if it was real.

Her head cocked to the side, and her brows drew together. "What do I have no idea about?"

He stepped closer to where her body was pressed tightly between him and the wall. "The allure you have." He purposefully lowered his voice, and when her eyes moved to his mouth he all but smiled. "It's in your eyes," he continued in his low voice and kissed each eye. "Where innocence meets the fire burning inside."

His knees bent until his mouth touched her chin in a light nip. "The way your chin turns up with stubbornness and your refusal to give in."

Next, his mouth moved to just over her left breast where her heart was. "You have more giving and kindness than I have seen in a very long time," he whispered before he rose and looked down at her.

Her eyes had darkened, and her chest rose and fell rapidly as if she had run a great distance. He had purposefully left her mouth for last. Now, he leaned close and saw her eyes close.

"But this," he said and lightly licked the corner of her

mouth. Her lips parted instantly, but he didn't taste more of her. Yet. "This mouth of yours is the sweetest part of you. Despite all that you have been through," he paused and kissed the other side of her mouth, "you haven't cursed anyone."

His lips kissed all around her mouth but never fully on. "Only given, sharing your life and any ideas you might have."

She shook her head. "I'm not good. All I have thought about was having you kiss me again."

It was Roderick's undoing. He had wanted to tease her until she begged for him, then he would love her until she couldn't move. But instead of him having the upper hand, she had gained it without even knowing it.

"Elle," he whispered just before he crushed her against him and wrapped his arms tightly around her while his mouth gently coaxed and teased some more.

"Please," she begged, her hands clawing at his shoulders.

He knew what she wanted. He wanted it, too. Desperately. With a firm grip of control over his body, he pulled away from Elle until she looked at him. "No more misunderstandings. I want you."

She swallowed and licked her lips that were swollen from his kisses. Possessiveness overtook him in a raging storm. He would defend her to the death. Not because it was his duty as a Shield, but because of the way she made him feel – as if he were almost whole again. Something he hadn't felt since before his brother's death.

"I want you as well." Her voice broke over the words, but it was the sweetest thing she could have told him.

"There will be no stopping this time," he warned. "I was barely able to the first time, but now that I've had a taste of you, I want it all."

She shivered in his embrace. "I'm offering it all. Take what you want."

Chapter Twenty-Two

Elle couldn't believe it was happening. Roderick wanted her, really wanted her. He, the most handsome man she had ever laid eyes on, wanted her, plain old Elle. It had to be a dream.

Yet, when he laid her down on the bed and his weight fell on top of her, all she could do was sigh. Loudly.

"By the gods, you feel good," he murmured against her neck as his mouth placed delicious kisses along her throat and jaw.

She wanted to tell him how good he felt on top of her, but her words lodged in her throat as his legs moved to either side of her and he rose up on his knees to move his mouth down her chest. Her breasts grew heavy just knowing he was about to touch her. Then his hands cupped her breasts. His mouth placed kisses everywhere but her aching nipples.

"You've too many clothes on."

She agreed, but had no wish to move to discard them. When he moved away from her, she reached for him to stop him. Gingerly, he dodged her hand, a small smile pulling at the corners of his lips.

"Impatient are you?" he asked as he removed his jerkin.

Elle would never tire of looking at his chest. It was picture perfect, what men at gyms worldwide tried to achieve, Roderick had naturally. Her hands itched to run along the silken skin, to feel his chest hair spring against her hands and his muscles bunch and flex.

When his hands went to his pants, she bit her bottom lip in anticipation. She knew just how muscular his legs were from riding with him on the motorcycle and the horse, but to see them bare, now that was something she was dying to see. Not to mention the most sexual part of him –his cock.

Her tongue grew thick in her mouth, her palms began to sweet, and liquid heat pooled between her thighs when he discarded his pants and stood before her in all his glory.

"Oh, my," she managed as he walked closer to her. She reached for him, but he took her hands and shook his head.

"If you touched me now it would be all over. I want this to last at least a little while."

And who was she to argue. "Later?"

"Later," he promised and pulled her to her feet. His fingers reached for her gown, but she quickly halted him. "My turn," she said and pushed him down onto the bed.

She had never stripped in front of anyone before, but the idea had taken root at seeing him disrobe. She wanted to see the desire burning brightly in his eyes. Deftly, her hands began to unlace the back of her gown. She bared one shoulder and saw him take a deep breath. With a gentle tug, the gown slid from her other shoulder. Her hands were locked over her breasts, so the material couldn't go lower.

His gaze lingered on the straps of her bra. Elle wasn't afraid to try new things, but she liked her bra and panties and preferred those to what was worn at the time. She glanced at the apricot straps of her bra and then lowered her eyes to catch just a hint of lace showing at her breasts. She lowered her arms and the gown fell to her hips, exposing her upper body.

When Roderick licked his lips, Elle grew bolder at the knowledge she turned him on. Thanks to the belly dancing

DVDs she had ordered, she knew just how to jerk her hips to send the gown falling into a pool of material to her feet.

He rose, but she raised a finger to stop him. Roderick sank back onto the bed with a small curse, though his eyes never left her. The only thing between her and Roderick was the expensive Italian lace bra and panty set she had bought from Victoria's Secret. It was a secret pleasure she indulged in often and something she was going to miss dearly.

She turned until her back was to him, then reached around and unclasped her bra, sending him a seductive smile over her shoulder. His eyes smoldered, and his cock jerked in reaction. A thrill raced through her as a delicious heat began to pulse at her core. She turned toward him, her hands cupping her breasts to keep her bra in place as the straps slowly fell from her now bare shoulders.

When his lips parted and his breathing increased, she became bolder. A seductress she was not, but apparently she was doing something right. She followed what she wanted to do, what felt right, and had hit the mark so far.

With a roll of her shoulder, she removed one arm from within her bra, careful to keep her breasts covered. She replaced that arm, and with the other she let the bra dangle from her fingers before dropping to the floor.

"I cannot stand much more," Roderick warned.

She repressed her giggle of excitement. "There isn't much left."

With a deep breath for reassurance, Elle dropped her arms. She hadn't known what he would do, but the painful moan that came from him wasn't it. If it wasn't for his bulging arousal reaching up to the sky and his eyes such a dark blue they looked nearly black, she wouldn't know if he liked what he saw or not.

"More?" she asked and gave him a wink.

"You're going to kill me, woman."

She laughed. "Not likely."

"Elle," his voice warned.

She knew he wouldn't stay on the bed much longer, but she really wanted to finish undressing. Watching him watch her was a new excitement, and one she wanted to repeat very soon.

With her fingers hooked in her panties, she ran her fingers around the edge, skimming her stomach and hips. Since the panties were a thong, she realized he might never have seen one before, and she wanted to see his reaction. She turned around until her backside faced him, and instantly his hands reached out to touch her.

His finger scorched a trail from her lower back over one cheek and then the other. "Very…beautiful."

His voice was thick, as if he found it difficult to speak. With his eyes downcast, he watched his finger play over her derrière.

"More?" she asked over her shoulder.

He nodded and raised his gaze to her face. "I want to see all of you."

She easily slipped her thong off and then turned to face him. He kneeled before her, his hands tracing a line from her waist, down her legs, and back again. His touch was light, admiring, and she wanted more. Much more.

"Spread your legs," he said as he bent down and placed a kiss next to her belly button.

Elle was quick to obey. The throbbing at her sex doubled, and her breasts cried out for attention as she wondered where he would touch her and what he would do.

"Wider."

She was afraid if she opened them too far she wouldn't be able to hold herself up if he did touch her, yet she did as requested and spread her legs wider.

His hands never left her. If they weren't skimming over her legs, they cupped her backside or her waist, learning her as she wished to learn him. His hand caressed her breasts many times, but never did he fondle them or touch her nipples that were so hard they hurt.

Nor did he touch her sex. And she ached as she had never

ached before. The need for release continued to grow, and he hadn't even touched her yet. When his finger ran up her leg toward her core, she eagerly waited to feel him dip into her, yet he left her waiting. His finger grazed her nether lips as he explored the flesh between her thigh and her sex.

"So soft," he mumbled and blew his hot breath on her.

She jumped and sighed at the sensation.

"So responsive, and I haven't touched you yet."

She wanted to say 'I know', but it was lost on a moan as he blew on her again. "Oh, God," she whimpered.

And then finally he gave her some relief. One hand reached up and found her breast and her aching nipple while his other hand continued to fondle her sex. He rolled her nipple in his fingers making it even harder than before. With his mouth, he licked and kissed around her stomach and inner thighs, but never touched the place that ached for him the most.

She was so wrapped up on if his tongue would find her that when his finger skimmed over her swollen, sensitive sex she gasped. But she wasn't given long to think about it as his tongue reached out and flicked over her clitoris.

"Roderick," she cried as her legs gave out on her.

He easily caught her and rose to place her on the bed. "It's just beginning," he said with a twinkle in his dark blue eyes.

He didn't waste any more time talking. Sitting on his knees between her legs as she lay on her back, Elle found herself completely exposed to him. She should have been embarrassed, but instead she found herself feeling sexy, alive.

His finger traced the sensitive skin between the juncture of her legs and her sex and sighed with pleasure as he continued the assault. Every once in awhile his finger might touch her sex, but it was just the slightest of touches that left her aching for more, wondering when he might touch her again.

She arched her back off the bed as he reached up and claimed a breast in his hand. They were heavy and swollen, her nipples begging for attention that he gladly gave them. He did things to her nipples that she had never experienced before.

The pleasure was intense and immediate. She moaned for more the same time she begged for release.

"Not yet," he whispered and kissed her stomach.

Her fingers threaded in the covers as she strained against the pleasure building inside of her. Until finally he parted her nether lips and his tongue ran across her clitoris. She cried out from the sensation and the fact he wouldn't repeat it.

"Please," she begged.

With one hand still on her breast, he moved the other until he cupped her sex and lightly pressed. Elle sighed and rubbed herself against his hand. Just when she had found a tempo, he removed his hand. She bit her lip to keep from crying out again, knowing whatever he did next would send her even higher.

He didn't disappoint.

With his thumb he ran it back and forth over her swollen clitoris, barely touching, just the hint of something there while at the same time squeezing her nipple. The pleasure/pain sent her spiraling to another plane. Time and place were forgotten as he played her body as if he had known her forever, and her body welcomed him, eager for more delights he might share. Just when she was about to find release, he stopped.

This time she did cry out.

He leaned over and took her mouth in a kiss that awoke desires deep inside of her. She opened her eyes to look at him as he pulled away. "What have you done to my body?" she asked as she pulsed and squirmed for more.

"Awakened your desires."

"More," she said and heard his laughter.

He moved back between her legs. "There will be more. Much more."

There was no more time for talking as his tongue replaced his thumb on her sex. Bliss swept through her with each lick. He explored every inch of her sex with his tongue, then circled back up to concentrate on her clitoris.

She moaned and writhed on the bed as he increased the

tempo, and just as she was about to come, he would stop and kissed her thighs or fondled her breasts. She didn't know how much more she could take.

And then it started all over.

Elle lost count of the many times he would take her to the edge only to bring her back. She was mindless with desire, searching for the fulfillment she knew he could give her but kept just out of reach.

And just when she expected him to pull back again, he kept the tempo. As her orgasm continued to build, she let herself go and experienced the most mind blowing climax she had ever known. Yet it didn't end.

Roderick never stopped moving his tongue. As she reached peak after peak, he brought her higher and higher, and then he rose above her and entered her in one thrust. He was large, and it took her a moment to stretch to accommodate him, but it was well worth it to feel his thickness inside of her.

Then he began to move within her. Elle wrapped her legs around his waist and met his thrusts. She never knew it could feel so wonderful. He stroked her long and slow, then quick and short, each time building the tension in her sex. To her surprise she felt yet another orgasm building.

And when it hit, she cried out and clutched Roderick's shoulders as the waves of pleasure consumed her. She felt him plunge deep inside of her, touching her womb as he threw back his head and his seed emptied into her.

Roderick looked down at the woman in his arms. She lay spent, just as he wanted her, but it wasn't enough. He wanted her again, and he began to fear there would never be enough.

He slowly pulled out of her and rolled to his side, taking her with him. As he gazed at the top of the canopy, he found himself smiling. He had never given so much to a woman before, never wanted to please one so desperately, yet she had satisfied him more than he had expected or hoped for.

She had touched a part of him he had locked away at his brother's death. A piece he thought forever dead. Now he wondered otherwise.

"Roderick," she whispered and snuggled closer.

He ran a hand down her bare arm and kissed her forehead. Whatever happened now, Elle Blanchard was his.

Chapter Twenty-Three

Elle awoke before Roderick. She had expected to wake to find him gone, and it pleased her immensely to discover him still in her bed. Slowly, she moved out of his arms until she was between his legs. Thankfully he slept on his back or her plan would have had to wait for another time.

After all the pleasure he had given her, she wanted to give some to him, so she planned to do something she had never done before.

She admired his perfect form, letting her hands trace over his slim hips and bulging thighs. And to her amazement, as she watched, his rod had begun to thicken. It wasn't hard yet, but she planned to take care of that. She bent forward and took him in hand. He was smooth and partially flaccid. She blew on him as he had done her and saw him grow a little more. She repeated the action twice more, and though he wasn't fully erect, he was half way there.

Next, she cupped his sacs as she closed her other hand on his staff. He moaned. Instantly, her gaze went to his face, begging him to sleep yet. When he didn't open his eyes, she moved her hand up and down his rod until he grew stiff. A smile pulled at her lips when he issued another moan and turned his head.

Her breath caught in her throat, for she wasn't done yet.

With one hand still on his rod, she bent until she took him in her mouth. Silky smooth, hot and hard as granite. How something could be all three was an amazement to her, but she enjoyed learning him.

Since he was so large, she couldn't take him into her mouth as far as she would have liked, but she found licking him like he was a sucker was what he liked best by his moans. It wasn't until she felt his hands on her shoulders that she knew he was awake.

"By the gods," he groaned. "I've never felt anything so good."

It was just what she wanted to hear, so she doubled her efforts.

"Stop or I spill now," he said between clenched teeth.

But Elle didn't want to stop. She wanted to pleasure him.

"Elle." He sounded pained, but still she didn't stop. She used her other hand to cup his sacs again.

"I want to take you with me," he begged, but nothing he could say would stop her.

He stiffened beneath her, and she assumed he was about to orgasm. She should have known better. He moved with lightening speed, and Elle next found herself face down on the bed and Roderick on top of her.

"I just wanted to please you," she said, wishing she had managed it somehow.

"You pleased me more than you know, but I want to take you with me when we climax," he said huskily in her ear.

Chills of anticipation ran down her body. After the lovemaking last night, Elle didn't know what he could possibly do different, but then she realized what she knew of sex could be held in a thimble. Obviously, Roderick knew much more.

Which was quickly grasped when his hand reached down between her body and the bed and found her pulsing bud. Since she was already turned on by playing with him, it took just a few flicks of his finger to bring her to the edge. Her sex clenched as she eagerly awaited the feel of him inside of her.

His laughter rumbled around her. "Not yet," he said.

She was really beginning to hate those words, yet how could she when he brought her such pleasure?

He nudged her legs open with his knee, and with his hand against her womanhood, he urged her hips up. His finger slipped inside of her heat, and she groaned.

"Yes," she whispered, her hands tangled in the sheets.

He removed his finger and rubbed it against her bud while his hand grasped her hip to keep her still. She was breathless and begging for more when his finger again dipped inside of her. This time another joined the first, spreading her. She closed her eyes and rocked back against him as her pleasure built. Then, his hands were gone, replaced by his long, thick staff. She bit her lips and moaned as he filled her slowly.

He eased out and pushed farther inside of her. He repeated the process until he was fully sheathed. Elle waited for him to begin pumping inside of her, but he didn't move. Instead, he reached around and fondled her clitoris.

She tried to move her hips, but he kept her locked in place. She cried out at the pleasure and not being able to move. Then, his hand shifted to her backside. He used both hands to rub her cheeks, and she used that time to slowly move her hips so that she might reach orgasm. She should have known better.

Just as she thought he didn't know what she was doing, he put one hand on her hip and the other he placed on palm down just below her lower back. He began to slowly move inside of her. The pressure built yet again, and she moaned low in her throat when he began to thrust faster. The feel of him against the back of her legs only added to the sensations assaulting her.

It was all it took to send her over the edge. She splintered into a million pieces as Roderick thrust inside of her, his tempo ever increasing. She was just coming down from her climax when he cried out and thrust deep within her.

She was slow to return to reality, but when she did it was to find Roderick on his stomach looking at her. She returned his smile and linked hands with him.

"Wow," she said.

His smile broadened. "I think we woke the castle."

"I don't care." She laughed because it was true. "After the way you've made me feel, I wouldn't care if the entire realm knew what we were doing."

"Did you sleep well?"

"Extremely well, thank you," she said and kissed his lips. "How about you?"

"Very well."

"Since no one woke us, I think it's safe to say the harpies didn't arrive last night." She shouldn't have mentioned them. As soon as the words were out of her mouth his smile slipped, and he frowned. She parted her lips to say more, but his finger over her lips quieted her. Sounds from the bailey drifted through the arrow slits, and she felt Roderick relax beneath her.

"There is much we need to do today," he said as he sat up and leaned against the headboard.

Elle sat back on her haunches, her hands on her knees. "I know."

"Are you worried?"

She nodded. "For the safety of the people of Stone Crest. I know you, Val, and Hugh can take care of yourselves, but you can't watch everyone."

"Nay, we can't. If I were able to save everyone, I would."

"I know," she said and took his large, calloused hand into hers. He had a man's hand, not smooth and womanly, but rough and beautiful.

"Did you speak with Aimery last eve?"

She nodded and raised her gaze to Roderick.

He grinned. "Are you going to tell me what happened?"

"Of course. I asked, but he wouldn't give me an answer right then. He said he needed to think on it."

"Hmmm," Roderick said and leaned up to give her a kiss. "Just like Aimery.

You may not know the answer until the last moment. What kind of weapon did you ask for?"

She gulped. "Was I supposed to be specific? Mina didn't tell me that?"

He shrugged. "I don't think it matters. The Fae give you a weapon they think will be the most useful to you."

"Then I'm in trouble."

"Why?" he asked, his brow furrowed.

Elle turned and scooted off the bed. "I don't know how to use any weapon, and if he waits, it's as useless to me as if I didn't have one at all."

Roderick didn't answer her right away. He swung his legs over the bed and stood. He didn't bother with clothes as he walked to her. "I know you would feel safer with a weapon, but I'll protect you with my life."

"I don't want it to come to that. I would much rather have you alive."

"Me, too," he answered with a grin.

His gaze shifted over her shoulder, and he murmured something in a language she had never heard. Elle turned around to find three weapons propped against the wall near the bed.

"I didn't hear anyone come in," she said as Roderick walked to the weapons.

"These are my weapons that were left in your time."

"Then how did they get here?" His answers were only confusing her more.

"Aimery."

She looked around the room, expecting Aimery to jump out, and she quickly reached for a blanket to cover herself.

"He's already come and gone," Roderick said over his shoulder. "There's no need to hide yourself now."

"You mean he saw us?" she asked as she looked under the bed.

A chuckled was her answer. "I'm sure he did."

"Oh, God," she moaned and buried her head in her hands. How could she face him now? And what if he told the others?

Strong hands took hold of her shoulders and raised her to her feet. "Don't," Roderick said and moved a lock of hair from her face. "Aimery will say nothing, so do not worry yourself."

Easy for him to say, she thought. She nodded and glanced at the weapons. "I thought you only had a halberd and a sword."

"I did," he said as he crossed his arms over his chest and stared at her.

"Then were did the other weapon come from?"

"I think it's yours."

Elle studied him a moment before she turned toward the weapon. It looked somewhat like a bow and arrow but much smaller.

He moved beside her and picked the weapon up. "The Fae have many weapons. This is one that Aimery thought would suit you."

"But I don't know how to shoot a bow and arrow."

He shrugged and smiled. "Looks like you better learn."

She held the magnificent weapon in her hands. It was light but sturdy. She pulled back on the string as if she had notched an arrow. It fit her hands perfectly, as if someone had measured her.

Upon closer inspection, she saw many designs that looked like Celtic knots that were so popular in her time, but different, more fantastical and intricate.

"It's beautiful," she said and ran her hand over the wood.

"Everything the Fae does is beautiful."

She raised her eyes at his tone, as if he were remembering something. "Have you ever been to their realm?"

He nodded, a sad look on his face. "Few are allowed there. I was one of them. Hugh has been summoned to the palace a few times, and his descriptions are incredible. I would love to see it sometime."

"I bet you'll get your chance."

A knock sounded on her door then.

She glanced at Roderick who stood stock still. Since he refused to look at her, she padded across the cold stone floor to the door.

"Who is it?" she asked.

"Lady Mina said you might need a bath this morning."

"Yes, please," Elle replied and unbarred the door.

The servant hissed and ran towards the hearth. "The fire went out, milady," the maid said.

"I'll tend to that," Roderick said.

Elle jerked around, hoping he had covered himself, only to find him standing with his clothes on. She shivered in the blanket, not used to the cold climate of England. A fire would be nice, not that she had noticed while snuggled up against Roderick.

The maid hastily moved out of the way as Roderick bent down and began to rekindle the fire. While the wooden tub was brought in and filled with water, Elle stood back and watched.

With steam rising from the tub and a fire crackling, all Elle wanted was to be alone with Roderick. And it seemed he was of like mind.

"Out," he ordered the servants.

When the door closed behind the servants, Roderick walked to her and took her in a toe-curling kiss. She sighed and melted against him, letting the blanket fall at her feet.

He pulled back and gazed down at her. "I need to see Val and Hugh."

"I understand," she said, hoping he didn't see too much disappointment in her eyes.

He made a sound much like a growl. "You must know I wish to stay."

She laughed when he rubbed his stiff rod against her. "I know. I just didn't want the night to end."

"It won't," he promised and released her to retrieve his

weapons. "I must go before I throw you on the bed and ravage you again."

"If I can't tempt you, then you had best leave," Elle taunted as she lifted one leg and placed it on the edge of the wooden tub.

"Don't be long," Roderick said before he slipped out the door.

Elle sighed as she sank into the hot water. Not because the heat helped melt some of the iciness from her bones but because she looked forward to seeing Roderick.

Chapter Twenty-Four

Roderick raced to his chamber. He stripped his clothes and tossed them in a corner as he hurriedly washed with the cold water left in a bowl for him. He and the other Shields never worried about clothes. The Fae took care of all of that.

He lifted the lid to the trunk by his bed and found clothes just to his taste. And as he knew they would, they fit perfectly. With his boots back on, he stood and gazed at his bed. Images of the night before flashed in his eyes, and he longed to return to Elle, but there was much to do. Just as he reached for his sword, he felt something behind him. His hand closed over the hilt the same time he swung around.

Aimery easily sidestepped the blade and cocked a brow at Roderick. "Do I take that to mean you didn't want your weapons returned?"

Roderick cursed and lowered his sword. "I had no idea it was you. I felt something and attacked."

Aimery frowned. "Have you ever felt my presence before?"

"Nay," Roderick answered as he strapped on the scabbard and sheathed his sword.

"Strange, don't you think?" he asked.

Roderick raised his gaze to the Fae commander. "Aimery, things stopped being strange the moment I became a Shield."

Aimery chuckled, a sound Roderick rarely heard. He eyed the Fae again as he ran his hands through his hair.

"Thank you for giving Elle her weapon," Roderick said after several moments had passed and Aimery hadn't spoken.

He shrugged. "There was no real reason to deny their request. If able, it's her and her people that will end the evil here, as well as giving you a clue as to how to end it on your realm."

Roderick closed his eyes. While he had been with Elle, he had forgotten the awful pain he lived with every day, the yearning to return to his realm to see his family again, but more than that, the forgiveness he needed to beg for. Instead, he had only thought of her and the happiness she had given him.

He opened his eyes and looked at Aimery. "You delivered the weapons?"

Aimery nodded.

"Aren't you going to say anything?"

"What is there to say?" Aimery asked. "You are grown men. I don't stop any of you from finding what little happiness you can while doing your duty."

"But this is different," Roderick argued. "Elle is different."

Aimery dropped his arms and took a step toward him. "Aye. She is. More than you realize."

"What's that supposed to mean?" Roderick hated it when Aimery gave hints to things but never spoke. "Don't do this, Aimery. Tell me."

"You already know," the Fae said.

"By the gods," Roderick hissed and turned away to pace. "Lecture me on keeping away from the very women that could aide us, reprimand me on keeping my mind on my duty and not on…other things."

"It wouldn't do any good," Aimery spoke calmly. "Besides, what you and Elle shared was mutual. You didn't take advantage of her. She wanted you as much as you wanted her."

Roderick stopped pacing and ran a hand through his hair. "Then why do I feel as though I've betrayed you and the Shields."

"Only you can answer that," Aimery said.

"I want her."

Aimery nodded. "I know."

Roderick sank onto the bed. "Yet, I cannot have her, can I?"

Aimery didn't reply, which was all the answer Roderick needed.

"No one really knows the future," Aimery finally said. "Only time will tell."

When Roderick raised his gaze, Aimery was gone. There was no use cursing the Fae since he wasn't there to hear it. Instead, Roderick rose and walked from his chamber. He had a sinking feeling that the harpies would attack very soon.

"There you are," Val called as Roderick stepped into the great hall. "Hungry?"

"Starving," Roderick answered, though it wasn't food he wanted. What he yearned for sat in a hot bath upstairs.

He tried to ignore Val's watchful gaze as he helped himself to the platter of food on the table. Finally, he could take it no more.

"What?" he asked.

Val shrugged. "I know not. You look...different."

"What are you talking about?" he asked before taking a bite of the warm bread.

"I have no idea," Val said with a grumble. "Have you spoken to Elle this morning?"

Roderick stopped chewing and glanced at Val. "Aye. Have you?"

Val shook his head as he took a drink. "I wondered how she fared during the cold night. She isn't used to this weather."

"She fared fine."

He waited for Val to ask him how he knew that, but

thankfully, his friend didn't. "My weapons were returned last night."

"I figured they would be," Val said. "I also think we need to finish preparations."

Roderick set down his knife and turned to Val. "I agree. I think our time is about to run out."

"Do you know something?" Val asked, staring at him closely again.

"Nay," Roderick answered and turned away. "I just have this...feeling that the harpies are closing in."

"You have never had anything like this before."

Roderick rubbed his neck. "I know."

"What do you think it is?"

"I haven't a clue, but I sincerely hope I'm wrong."

Val tapped his finger on the table. "I don't think you are. In Rome, we learned to listen to the instincts of the people that were able to channel certain things."

Roderick chuckled and looked at him. "I am not a seer, Val."

"This I know," Val said. "However, you sound convinced of your feelings, and I have known you long enough to trust you."

Hugh walked up and stood between them. "Trust Roderick for what?"

"He thinks the harpies will be here soon," Val answered.

Roderick turned his face to Hugh and his questioning gaze. "I cannot explain it."

"No need," he replied. "Let us start immediately then."

Val and Roderick scooted their chairs back and rose from the table to follow Hugh from the hall. Suddenly, Hugh stopped and turned to them.

"Roderick, did Elle receive something this morn?"

"Aye," Roderick answered. "Aimery gave her a weapon. And Mina?"

"Her as well."

"I knew he would," Val said and walked from the hall.

Roderick waited for Hugh to continue for it was obvious something bothered him. "What is it?"

Hugh shrugged. "I am not comfortable with Mina being involved with this."

"Nor I, but we need both her and Elle. If it were up to me, I would lock them away until it was all over."

Something changed in Hugh's gaze as he stared at him, and it made Roderick uncomfortable. It was as if Hugh could see into his soul and what he and Elle had done the night before.

"How did Elle fare last night?"

Roderick ground his teeth. "She fared well."

"Good," Hugh said and smiled widely.

Thankfully, Hugh ended the questions and turned to exit the castle. Roderick followed but stopped at the door and looked back. He had hoped Elle would have come down by now, but he suspected Mina had trapped her.

He shut the door behind him and stepped out into the chilly air as snow began to fall. His gaze lifted to the sky, listening for anything odd. So far, nothing, but he knew, knew just as he knew the moon would rise that night, that the harpies were on their way.

"Roderick," Hugh called.

He hurried to Hugh and Val and the handful of knights that Hugh had personally picked.

Elle hated to rise from the warm water, but she had no other choice if she didn't want to turn into an icicle when the water began to turn cold. She jumped out of the tub and stood before the roaring fire on a rug and hurriedly toweled off.

The towel wasn't the fluffy, soft cloth she was used to, but she made do. Her teeth were chattering as she wrapped her arms around herself and ran to where she had discarded her clothes and lingerie the night before, only to find them gone.

Since she was turning blue, she grabbed the blanket she had used earlier and wrapped it around her. That's when she spied her clothes neatly folded on a stool near the wall. They looked clean, as if someone had washed them.

Remembering how Aimery had taken care of the weapons, something urged her to check the chest at the foot of the bed. She opened it to find her lingerie inside. She squealed with delight at spying her expensive garments.

"Thank you, Aimery," she said.

"What are you thanking him for?" Mina asked as she stepped into the room.

"Your weapon?"

Elle laughed. "Well that, too, but this," she said and held up a sapphire blue bra.

Mina's eyes widened. "What is that?"

"My lingerie."

"What?"

Elle laughed again and decided it best to show instead of tell. She dropped the blanket, not caring that she was nude beneath and clasped her bra in place and tugged on the matching panties.

"The saints," Mina said in awe.

"They are wonderful," Elle said, delight pouring through her.

Mina knelt at the chest and shifted through them. "So, Aimery brought these to you?"

"I guess. And I didn't even ask for them."

"And the gowns?"

Elle was about to put on her gown from the day before but stopped at Mina's words. "What clothes?"

"These gowns."

She walked to Mina and the chest and looked inside to see the beautiful gowns. "Oh, my," she said as she held up a dark blue gown.

"Put it on," Mina said as she stood.

Elle hurried to comply and wasn't surprised when it fit. "Amazing."

"Aye, the Fae are like that. The color brings out your eyes."

Elle bit her lip as she thought of Roderick.

Mina laughed and began to lace up the back of the gown. "And Roderick will love you in it."

"What?" Elle tried to act as though she had no idea what Mina was talking about, but she knew she failed miserably.

Mina tied off the gown and walked around Elle until she faced her. "I'm not as blind as my husband or Val. I could practically see the tension between you and Roderick. And since you're smiling this morning, I gather everything has worked out."

Elle had never been so embarrassed. In her own time, sleeping with someone that interested you wasn't a bad thing, but this was Medieval England. Things were different. "Please, don't think badly of me."

"Why would I?" Mina asked, her lips turned down in a frown. "You are my friend."

"But things are different here."

Mina laughed and rolled her eyes. "Not so different."

Elle blew a breath out of her mouth, unaware just how much Mina's approval meant to her until that moment.

She sat and let Mina brush her hair and pull it into a thick braid that fell to the middle of her shoulder blades. Elle stood out with her bangs, but she didn't mind. She still loved the haircut, which was something that occurred maybe once every ten years for her.

"We must hurry," Mina said as she walked to the door.

Elle grabbed her new weapon and followed her. "Why?"

"The men are waiting for us."

"For what?" she asked as she lifted the hem of her skirt and prayed she didn't tumble down the narrow stairs.

"We must prepare for the harpies."

Elle stopped. The harpies. How had she forgotten about them? She looked around the great hall and thought of Mina and Hugh and the people of Stone Crest. Her thoughts then skidded to Val and Roderick. Would they all come out of this alive?

"Elle?"

She looked down at Mina's questioning gaze. "I don't know how to use my weapon."

"That will be rectified this morn."

Chapter Twenty-Five

Elle followed Mina into the bailey, quickly tying her cloak while juggling her bow and arrows. Her eyes immediately scanned the crowds until she found Roderick. The sun glinted off his golden waves, and she itched to run her fingers through the shoulder length locks again.

Suddenly, he turned and looked at her. They shared a secret smile before he and Val walked toward her.

"Up already?" Roderick asked.

Elle was hard pressed not to laugh while she shivered. "Actually, I've been up awhile. I found a few...interesting...items in my room."

"Aimery brought her a few things," Mina explained. "The chest is filled with gowns and a few other things."

"Other things?" Val asked. "Like what?"

"Personal items," Elle said and glanced at Roderick.

Val grumbled beneath his breath. "We need to go."

Roderick turned and motioned to someone Elle couldn't see. He turned back to her. "We are going to the monastery and the Druid ruins."

Elle didn't answer him, just looked at the horses being brought to them. It had been a long time since she had ridden, and only with a western saddle. She didn't know how she was going to manage in a dress.

"You'll do fine," Roderick whispered as he walked her to a small gray mare and hooked her bow and arrow on the saddle. "She has a sweet disposition, and I promise that I won't let anything happen to you."

"You better not," she said over her shoulder as she reached up to pat the mare. "She's pretty."

"Not as beautiful as you," Roderick whispered right before he lifted her onto the horse.

Elle didn't have a chance to reply as he walked to the white horse beside her and mounted. Butterflies flew madly around in her stomach, and all she could think of was leaning over and tasting his scrumptious mouth again. Lord, the man could kiss.

Just thinking about it made her a little dizzy and managed to warm her a tad. He should have a warning label next to lips. She giggled at her thinking that turned into an outright laugh as Val looked at her strangely.

"Nothing to worry about. My wits are about me," she told him.

"I hope so," Val said as he nudged his horse and rode out of the gates.

She turned to Roderick. "Isn't he going to wait for us?"

"He'll scout the area to make sure no one is lying in wait."

"Oh. All right." She was so ignorant of the goings on of a castle, but she realized most twenty-first century women would be as well.

They waited a moment longer until Hugh joined them with five other knights. Elle had the suspicion that they were going to be doing more than just looking at the monastery and the ruins, but she could be patient when needed.

She not so eagerly nudged her gentle mare to follow Mina out of the bailey. A glance over her shoulder showed Roderick behind her as well as half of the knights Hugh had picked. The other half were with Hugh in the lead.

Since this was her first time out of the castle walls, her

arrival not counting, she soaked up the beauty. Despite the icy fingers of winter grasping at her, the snow atop the trees and on the ground was a marvelous site. On the road, the snow had turned from white to brown with all the travelers, but Elle didn't mind. It was a part of life, a life that everyone accepted and made the best of.

In truth, there wasn't much about Houston that Elle missed. A toilet, hot shower, and her Diet Dr Peppers were the most missed. She wondered how long it would take her body to realize it was without caffeine and hit her with a headache.

She blew out a breath and watched it cloud in front of her. This kind of cold she rarely experienced in Texas. With the high humidity and nearly constant ninety-degree heat, it was no wonder she was a walking icicle.

"Is the cold bothering to you?"

She turned to find Roderick had moved up beside her. "What clued you in? My teeth chattering or the fact that I can no longer feel my toes and fingers?"

He chuckled and unlatched his cloak. With only his knees as a guide, he moved the stallion to her mare and threw his cloak around her.

Instant heat surrounded her. She sighed and gave him a grin over the fur at the collar of the cloak. "Thank you."

"Think nothing of it."

"Won't you become cold?"

"I am accustomed to this weather. You aren't."

She couldn't argue with him there. How she wished for a hand warmer and thick, wool socks for her feet. And a hot cappuccino.

"I gather Aimery left you something you greatly approve of?"

Elle chuckled. "Oh, yes, and I think you will like it as well."

His eyes darkened, and he leaned closer. "Is it your lacy underthings?"

She nodded and heard him growl low in his throat. "Wait

until you see all of them. I don't know how he knew, but I could kiss him for it."

"Don't say that too loud, he might just ask for that."

"Trust me, Roderick. A kiss would be a small thing to ask after bringing me something like my bra and panties."

He smiled. "He did me a service as well. Think you he might wish for a kiss from me as well?"

"I doubt it," she said through her laughter. She sobered as they entered the forest.

"What is it?"

She glanced at him to see his face lined with concern and shrugged. "I don't really know. I've always loved trees. Where I grew up it was nothing but trees, sometimes so dense you couldn't see but a few feet in front of you."

"And now?" he prompted.

"This forest doesn't seem to be," she searched for the right word and finally settled for, "normal. I can't name it, but there is something off."

"Aye, I feel it, too," Mina said over her shoulder.

Roderick tightened his fingers on the reins. He had felt it before they entered the forest, but the deeper they ventured the more it penetrated him.

"What is it I'm feeling?" Elle asked him. "Is it the harpies?"

He shook his head. "Nay. Evil lingers here." Which was odd since it had been several months since the gargoyle had been killed.

Elle slowed her mount. "There is something here then?"

"Nay. Just a lingering presence of evil," he told her.

"What fun," she mumbled sarcastically, yet Roderick still heard her.

By the smile on Mina's face, she too heard Elle.

Finally, they reached the Druid ruins. He saw Elle press her lips tightly together as he dismounted.

"I don't like it here," she said.

Mina quickly dismounted and looked at Elle. "Really? This

has always been a favorite place of mine, except for the fact my brother and sister brought one of the creatures from here."

"Wow. Really."

Roderick hid his chuckle at Elle's dry tone. "We won't stay long. Hugh wants to get the men set up in their positions so everyone will know where they are supposed to be when the time comes."

She turned her clear blue eyes to him. "Don't leave me."

Her words hit him like a battering ram. He lifted his arms as she easily went to him. With a gentle tug he brought her against his chest and slowly lowered her to the ground. "I'll only leave if you ask me to."

"That won't happen. I need you."

And he needed her, more than she realized. Maybe later he would tell her, once the harpies were taken care of and he had a few moments before another assignment was given to him.

"Roderick. Elle. Over here," Hugh called.

Roderick gave her a little shove to get her going as he quickly grabbed her bow and arrows. He caught up with Elle before she reached the others. It was then he noticed the smaller version of Hugh's massive crossbow.

"How did I know Aimery would give you that?" he asked Mina.

She shrugged and glanced at her husband. "Aimery knows me well."

"Not to mention she has talked me into firing my crossbow on a few occasions," Hugh added.

Roderick turned and handed the small bow and quiver of arrows to Elle. "It's time."

"For what?" she asked hesitantly.

"To start your training."

She visibly swallowed. "In front of all these people?"

"The knights will not stay here," Hugh said as he walked towards her. "It'll be just the five of us."

Roderick waited for her to agree. She gave him a small nod, and Hugh and Mina walked some distance away to start her training. "It'll be Val and I that teach you how to use the bow."

"Too bad Gabriel isn't here," Val said as he approached. "He is a master at the bow."

At Elle's worried look, Roderick was quick to assure her. "We are also good, Gabriel is just better. Just as we can all use the weapons, we each excel in something."

"Makes sense," she said and fingered the bow.

Val handed her his bow. "First, I want you to try and use mine."

Roderick crossed his arms over his chest and watched as Elle took the bow from Val.

"I've seen people do this on TV, and I even held one at a Renaissance Faire, but I've never used one."

"Here," Roderick said and walked to her side, molding his body to her back. He placed her hands on the bow and used his hands and body to show her proper placement.

He found it hard not to lean down and place a kiss at the hollow of her throat or cup her shapely breasts. His rod, having a mind of its own, had grown hard at the thought of contact with her, and now that he was snuggled against her back he was finding it hard not to rub his aching rod against her.

"I feel you," she whispered.

Ah, ye gods, Roderick silently moaned. He squeezed his eyes shut and tried to focus.

"Do you need me to instruct her?" Val offered.

"Nay," Roderick all but yelled.

At Val's chuckle, Roderick knew Val knew just what he was going through. But Roderick would have his revenge later.

"Now, steady your left arm and pull back on the string with your right," he instructed Elle.

She tried three or four times. "I can't budge it."

Roderick took the bow from her and handed it to Val. "Let's try yours," he said and retrieved it. He realigned himself at her back and turned her until she again had the right bearing.

"Do you remember where your hands go?" he asked.

"Of course," she said through her chattering teeth.

He really was going to have to do something about keeping her warm, he realized. Maybe he could find some thicker socks for her or gloves to keep her hands covered but nimble enough to still use the bow.

When she had placed her hands correctly, Roderick raised her arms until she was in position. "Now, pull back on the string."

This time she was able to not only move it but pull it back as far as she needed to. She let out a little squeal of surprise and happiness.

Roderick released her as she turned towards him.

"How?" she asked.

"My bow," Val explained, "was made on this realm. I have had it since my days in Rome. 'It was made for a man's strength."

"So mine is made for a woman?" Elle asked.

Roderick shook his head. "Not necessarily. The Fae make each weapon for a particular person. Not everyone can use all their weapons. Aimery took into account your size, what strength you have, and also just why you would need this weapon."

"For example, you could easily use my halberd," Val said as he tossed her the weapon. "And you might even be competent enough to wound or kill someone, but because it is my specialty and because that weapon was made for me in particular, it responds better for me."

"There is magic in them?" she asked, her eyes wide.

Val smiled widely. "Of course."

Roderick turned her back around and handed her an arrow. "In other words, Elle, this weapon knows what you can and cannot do. It senses if you are hurt and can't ready it as you normally do."

"So the more I use it, the better it'll know me."

He smiled down at her. "Exactly."

"Then show me," she urged him.

Roderick and Val spent the next half hour showing her how

to correctly notch an arrow standing, sitting, lying on the ground and even rolling. Elle was a fast learner, impressing Roderick tremendously.

"I could do this better in pants," she grumbled as she yanked her skirt out of the way. "This is such a beautiful gown, too."

"Don't worry," Val told her. "The gown will be as good as new tomorrow."

She stared at him a moment as if seeing if he was jesting or not. When she turned to him, Roderick nodded. "It's the way of the Fae."

"I see," she said. "Can I shoot the arrow now?"

"Aye, I think it's time." Roderick unclasped his hands from behind his back and again placed himself at Elle's back. And just like every time before, his body raged to life.

"I think we'll have to do something about that."

He groaned at her words, happy Val couldn't hear them. "Hush or I'll take you now."

"Promises, promises," she taunted.

"Ready yourself," Roderick said. Once she had complied, he moved his right hand from her arm to his side. "Keep your left arm steady, pull back on the string until your right hand is even with your ear, and think about where you want the arrow to go."

"Anywhere I want it to go?" she asked.

"Anywhere. Line up the location with the end of the arrow and release."

She took a deep breath and did as he asked. They watched as the arrow embedded itself in one of the enormous fallen pillars.

Roderick looked at her. "Is that where you aimed?"

"Sort of. Beginners luck?" she asked.

"Not exactly," Val said with a laugh.

"Try again," Roderick said.

This time he stood back and let her do it herself. Each time she came closer and closer to her goal, until finally she hit her mark.

Roderick caught her as she flew into his arms and kissed his cheek, but his smile vanished when she kissed Val's cheek as well.

Chapter Twenty-Six

"I did it," Elle said as she danced around the ruins.

"Keep at it," Val advised as he walked to the horses, a huge grin on his face as he winked at Roderick.

Roderick glanced at Hugh and Mina and found her progress had gone just as well. He was anxious to see the monastery and plan their attack now that Elle had learned her bow well enough. She still needed practice, but she had skill, and the bow reacted to her nicely, which helped.

"Thank you," Elle said as she stood beside him, her breath coming in great gasps and billowing between them.

Roderick put his hands on his hips and regarded her. "How will you thank me?"

"Oh, I'll think of something," she teased.

"Ready?" Hugh asked from the horses.

"Ready," Roderick answered. With his hand on Elle's back he guided her to the horses and helped her mount.

"To the monastery," Hugh said and kicked his horse into a run.

"About time," Elle said and followed Hugh and Mina.

Elle snuggled deeper into Roderick's cloak. If the harpies didn't kill her, the cold would. Thankfully she didn't have to guide her mare. The horse followed the others on her own, leaving Elle to gaze around the forest.

It really was a beautiful sight and was probably even more glorious in summer where she could actually see things instead of shivering. The elation she had of learning to use her bow had quickly worn off, but the trepidation of soon encountering the harpies was growing by leaps and bounds. At least she felt a little safer having a weapon and being able to use it.

They arrived at the monastery much sooner than she anticipated. By the looks of it, it had been abandoned for a very long period, and though Elle had little doubt that ghosts inhabited the crumbling stones, anything was preferable to freezing to death.

She didn't wait for Roderick to help her dismount, though she should have since she misjudged the distance and nearly fell. His large hands clasped her arms and held on until she regained her feet.

"Thank you," she mumbled.

He sighed and shook his head. "I'm really going to have to do something to keep you warm."

She could only nod in response. Her feet stumbled over rocks hidden beneath the layers of snow, and each time Roderick was there to help her. Finally, he kept his arm around her in an effort to keep her steady.

"Elle?"

She heard the worry in his deep voice and wished she could soothe him and tell him she was all right, but the fact was, she was far from all right.

"Cold," she said between her chattering teeth.

In an instant, she was lifted into his arms as he shouldered his way past the others and into the dark monastery. Though it was still cold inside, it held more warmth than the snow.

"Get a fire lit," Roderick thundered as he sat and wrapped his arms around her to lend her his heat.

She rested her head against his shoulder and tried to lick her lips. Big mistake. They were dry and cracked open immediately. Out of the corner of her eye, she saw men gathering wood to start a fire. As soon as the flames gathered enough strength, Roderick moved them closer. The heat penetrated Elle instantly. She sighed and let the warmth envelope her. When she had warmed enough, she raised her head to find everyone sitting around the fire.

"I'm sorry," she said and tried to scoot off Roderick's lap.

He held onto her tightly, refusing to let her move. "Stay and get warm," he whispered.

"I've kept everyone waiting."

"Nonsense," Mina said. "It's unforgivable of us to continue on when you aren't adjusted to our climate. I keep forgetting that you are from somewhere extremely hot."

Hugh laced his fingers through Mina's. "Once you've warmed yourself, we'll proceed."

"There isn't time," Elle argued.

"There is," Val said as he walked behind her and Roderick.

Elle was embarrassed and grateful to the people around her. Though she knew time wasn't on their side, they were waiting for her to thaw before going forward.

"Next time, warn me," Roderick said as he rubbed his hands up and down her arm.

She smiled. "I will."

"How many levels does the monastery have?" Val asked as he looked around the room.

"At least six," Hugh said. "Mina and I came through the underground tunnel the first time."

"Underground," Roderick and Val said in unison.

Elle nearly laughed.

"Aye," Mina said. "On the return trip to Stone Crest I will show you the entrance."

"Or what is left of it," Hugh said.

Roderick's face was thoughtful for a moment before he asked, "What is in the lower level?"

"Storage chambers," Mina answered. "It's very dark in them. No windows."

Roderick and Val exchanged a glance. "Could be useful," Val said.

"Most of what you see here is how the rest of the monastery is," Hugh said.

"Someone came in and tore through the place in search of something."

"A pity," Elle said, and everyone nodded.

Elle listened as Hugh, Val, and Roderick discussed different strategies to use against the harpies until she could no longer sit on Roderick's lap comfortably. She had more than warmed herself, and it was time to get moving.

She slid out of his lap, managing to evade his hands. "I'm much warmer," she told him.

"Are you sure?" he asked as he stood.

She smiled, loving the concern he had for her. "I'm sure."

"Then let us explore," Hugh said as he walked to a door towards the back of the large room.

Elle hastily looked around her. The room was at least three stories high with gorgeous stained glass windows, though the majority of them had been broken.

She didn't mind when Roderick put his hand on the small of her back to guide her. His strength gave her comfort on a level she couldn't begin to describe. With all the twists and turns they took going into each room, up the stairs and down the stairs, Elle had lost her sense of direction. All the rooms began to run together in her mind. It wasn't until they ventured to the level below ground that Elle knew where she was.

The hallways were extremely narrow and short. The men had to duck their heads for the most part. They came to the first room to see the door broken into pieces.

"I was in here," Mina said. "My brother, or who I thought was my brother, had me locked in here."

"How awful," Elle said as she peered inside the tiny room.

Mina visibly shuddered. "It was."

They moved on, and every room they came too looked exactly as the first one did. Elle lost count of how many rooms, but she estimated about a dozen or so.

"To the roof," Val said as he hurried out of the tight hallway.

The last thing Elle wanted to do was venture back outside, but she wasn't about to complain. It might take her a while, but eventually she would become accustomed to the weather.

If you live that long. Not to mention, no one said you would be staying.

True, but it wasn't as if she could easily return to her time. And she wasn't sure if she wanted to anymore.

She climbed the stairs to the roof, Roderick at her back. Several times she thought she heard him say something, but each time she looked back he would give her an innocent look.

Finally, she stopped and faced him. "I know I heard you that time."

He gave her a heart-stopping smile and turned her around, then gave her a gentle nudge to continue up the stairs. "I'm just admiring the view," he whispered.

Warmth spread through Elle like syrup over pancakes. The urge to turn and kiss Roderick was strong, very strong. And since she couldn't do that, she did the next best thing, she swayed her hips more as she climbed the stairs.

She heard his hiss as he sucked in air and smiled to herself. Teasing him was such a joy that she regretted when they reached the top.

"Thank the gods," she heard him murmur.

"Something the matter?" she asked innocently.

His gaze smoldered. "A few more of those stairs and I would've had to throw you down and ravaged you."

She lifted her eyebrows. "Sounds interesting."

He growled, causing her to laugh and draw the looks of the others. She left him and walked to Mina.

"So this is where you destroyed the gargoyle."

Mina nodded. "Aye."

"Show me," Elle urged her.

She followed Mina to the far left corner and looked over

the side, ignoring the biting cold of the snow on the edge. With the heavy snow she couldn't see anything though. Her toe hit something, and she looked down to find a piece of stone the size of a softball at her foot.

Her gaze rose to Mina. "The gargoyle?"

"Oh, aye."

Elle turned and braced her hip against the edge of the roof. "Aren't you afraid he'll return?"

Mina shook her head. "We ended his life. Another could come back to take his place, but this one is gone."

"I hope the harpies are as easy," Elle said, though she knew they wouldn't be.

"Don't fear," Mina said softly. "The Fae chose the men well. They'll succeed."

"They better," she said and let Mina pull her back to the group.

"It's big enough," Val was saying as they approached.

"For what?" she asked.

"Battle," Roderick answered.

She looked around, not liking the idea at all. "This gives them too much room to fly. I think we should keep them below, hinder them all we can."

"She has a point," Val said.

Mina turned toward the stairs. "Now that we have the layout of both the ruins and the monastery, let us return to Stone Crest and plan."

Elle was all for that idea. By the time they reached the main room, someone had put out the fire. She hurried outside to her mount and reached for the reins when Roderick's hand encircled her waist and lifted her.

"Thanks," she said breathlessly once she was in the saddle and had arranged both her cloak and Roderick's.

He gave her a wink and vaulted onto his horse. The journey back to Stone Crest took even longer since Mina and Hugh took them to the entrance of the underground tunnel.

Elle gawked at one wall that remained of the once small

cottage. "What happened?"

Hugh cursed, and Mina laughed nervously. "The gargoyle chased me here," Mina explained. "Hugh followed and while I found the door to the tunnel, Hugh kept the gargoyle out."

"I'd have loved to see that," Val said as he walked his horse around the cottage.

Roderick nodded in agreement and nudged his horse toward the cottage. "Where is the door?"

"Under the roof," Hugh answered.

Elle looked at the roof that now lay on the ground as if the walls had been kicked out from under it. She didn't fancy lifting it to find the door. The men, however, seemed to have other ideas. Roderick, Hugh, and Val talked privately far enough away that Elle couldn't hear.

"I hate being left out, too," Mina said from beside her.

Elle fidgeted with the reins. "Yes, but you'll find out later what they spoke of."

"So will you."

Elle turned to find Mina smiling at her. "Not sure if I'll remember to ask."

Mina burst out laughing, causing the men to stare at her oddly. Elle managed to control hers to only a giggle, but it was hard. Every time she and Mina would look at each other they would start laughing.

She watched Hugh roll his eyes and turn his mount away from the cottage. "To Stone Crest," he said and nudged his horse into a gallop.

Elle waited for Roderick to reach her. "What was that about?" he asked.

"Girl talk."

"Girl talk?" he repeated.

She nodded, a smile on her lips. "That's right. Girl talk."

"Think you can manage a gallop?" he asked.

She took a deep breath. "I'm willing to try," she said and clicked to the mare who instantly moved into a gallop.

Elle managed to hang on and after a few moments, she felt

comfortable enough to loosen the reins and give the mare her head. The horse didn't bolt, but she moved from a gallop into a run.

The cold air pierced Elle's face like little needles, but it was worth it to ride again. She had forgotten just how much she missed it until that moment. She pulled gently on the reins to slow the mare to a cantor as they neared the giant gate of Stone Crest. The mare again responded instantly, never giving Elle the least bit of a problem.

"Impressive," Roderick said as he came up beside her.

Elle laughed. "I used to ride when I was younger. It's different here, especially with a dress on. I had forgotten just how much I loved to ride."

"We'll have to remedy that," he promised.

A smile pulled at Elle's lips and stayed there until they were seated in the great hall. She stayed huddled in hers and Roderick's cloak, wishing for a hot cup of anything to drink. She would even take hot chocolate if they had it, despite her dislike of chocolate.

But hot drinks were dismissed as they began to plan.

"We all ride to the forest where the rope is," Hugh said.

Roderick steepled his fingers. "Once we get one of the harpies to follow us-"

"And hopefully beheaded," Val interjected.

"-then we split up as planned."

Hugh nodded. "I think we need to lead them on a chase, tire them out if we can."

"They fly faster than the horses run," Elle pointed out.

"Not through the trees," Roderick answered.

Chapter Twenty-Seven

Roderick barely tasted the food at the noon meal. He inhaled and breathed Elle's sweet fragrance that was solely hers. After the morning riding through the forest and inspecting first the Druid ruins and the monastery, he was eager for some time alone with her, though he knew it wouldn't come until night.

Which wasn't good for his aching cock. He closed his eyes and recalled the feel of her tight sheath as he thrust in her. Sweat beaded his upper lip as he clenched his hands under the table in an attempt to gain control of his raging body. No one had ever affected him like this. A feather light touch brought him back from the brink. He cracked open his eyes and turned to find Elle watching him.

"Everything all right?" she asked softly.

He shook his head.

"What is it?"

"You. I need you."

A slow smile spread across her face. "Not any more than I need you. I'm not sure what you did to me last night," she whispered, "but I want more of it."

A heady dose of male pride swept through him. He may not

have been her first, but he was the first to bring out the real woman in her, the passion that longed to be freed. He leaned towards her. "I will do that to you every night."

She sighed as her lips parted and her eyes closed. "How is it just your words set my blood afire?"

"Just think what my mouth can do."

Her eyes snapped open, her pupils dilated, and her breath came faster. "Stop," she begged. "I can't take anymore."

"I haven't even begun."

"I know," she said and grabbed his hand under the table.

For long moments they sat as they were. Roderick straightened and turned to talk to Val as Elle spoke with Mina. Elle's hand moved over his, her nails softly raking across his skin, sending chills racing through his body. He squeezed his eyes shut and tried to concentrate on what Val was saying but didn't succeed.

"Roderick?" Val asked. "Are you feeling well? You look a bit…green."

"Fine," Roderick managed to get out. "Just fine."

Val gave him a look that said he knew Roderick was lying and rose from the table.

Roderick turned toward Elle. "You've got to stop."

Her clear blue eyes turned to him. "I can't. I can't stop thinking of you or touching you."

It was more than he could take. He wrapped his hand around hers and rose from his chair, taking her with him. She didn't shout or complain when he all but dragged her from the hall and up the stairs.

"The others saw," she said as she lifted her skirts to match his stride.

He waited until they reached the hallway before he answered. "I don't care. Do you?"

"No."

Roderick stopped at his door and opened it for her. "Good, because I want everyone to know."

"You do?" Her chest rose and fell rapidly from their hasty

trip up the stairs.

He nodded and pulled her into his chamber. "I do."

When he tried to pull her towards the bed, she pulled back. "Why?"

"I want them to know you are mine."

She raised an eyebrow and cocked her head to the side. "Yours?"

"Mine," he said and drew her into his arms.

She didn't resist as he lowered his head and kissed her. White-hot passion streaked through him at her sweet taste. The need to feel her, to be inside her overwhelmed his good intention of taking her slowly.

"I need you now," she said against his cheek.

He shook his head. "I'll hurt you."

But she didn't listen to him. Instead, she lifted her gown to her waist letting him see the dark blue lacy underthings she wore. He nearly swallowed his tongue.

"By the gods, Elle," he said and pushed her against the wall.

Raw desire snaked through him as he unfastened his trousers and released his aching rod.

"Oh, my," Elle said and licked her lips.

In one motion, Roderick lifted her until her legs fitted around his waist, pushed aside the lace at her sex, and drove inside of her. She screamed and clung onto him as if he were life itself. He knew exactly how she felt. He held steady for a few moments, knowing he wouldn't last long, yet wanting to take her with him.

"Please," she begged while trying to move her hips.

Roderick gave in and began to move inside of her. Slow at first, but his tempo quickly increased until mindless passion and the need to feel her clenching around him filled his mind. The closer he came to his climax the more he knew there was something distinctly different about Elle, something he wanted to hold on to.

She shouted his name and spasmed around him, sending

him over the edge, to a climax so powerful it nearly brought him to his knees. With Elle still clenching around his spent rod, he walked to the bed and laid her down. He pushed inside her once more, and she whispered his name as one last shudder left her body.

Elle was really starting to hate the harpies. If it hadn't been for them she might never have met Roderick, but now, because of their impending attack, the time she could have spent with him was next to none. She stopped as they walked from his chamber and glanced at him.

"What is it?"

"Well," she said and blew her bangs off her forehead. "I'm a little worried about returning to the hall."

He smiled and leaned a shoulder against the stone wall. "Why? Because they know what we were doing?"

"Well, yeah," she answered and almost gave him a "duh".

He laughed and took her hand to bring it to his lips to kiss. "Don't be. They're all adults."

"Which means nothing. Trust me, Roderick. I know how some people react to a couple…together…outside of marriage."

His eyes narrowed slightly on the word marriage, and she inwardly cringed.

"And this bothers you?"

She sighed and tried again. "What bothers me is that they might look at me differently."

"I'm sure they will."

She was about to scream. Needing to burn off the growing frustration, Elle paced for a minute. Once she had calmed down, she faced Roderick again. "I know they will look at me differently. I'm more concerned with how they will treat me." Before he could speak, she went on. "I don't want them to think badly of me or treat me unkind because you and I are sleeping together."

"They won't."

She waited, hoping he would say more. "That's it? 'They won't' How are you so sure?"

"You'll have to trust me."

She let him guide her to the stairs since she knew she couldn't shake his confidence in the matter. With a silent prayer that he was right, Elle descended the stairs to find everyone still at the dais.

"How long have we been gone?" she whispered to Roderick.

"An hour or so."

"About time you two returned," Hugh said as they approached the dais.

The great hall with its warmth from the fire in the humongous hearth, beautiful tapestries, and various displays of weapons was one of Elle's favorite places. Even the many candelabras hanging from the walls or standing amid the great hall added a touch of ambiance that a light fixture had never done in her time. Yet, despite her love of the castle, she couldn't dispel the anxiety she had returning after leaving with Roderick.

Elle searched his eyes for any hint of cruelty but found only the same open friendship she had first seen. A glance at Val and Mina showed the same thing. A smile pulled at her lips at her unfounded worries. She sat when Roderick held out her chair.

"I told you," he whispered to her just before taking his chair.

For several minutes, Elle sat back and watched the other four talk amongst themselves. Every so often, Roderick would glance at her and smile. And for the first time in her life, she felt truly sated. Not because of the great lovemaking she and Roderick had shared, but because she was with people that understood her. She longed to speak of her future and just what would happen to her once the harpies were dead, but she couldn't bring herself to do it.

One thing at a time. First, we need to kill the harpies and destroy the stone.

"He'll come with them," she blurted out.

Roderick turned his head to her. "Who will?"

"Alex," she said, remembering the way he laughed as Jennifer fell to her death. "He has the stone. If the harpies come, so will he."

Hugh nodded solemnly. "We know.

Elle's eyes looked from Val, who refused to meet her gaze, to Roderick. "Why didn't you say anything to me?" she asked Roderick.

"We thought you might forget about Alex, and after what happened, that wouldn't be a bad idea."

"I can't forget him," she said. "At least not until he is dead and the stone destroyed."

"He'll die," Val said, his voice low and deadly.

Hugh grinned with excitement. "And the stone will be destroyed."

Elle was lucky to know such good people, but she couldn't help but worry. "Is there already a plan for Alex?"

"It depends on who he follows," Hugh answered.

Roderick leaned back in his chair. "And if I'm correct, he'll come after you," he said to Elle.

"Great," she mumbled.

"Between Val and I, we will get him."

Elle prayed he was right. "All right. Once we split up after the first harpy is beheaded. What happens?"

The three men smiled and leaned close.

Chapter Twenty-Eight

Roderick scratched his whiskered face as he walked into the stables. He had seen the red marks on Elle's soft cheeks after their lovemaking, and he would be sure to be clean shaven from now on so as not to harm her.

Her wild abandonment just hours earlier still brought a smile to his face. Even now his body wanted her again, and with each taste, his hunger for her grew. He glanced at the gray sky, hoping he would see the harpies. He was anxious to get the battle started so he and Elle could speak of the future. After so many years in the Shields, he knew better than to talk of the future before a battle. Better to wait until he defeated the enemy.

A quick check of the saddles and weapons let Roderick know everything was in order. He stood against the stall of the white stallion he had ridden earlier and rubbed his velvety nose.

It was then he found himself wanting to return to his realm. He wanted to see his family and introduce them to Elle. The guilt he had carried with him, for what seemed like an eternity, no longer weighed as heavily as it did before.

"I see some things have changed."

The cool voice of the Fae commander reached Roderick's ears. He didn't turn to Aimery but continued to stroke the stallion's muzzle. "What do you mean?"

Aimery walked around until he stood in front of Roderick. "Your guilt has lessened."

"Not really. I have much to pay for, but I have a different outlook now."

"Because of Elle."

Roderick sighed. "I wondered when you would speak of her."

"I do not pass judgment," Aimery said. "I have always told you all to take what pleasure you could find."

Roderick looked away, not yet ready to speak of just how he felt about Elle since he really didn't know what it was he felt.

"Yet, I sense that she is more than just a passing bed partner," Aimery said softly.

"Probe into my mind all you want," Roderick said and raised his gaze to the Fae. "The fact is, I don't really know."

The smile vanished from Aimery's face. "Though I do."

Roderick's stomach fell to his feet like a leaded ball. "Tell me what you know."

"I cannot, and you know it."

Roderick turned away in disgust. "Did you come here to torment me or for some other purpose."

"Actually, I came to warn you that the harpies will be here before nightfall."

Roderick spun back to face the Fae. "How do you know?"

Aimery's upper lip turned up in disgust. "We can smell their evil soaked bodies hours away. I hope all has been prepared."

"Of course. You know Hugh. Everything has been thought of."

"Good, good," Aimery said and walked to the stable doors.

Roderick could stand it no more. He had to know. "Aimery, will she live?"

For long moments the Fae didn't answer. Slowly, he turned to face Roderick. "There is a slim chance," he said, the sadness pulling at his handsome features.

"What can I do to ensure her safety?"

"There is nothing you can do. You are doing everything there is to be done."

"Then that isn't enough," Roderick said and strode to Aimery. "If there is a chance she will die, I want to know how to deal with it."

"That I know not. If I did, I would most certainly tell you." Aimery sighed and looked away. "You have to understand, that although we are able to see many things, some things are fuzzy, unreadable at times."

Roderick flexed his clenched hands. "And this is one of them."

"Aye. It must be because of how closely Elle and Mina are to us and our future."

"You need her," Roderick tried. "She is important to Earth, to your realm, and to mine. She cannot die."

Aimery reached up and clasped Roderick on the shoulder. "Then keep her safe."

"I will guard her with my life," Roderick promised.

Aimery lowered his hand to his side. "I have news from your realm."

"I don't want to know," Roderick said and turned away.

"Your father is dying."

Roderick's feet stopped as emotion welled up inside of him. "Not yet. I haven't redeemed myself to him and the rest of my realm."

"You have served the Shields faithfully for many years. King Theron and Queen Rufina have agreed that you may return to your realm immediately."

Roderick squeezed his eyes closed. Either Elle or his father. How could he choose?

"How long does my father have?"

He felt more than saw Aimery's shrug. "I know not. I know

what happened, Roderick. Face your father again and receive his forgiveness so that you can go on."

"When must I leave?" he asked and opened his eyes.

"Now."

Roderick swallowed hard, picturing Elle's lovely face as she called his name as she climaxed. "I need time."

"There is no time," Aimery said as he walked to him. "I don't envy you the decision you must make. Your father or the woman who could be your heart's match."

"Is there anyway I could leave now and return before the harpies arrive?"

Aimery stared at him for several heartbeats. "We could try, but I don't think so."

But it was worth a try. "Listen for my call," Roderick said and rushed from the stables to find Hugh and Val.

Val sat alone next to the tall stone wall that surrounded the castle, sharpening the point on his halberd. He looked up as Roderick approached and frowned. "What is it?"

"I have just had a visit from Aimery."

Val cursed and jumped to his feet, shook off the snow, and headed towards the castle doors. "Best to find Hugh so you need only tell it once."

They found Hugh inside the armory as he inspected weapons his knights would use. "Aimery," he said as Val and Roderick approached.

"How did you know?" Val asked.

Hugh shrugged. "I know that look. What happened?"

Roderick took a deep breath. "The harpies will be here before nightfall."

Both men cursed long and loud.

"We need everyone in place, especially a lookout," Roderick continued.

Val nodded. "Three are already in place."

"That is not all Aimery told you," Hugh said as he searched Roderick's face.

Roderick sank onto a barrel and looked at his two friends.

"My father is dying, and there is a chance Elle will die this night."

Val whistled and propped his foot on another barrel. "You must choose."

Roderick nodded.

"Go," Hugh said. "We will watch Elle for you, keep her alive until you return. You need to see your father, to explain what happened."

Roderick looked at his leader. "How do you know?"

Hugh smiled ruefully. "I pieced things together through the years. I don't know what happened exactly, but whatever it was needs to be explained so you can receive your family's forgiveness."

"There is a chance that I can go to my father and return before the harpies arrive," Roderick said.

"Then do it," Val urged. "Find Elle and explain to her."

Roderick put his head in his hands. The last thing he wanted to do was tell Elle why he had no other choice but to return to his father before died. If she didn't hate him for leaving her, she would hate him for what he had done.

"I cannot," he mumbled.

The armory grew silent as the three men turned to their thoughts.

"Do you love her?" Hugh finally asked.

Roderick lifted his head. "I do not know. What I feel for her is hard to put into words, but is it love?" He shrugged.

"I'll tell her," Val offered. "Go to your father."

Roderick turned to Val. "I can't ask you to do this."

"You didn't. I offered," Val said with a smile. "I give you my word that I'll keep Elle safe. Go so you can hurry back."

Roderick knew he would forever been in Val and Hugh's debt. He stood and gazed at the two men. "I cannot thank either of you enough."

"Don't try," Hugh said and pushed him towards the door. "We'll be waiting for you."

Roderick hurried from the armory and out of the castle to

the stables. Just as he reached the stables he called out for Aimery who appeared instantly.

"Well?" Aimery asked.

"Let's go so that I may return."

Aimery smiled and then glanced over Roderick's shoulder, his smile slipping.

"What is it?" he asked as he looked over his shoulder.

And spotted Elle.

She was coming towards him, but Val quickly intercepted her. Yet, Roderick couldn't take his eyes from her beautiful face. And when the anger and surprise shown in her eyes, he knew then he had lost her.

"Fight for her when you return," Aimery said.

Roderick knew he was right. He turned back to Aimery and nodded. "Take me to Thales."

And that's when it happened. The instant Aimery touched him, Roderick smelled the evil.

Chapter Twenty-Nine

Elle blinked, her mind barely registering that Roderick had left her. What was it Val had said? That Roderick needed to return to his realm.

"Elle," Val yelled and pulled at her arm.

She turned and looked at him as if through a fog. Her mind had stopped working the instant she heard Roderick was leaving her. After he had sworn never to.

Val grabbed both her shoulders and shook her. "Elle, look at me."

She blinked again and focused on his face. "He left me."

"He'll return," Val promised. "We must leave. Now."

"Why?"

"The harpies are here."

And then she heard their unmistakable screams, screams she never wanted to hear again. Like nails on a chalkboard, their cries would rival that of a banshee. She lifted her skirts and followed Val into the stables. While Val began to saddle the horses, she barred the door after Hugh, Mina, and the knights ran inside.

"Did the call go out to the others?" Hugh asked as he saddled his horse.

"Aye," two of the knights answered in unison.

Elle ran to her mare and gathered her weapons to place on her saddle now that Val was done. She tossed him the bridle to his horse and then moved to mount hers. It was on her third try that she felt hands on her waist.

Once in the saddle she looked down at Val. "Thank you."

"We'll take care of you," he promised as he vaulted on his horse.

The small group looked at each other in the stables before Hugh gave a nod.

"Ready?" he asked.

Elle was anything but ready. She knew Val would keep her safe, but they needed Roderick. As the group burst from the stable, Elle tried to recall just what reason Val had said Roderick needed to leave.

"Stay with me," Mina said as she rode beside Elle.

Elle nodded, her throat unable to make a sound as the harpies flew towards them. The clank of their wings as they grew closer drowned out the sound of the horses' hooves as they rode through the bailey and out the gates.

Elle glanced over her shoulder to see the gates closing behind them. At least the people of Stone Crest would be safe, she thought.

Her horse veered to the left as she struggled to hang on. The oak trees where the rope was strung were only a short distance ahead. They could make it. They had to make it.

A man's terrified scream sounded around them.

Elle glanced back to see one of the harpies had taken a knight off his horse and tore him limb from limb. She choked on her bile and turned to lower herself over the mare's neck. Snow had been falling all day, but the flurries grew larger and heavier, obscuring her view. She kept Mina in her sights at all times, and a glance to her right showed her Val stayed with her. His horse could easily outrun hers, but he held back, protecting her.

And then she saw them.

She could just make out the giant oaks through the blinding snow. Their small group plunged their horses through the two trees.

🙢✖🙠

"Take me back. Now," Roderick demanded.

Aimery raised his nearly blonde brows. "You are on Thales. Do you not wish to see your father?"

Roderick sighed. "More than anything."

"You are here, Roderick. See your father."

But Roderick didn't budge. "The harpies attacked as we left. I must return."

For several moments Aimery didn't speak. "You realize, that if you leave now, there is a chance you might never see your father again."

"I knew that chance when I left Thales all those years ago. It's the chance I must take again."

"All right," Aimery agreed and started to reach for Roderick.

"Wait," Roderick stopped him. "I would ask for one thing."

"Ask. If it's in my power, I'll give it."

Roderick turned his head to look at his beloved city, the home he yearned to return to. "Go to my father. Explain to him why I couldn't be with him."

"Is that all?" Aimery asked. "Isn't there more you would like him to know?"

"Aye," Roderick nodded sadly. "If he won't last until I can return…tell him for me."

"Consider it done," Aimery said and gave him a sad smile.

Roderick blinked and found himself once again on Earth. He looked around the stables and recognized Stone Crest. "Thank you, Aimery," he said as he vaulted onto the white stallion. "Ride," he whispered as he rushed from the stables.

Only to find the gates being shut.

"Open them!" he shouted. "Now! Open them."

They heard him just before he reached the gates and gave

him room enough to ride through. As the stallion's hooves thundered over the snow-covered ground, he heard the boom as the gates closed and locked.

Up ahead, he saw the three harpies flying over the trees of the forest, as if deciding if they should venture down or not. Finally, they swooped down, and Roderick lost them in the trees. But he knew where they were headed.

The oaks.

He leaned low over the stallion's neck, and the horse increased his pace, nearly flying over the ground. And all the while Roderick prayed he reached Elle in time.

Elle raced through the two oak trees and didn't turn around until she heard one of their screams. Hugh and Mina slowed to look, but she and Val continued on. Elle glanced over her shoulder and saw one of the harpies had fallen for their trick.

And by the screams of rage resonating above them, she knew her terror had just begun.

"Ride," Val yelled over the drone of the horses' hooves.

She followed him down the narrow trail to the monastery, her breath burning like ice in her throat. Her heart beat like a drum as her stomach ran with the acid of fear. She wanted to look and see if the remaining two harpies had been separated, but mind-numbing fear kept her head straight.

And then, just up ahead through the snow-laden branches, she saw it. The monastery.

Val never slowed as he thundered through the low, crumbling gates of the monastery. Elle ducked just in time to keep her head from being removed from her body as she passed through the stone gate.

"Jump," Val said over his shoulder as they reached the door.

Elle might have gained some confidence from riding, but there was no way she could jump off a moving horse and not break something. She watched in horror as Val did just that and rolled to his feet. Mere seconds was given to her to make a decision.

"Elle. Now," Val said from the doorway.

He glanced over her, and Elle knew. At least one of the harpies had followed them.

Kicking free of the stirrups, Elle tried to mimic Val's jump but only managed to get her legs tangled in her skirts and fall in a heap on the ground. At least there was snow to break her fall.

One of the back hooves of her mare grazed her temple as she landed, but she shook off the injury and scrambled to her feet. Val's hands closed over her arms as he hauled her into the monastery.

"Do you remember the plan?" he asked as he raised his halberd.

Elle stared in horror at the weapons hanging from her saddle.

"What is it?"

"My bow. It's still attached to my saddle."

Val cursed. "Wait here," he told her and slipped out of the monastery.

Elle tried to catch him, but he was out the door before she had even lifted her hand. Luckily for them, her mare had stopped almost immediately after she had fallen. How Val made it to the mare and back without being attacked, Elle would never know.

He handed her the weapon, and she wrapped her arms around his neck. "Thank you," she whispered and stepped back.

His cocky smile nearly brought a laugh from her. "Any time." Then the smile dropped as a harpy scream reached them. "Do you remember the plan?" he asked again.

She nodded.

"Good. Keep to the plan, Elle. Everything will be fine."

But she knew it wouldn't. Roderick wasn't there. His departure made ragged gnashes on her soul so deep she couldn't even think about it without bursting into tears, and tears would do her no good now.

First, she had to live through the harpy attack, then she would face the hollow in her chest.

Her feet stumbled several times over the fallen stones and bookshelves that littered the main room. Even in her haze of fear and glum she managed to recall where the door was that led down to the lower rooms. Through the cold she could smell the mold and mildew from long decades of lack of use. She pushed away her growing panic of being alone in the dark of the lower level and grabbed the torch they had made for her.

After several attempts, she managed to light the torch and held it high overhead. Long, silent shadows met her gaze.

"You're being silly," she said to herself and took her first step into the narrow hallway.

Roderick heard the startled screams of the harpies and smiled. Elle's plan must have worked, but just as they expected, the other two hadn't fallen for the trick. His eyes darted up to see two of the harpies circling over the trees just as he reached the forest. He tried to keep his eyes on them as he rode, but the snow and trees hindered his view. He reached the fallen harpy and nearly choked on the rancid smell of evil. His stallion pranced and tried to turn away, but he was trained well, and with Roderick's expert handling, the stallion calmed, though his withers twitched to be away.

Roderick didn't take long to scout the area, but enough time that he saw where Hugh and Mina had nearly stopped and two other horses rode past.

"Elle and Val," he whispered and looked in the direction of the harpy.

The creatures had grown silent, and even in the stillness of the day, he could barely hear their wings beating. He wished he knew if the second part of their plan had succeeded.

He turned his horse toward the monastery and urged him

211

forward. The stallion lurched into a run, as if sensing Roderick's urgency. In his mind's eye he could see Elle's expression of surprise and anger at his leaving. And she had every right to be. He had given his word he wouldn't leave her, but he had hoped, nay prayed, that he could go to his father and return before the harpies attacked.

Inwardly, he cringed as he wondered what Elle thought of him now. But he would make it up to her, and explain everything. It was time she knew his dark secret, the secret that had sent him running like a coward from Thales and his beloved family. Finally, he reached the monastery and spotted Elle's mare. He raised his eyes and scanned the skies but saw no trace of a harpy. Or heard her.

Which wasn't a good sign.

He kicked free of the stirrups and pulled back on the reins. The stallion slid to a halt as Roderick landed on his feet. "Hide," he whispered to the stallion and slapped him on the rump.

Roderick spared the animal just a glance to make sure he would indeed find a place to hide, and thankfully, Elle's mare followed him. He stepped into the monastery and wrinkled his nose at the scent of evil. The harpy was here but where? He knew Val and Elle would stick to the original plan unless something had gone terribly wrong. Silently, Roderick unstrapped his flail, the weight of the spiked balls tugging at his hand. He yearned to use it on the harpy, to feel the spikes sink into its skin.

With a skill long learned, he picked his way through the large chamber, never making a sound. Not even the chain from his flail clinked as he walked. It was as if he were a spirit, and what better way to sneak up on evil than a spirit? His heart urged him to follow the stairs below to let Elle know he was here, but his head told him to go to his arranged spot and carry out the third part of the plan.

With his back to the stones, Roderick climbed the stairs as if he had all the time in the world, all the while listening for any hint of sound from a harpy or anything else. Just as he stepped onto the landing of the third floor, a soft sound reached him. He ducked to the right as a weapon came at him.

Chapter Thirty

Elle's skin began to crawl, but she told herself that it was her imagination running away with her. The harpies were outside. Val would take care of them. All she had to do was stay safe until someone came for her.

She could do that. It was easy. Or, at least, it should be easy. But she had never liked being alone in scary situations, which is why she never watched horror or thriller shows. She was much more comfortable with a drama or a comedy.

"Buck up, Elle," she told herself and took a deep breath.

She came to the designated room and opened the door. It creaked once, but otherwise was quiet. As far up as Val and the harpy were, she was sure they hadn't heard that small sound. After she shut the door behind her, she turned around.

Only to find she wasn't alone.

Roderick ducked just in time to miss being speared by Val's halberd. Neither man made a sound as they gawked at each other. Val hastily lowered his weapon and held out his hand. Roderick accepted it and gave a nod to let Val know everything was all right.

Val pointed upwards, and Roderick followed his finger. He signed. Somehow he had known the harpy wouldn't willingly come inside the monastery. Not because it was a holy place, but because the creature was no a fool. He held his hand for Val to stay in place, then hurried up the stairs to the roof. As he opened the door, he spotted the harpy leaning against the bell tower as if bored.

She perked up at seeing him.

"Ah. My favorite. I had hoped I would see you again," Kaleno purred as she took a step toward him.

Roderick glared at the black-haired harpy. "I don't suppose I could talk you into leaving?"

She shook her head. "Even if I wanted to, I couldn't. You know that. 'Tis the rules."

"Then let us begin," he said and braced his feet apart, his weight evenly distributed.

Just as she attacked he fell backwards and rolled away from her. Kaleno stood in the doorway and eyed him as if she wanted to devour him.

"If you want me, come and get me," Roderick taunted and ran down the stairs.

Elle couldn't stop the scream that erupted from her. She fell back against the door and eyed Alex.

"Surprised to see me?" he asked, his arms folded over his chest. "I knew they would bring you here. So very typical. Anything to save an innocent life."

"Something you wouldn't understand," she couldn't help saying.

He shrugged. "I don't pretend to. Power has always been my game, Elle. You can have part of that power. It's a heady thing."

"I'll pass, thanks."

He cackled as he pushed away from the wall. "You were

never as smart as you pretended to be. Let me put it another way." The smile vanished as his lips lifted in a sneer. "Join me or die."

She rolled her eyes, feigning courage. "Now that's not very original. How many movies and TV shows was that in?"

As soon as the words left her mouth she knew she had pushed Alex too far. In two strides he was before her, a knife at her throat. "I don't have to be original. I'm the one with the power." He stared down at her.

"Do you want to live?"

She nodded, hating the feel of the steel against her throat.

"On your knees then."

He removed the knife, and she slowly sank to her knees. To her astonishment, he rubbed the bulge between his legs.

"I don't know why I have wanted a taste of you, but I always have. Even from that first day I met you. Now, I think its time you showed me how much you want to continue living," he said and began to unzip his blue jeans.

Bile rose in her throat. Before he could free himself from his pants, Elle rose up on her feet the same time she elbowed him in the groin. Without looking back, she flung open the door and raced down the darkened hallway.

Roderick stopped on the third level, Val still in the shadows, and waited. Kaleno didn't keep him waiting long as she flew toward him.

"Running from me already?" she asked sweetly as she flexed her massive claws.

Roderick shrugged. "I like to stay conditioned."

She smiled. "I really am going to hate killing you."

Just then Roderick heard a very human howl of rage and pain. He looked over his shoulder and spotted Elle running up from the lower level. When Roderick turned back around, he saw Kaleno had also spotted Elle.

"Leave her be," he warned the harpy. "You want me.

Remember?"

Kaleno licked her red lips. "Oh, I want you, Thalean. But my orders were clear."

When the harpy tried to fly down to Elle, both Roderick and Val attacked. Roderick swung the flail over his head before burying it in Kaleno's back. She howled in rage yet yanked free. Val speared her through the leg with his halberd, but again, she quickly pulled free and flew away from them. Roderick saw Elle look up and spot the harpy.

"Run," he yelled at her, but she couldn't hear him over the loud beating of Kaleno's wings.

With Val at his back, Roderick raced down the stairs in an attempt to reach Elle in time. Just as he reached the last step, he saw Alex hobble from the stairs that led to the lower level. He held his groin, which made Roderick smile.

He and Val stood in front of the exit, their weapons poised and ready. When Kaleno moved, he caught Elle's gaze and wished he could dispel the fear he saw cloud them. Suddenly, Alex had a knife at Elle's throat as he pressed her back against him and spoke to the harpy. Kaleno had finally stopped beating her wings, but by that time Alex had finished speaking.

"You have nowhere to go," Val said.

Alex laughed. "If you want Elle to live, you will let us pass."

"Don't," Elle screamed. "He's going to kill me anyway. You know that."

Roderick's gut clenched. There was no way he was going to step aside and let them take Elle, but then again, he couldn't chance her being killed either.

"Roderick?" Val whispered.

He glanced over at his friend. No words were need. They each knew what needed to be done. He turned back to Alex and waited.

"So be it," Alex said.

At that moment, Kaleno threw back her arms and howled. Everyone covered their ears as the harpy continued her screaming. It seemed nearly an eternity before she stopped. Roderick lifted his head as Kaleno, with Alex in one arm and Elle in the other, flew out of the monastery from a hole in the roof.

Roderick and Val ran from the monastery and watched as the harpy and her prey disappeared over the tops of the trees.

Val cursed in Latin.

Roderick closed his eyes and sighed. He had failed. Again.

"Don't blame yourself," Val said.

"I should have been with her."

He felt Val's hand on his shoulder. "You wouldn't have been in the chamber with her. The plan was for her to go by herself."

Roderick raised his eyes to Val. "Someone should have been with her."

He didn't know how long he stood staring at the last place he had seen Elle. It wasn't until Hugh stood before him that he realized someone had spoken.

"What happened?" Hugh asked again.

Roderick let Val explain since he could barely look anyone in the eye. A soft hand touched his arm, making him ache for Elle. He looked down to find Mina beside him.

"We'll get her back."

He tried to smile but gave up. "I failed her."

"You'll only fail her if you give up," Hugh said. "Have you given up?"

Roderick glared at his leader. "Nay."

"Good," Hugh said with a smile. "We killed the second harpy. The odds are getting better."

Roderick spotted Mina's crossbow and rushed back into the monastery. He found Elle's bow in the chamber she was supposed to hide in. His fingers clasped around the small weapon and gently picked it up. He would keep it with him since he knew she would need it later.

He refused to think of any other possibility.

෧⋊෨

Elle swallowed the bile that rose in her throat each time she looked at Alex. All she could see was Jennifer's frightened expression as she called her name right before she died.

The talon wrapped around her tightened, poking her sharply in the ribs. She didn't utter a sound. The harpy was furious for losing two of her sisters, and Elle knew better than to bait the creature or give her any reason to cause her even more harm.

"You'll thank me later," Alex yelled over the clanging of the harpy's wings.

Elle just glared at him. She might plunge a knife in his heart, but she would never thank him. She had no idea how long they flew. She lost track of time as she gazed down at the landscape and tried to figure out where she was, but she might as well have tried looking for a needle in a haystack.

Inwardly, she groaned.

She had always hated it when people had used that expression, but it fit so adequately she had no other choice but to use it. When the harpy suddenly dipped and Elle's stomach flew to her throat much like it did when on a roller coaster, she gripped the harpy's talon and braced herself for whatever might come next.

Instead of death, she was gently placed on her feet and released. She raised her eyes to the harpy and saw the sadness reflected in her big, beautiful eyes.

"I'm sorry you've lost your sisters," Elle said, and then wondered why she even bothered. The harpy was out to kill her and would do whatever she had to do complete that assignment.

"Are you?" the harpy asked. "I wonder."

Elle shrugged. "If there had been a way to stop y'all without the killing, we would've gladly done it. However, y'alls intention was to kill me, which left us with little choice in the matter."

"Enough," Alex said and stepped between Elle and the harpy. He took hold of her arm and turned her away from the harpy. "We have things to talk about," he told the harpy. "Keep watch."

Elle would have preferred to take her chances with the harpy rather than be with a snake like Alex. She let him lead her into a small cottage in the middle of nowhere. One glance out the crack in the shudders and she saw the open expanse of the hillside. Nothing to help hide her.

"Now," Alex said as he sat in a chair and looked at her. "Tell me how badly you want to live."

Elle slowly turned her head to look at her nemesis. Good looking he might be with his chiseled features and toned body, but his soul was as black as Satan's. "Why do you want me to live?"

"Its true I could kill you now, easily. As a matter of fact, that's what I'm supposed to do. But, I find myself intrigued by you."

"It'll wear off," she said and turned her back to him. "If you're orders were to kill me, then get it over with. I'd rather be dead than listen to you."

The scrape of the chair legs on the dirt floor let her know he had risen to his feet. She tensed, waiting for him to come up behind her. Instead, he walked until he stood in front of her. The fury in his eyes caused her to step back.

"That can be arranged." He took a deep breath and eyed her. "What are the lives of your friend's worth?"

Elle closed her eyes to hide her tears. She had wondered if he would use that tactic, because he knew she would do whatever he wanted for their safety. She opened her eyes and sighed. "What do you want?"

"You," he said and stepped toward her. "I want you."

Chapter Thirty-One

Roderick clenched his jaw as he rode his stallion at a breakneck speed through the forest. He had to find Elle. Every time he thought about Alex's hands on her, or what Alex might do to her, he went blind with fury. He managed to stop in time as Hugh and Val brought their horses around in front of him.

"What are you doing?" he demanded of them. "We cannot waste time."

"We won't," Val said slowly. "You've been a Shield a long time. You know we can't let emotion get in the way."

Roderick's gaze shifted to Hugh. "Did you let emotion get in the way when the gargoyle took Mina?"

Hugh sighed and nodded. "I did, but I pushed it aside. I had to, Roderick. If you want to save her, you have to think with your head, not your heart."

Roderick cursed and looked at the gray sky. He hated feeling powerless, and that's exactly what he was. He lowered his head and regarded his friends.

"What do you suggest?" he asked.

"We wait," Val said.

That's not what Roderick had in mind. "I don't think I can. He came to kill her."

"Then why didn't he do it at the monastery?" Mina asked.

Roderick had to admit she had a point. He turned his head and looked at her. "What are you thinking?"

"I saw the way he looked at her. He wants her."

Roderick fisted his hands, and it took all the control he had not to kick the stallion into a run and go looking for Elle and Alex.

"Why?" he finally asked.

Mina shrugged. "I don't know. I think we should wait and see what he wants."

"I don't have anything he wants," Roderick said and looked at his hands. All he had, Alex now had.

Hugh grunted. "I'm not so sure. Before, all the creatures immediately began killing. Why didn't the harpies."

"Power," Val said.

Every eye turned to him. Val lifted one shoulder in a shrug. "Alex wants power, and he's foolish enough to believe that since he controls the harpy, he has power."

Hugh laughed. "He has no idea someone has control of him."

"Oh, he will discover that soon enough," Mina said.

Roderick looked around at the people beside him. These people were family to him, and they were doing what they thought was best for Elle. He respected them for that and would go along for the time being.

"All right," Roderick agreed. "We wait."

For now.

Elle sat with her arms crossed at the table that had recently received a cleaning. It was evident by the still musty odor in the cottage that it hadn't been used in quite awhile.

"Just what kind of power do you have?" she asked Alex, hoping he would reveal something she could use against him.

He glanced at her and smiled. "More than you could imagine."

"I'm not so sure. All but one of the harpies is dead now."

He laughed. "Ah, but one harpy can still wipe out an entire village in a day. And a city like Houston? That could be annihilated in less than a week."

Elle shuddered. "That's supposed to impress me? What is power when everyone is dead?"

"It's what comes after."

Now she was confused. "These creatures are being brought here to destroy Earth. All of it. There won't be an Earth to rule."

But Alex only laughed at her words. Either he was delusional, or he had been told something else entirely. And if that was the case, then who was telling the truth?

"Who told you that you would have that kind of power?"

"I can't tell," he said and turned his back to her.

"Why? Is he afraid of me?"

Alex chuckled. "He isn't afraid of anyone. He isn't even from this realm."

Somehow that didn't surprise her. "What's his name?"

Slowly, Alex turned around to face her. "That isn't something you need to know."

"And what do I need to know?"

"Just what I've told you. Nothing more."

Elle hated being treated like less than a human just because she was a woman. "So," she said with a sigh. "What do we do now?"

"That is what I would like to know," the harpy said as she ducked and came into the cottage. "Why haven't you killed her as you were ordered to do?"

"I have my reasons, Kaleno," Alex said between clenched teeth.

"I do not think your master will be happy to hear you have disobeyed him."

Elle sat and listened with interest. Maybe she could turn Kaleno on her side and convince the harpy to help her.

And pigs can fly, Elle.

It was worth a shot though. She didn't utter a sound as the two continued to bicker, though she noted that Kaleno never raised her voice or advanced on Alex. And the reason was the stone hanging around his neck. Elle's eyes widened at seeing the stone. All she had to do was get the stone, and everything would end. Her mind began to form a plan.

Two hours later she was looking for a way to put her plan in motion. Night had begun to fall, and anxiety had set in.

"What are you doing?" she asked irritably.

"Waiting."

She rolled her eyes. "For what?"

"A visitor."

She crossed her arms over her chest and narrowed her eyes on the vermin before her. "Who? Your precious master?"

This time Alex laughed, his eyes shining with an intense light that sent a warning down her spine. "Oh, not anyone as special as that," he said.

With that, Alex turned and motioned to Kaleno who ducked out of the cottage and flew away.

Elle rushed to the window and threw open the shutters to see where the harpy was headed. Cold air rushed at her like a freight train, but she ignored it. "Where is she going?"

"On an errand," Alex said as he pulled her away from the window and closed the shutters. He turned her toward the roaring fire. "Warm yourself."

But there would be no warmth for her ever again.

Roderick stared at his feet. His hands itched to feel his weapons and attack Alex and the last remaining harpy. He seethed as he waited, yearning to find Elle. Out of the corner of his eye, he spotted Elle's bow.

His heart constricted, and the dull ache that had plagued him since she had been taken grew tenfold. He hadn't realized until she was gone just how much he cared for her.

Hugh had asked him if it was love. At the time, Roderick

hadn't known the answer. He did now. He loved Elle Blanchard, loved her so much that he knew he would never be whole again if he didn't save her. Even the guilt he had carried with him for decades didn't amount to a thimble full of what he felt for his woman.

His woman.

Aye, she was his. And he would tell her just as soon as he saw her.

Roderick sat back and took a deep breath, the fire's heat burning his cheeks. He wondered where Elle was and hoped she stayed warm. He looked around the hall and found men inspecting weapons and readying themselves. As soon as their small group had arrived at Stone Crest, Hugh and Mina had seen to it that everyone was safe in case they were attacked.

"Not much longer I suspect," Val said as he sharpened the blade on his halberd.

Roderick moved his gaze to Hugh who sat cleaning his crossbow.

"Aye. Anytime now," Hugh said, never taking his eyes from his weapon.

It was nearly too much for Roderick. Never had he been so anxious for a battle, so ready to kill. But then again, no one had ever taken his woman.

Mina walked into his line of vision and regarded him. "Will you tell Elle?" she asked softly.

"Tell her what?"

"How you feel?"

He noticed Val and Hugh stop their work and look up. Roderick had never liked being the center of attention. He preferred to stay in the background.

"Aye," he said, not recognizing the hoarseness of his voice.

"Good," Mina said and smiled. "She deserves to know."

"Did you see your father?" Hugh asked.

Roderick shook his head and pushed back the grief that threatened to overwhelm him. "There wasn't a chance. Aimery promised to talk to him for me. I only left because I thought there was time."

Val held up his hand. "There's no need to explain. We know. None of us expected the harpies to attack so soon."

"I swore to her I wouldn't leave." Even now Roderick could see the disbelief in her eyes.

"She'll understand once you explain," Mina said.

Roderick opened his mouth to respond when they heard the harpy scream. Each of them surged to their feet and grabbed their weapons.

"Knights. Take your places," Hugh bellowed as they rushed from the castle.

By the time they reached the bailey, the harpy had knocked down part of a wall and one tower of the gatehouse. Without thought, each raced to their places and waited. Roderick knew it was only a matter of time before Kaleno grew tired of knocking at stones. She wanted humans to kill, and he realized there was only one way to achieve what they all wanted faster.

He stepped out from his hiding spot and slowly walked to the middle of the bailey. He didn't try and shout to Kaleno. She would never hear him over her screams and the noise of her wings. But it didn't take her long to spot him. She dove down and landed on her feet several feet in front of him.

"What have we here?" she asked as she looked around her. "Where did everyone go?"

"You don't want them."

She cackled. "Oh, but I do."

"Well," Roderick said with a shrug. "You only have me."

Kaleno smiled. "You'll do."

He waited, yet she didn't attack, didn't kill him. "What are you waiting for? Aren't you going to kill me?"

She ran her hands through her long black hair. "Not yet. Master Alex wants to do the honors himself."

Roderick seethed. "Did you bring him?"

She snorted. "Of course not. He wouldn't dream of leaving his new prize."

"Is that what she is to him? I thought he was supposed to

kill her?"

"He will. Eventually. Right now he wants to have a little fun with her first."

It was all Roderick could do to keep a coherent thought in his brain upon hearing that. "Where is he? I'm just as anxious to fight him."

She cocked her head to the side, her black mane falling over her right shoulder.

"You won't win."

"That doesn't matter."

"It matters to everyone. Why would you fight if you know you will die?"

"I don't know that," he said.

She lifted her head, her black eyes intent. "There are some things that are meant to be. You and she shall both die."

Roderick refused to let her words deter him. "Everyone dies sometime."

"True, Thalean. Everyone and everything dies. Including realms. Your realm is on the brink."

He took a step toward Kaleno. "Where is Elle?"

She blinked once. "In the glen," she said and then flew away.

"What did she say?" Val asked as he ran up.

"Elle is in the glen.

Hugh rubbed his hands together. "Good. I've been itching for a fight."

Roderick wanted to go alone but knew how foolish that would be. He had no wish to see his friends in danger, but he needed all the help they could give. Though he was immortal, there was a good chance he could die, and he gladly would if it meant the survival of Elle.

He didn't know who got his stallion for him or who placed the reins in his hand. He secured his weapons and leapt onto the stallion's back. With one last look at Stone Crest, Roderick kicked his horse into a gallop.

Elle.

Chapter Thirty-Two

Elle stared into the fire, remembering her time with Roderick. Her chance of survival was slim to none, yet she clung to that slim chance. She knew Roderick and the rest would come for her. It was their duty, and they held duty above all else. Yet, she didn't want to see them die, and Alex would make sure they were all dead just for spite.

There were only two choices for her. Submit to Alex and become his sex slave, which appealed to her as much as clawing her own eyeballs out. Or, get the necklace for herself.

She wasn't what you would call a seductress, but it was worth a shot. After a glance in his direction near the window, she rose to her feet. Instantly, his gaze was on her. She kept eye contact with him, never wavering. She didn't try to appear sexy, she decided acting herself was the best role she could play. Her feet didn't stop until she stood in front of him. He came to his feet and looked down at her. His hand reached up and traced her jaw.

"Elle?"

"I've thought over your option."

He smiled. "Ah. You mean become mine so I spare your friends?"

She nodded. "Yeah. That one."

His hand traced down her shoulder to her breast then to her waist. She repressed a shudder and stood still.

"All right," he said. "We start now."

She wanted to scream no, but then she didn't have any other choice but to do as he said. He pulled her into his arms. When his lips moved to cover hers, she tilted her head so he found her neck instead.

His sloppy kisses made her skin crawl. Yet, she pushed that aside and moved her hands up over his shoulders to his neck. Her fingers brushed the clasp and yearned to grab it, but she held herself back. It was a good thing too, because Alex straightened and pushed her back onto the table. He ran his hands down the front of her body to her thighs. If she was lucky she would come away without having to experience him taking her fully. As it was, it was everything she could do to keep the grimace from her face.

But luck wasn't something that was usually on her side.

"Nice. Very nice," he murmured as his hands kneaded her legs, inching closer and closer to her sex.

She opened her arms, and he eagerly fell on top of her. Her fingers threaded into his hair, keeping careful to scrape her fingernails on his scalp and neck so that when she reached for the clasp he would think nothing of it.

No matter how many times he tried to kiss her, she continued to turn her head away. She wondered how long he would allow that before he forced a kiss on her. As it was, his lips were at her jaw, working their way toward her mouth once again.

To distract him, she raised her legs and wrapped them around his waist. He groaned and thrust his rod against her. She shuddered in revulsion, but he thought it was in anticipation. She wasn't about to tell him differently.

While he continued to grind his pelvis against hers, she wound her fingers around the necklace as she played with his hair. Luck, it seemed, was on her side when she found the clasp at her fingers.

Ever so deftly, she began to unclasp the necklace when Alex jerked his head up and eyed her.

"Is something wrong?" she asked innocently.

He growled and backed away. Elle didn't have time to unwind her fingers. His eyes narrowed dangerously as he reached up and jerked her hands from around his neck.

"Bitch," he roared as he backhanded her.

Even though Elle saw the fist coming, she couldn't move fast enough to dodge the blow, which sent her tumbling over the table to the floor on the other side. She sat dazed, as little lights flickered around her as she tried to stop the world from spinning. Her body began to shake, and a sheen of sweat covered her body. Her hand covered her cheek in an attempt to stop the pain, but there was no stopping it. It grew worse with each passing second until her stomach rolled violently and she worried that she might vomit.

"You're pathetic," Alex said as he yanked her up by her arm.

Elle licked her dry lips and tried to breath through her mouth to calm her racing stomach. It helped a little, but if she didn't sit soon, nothing would help her.

He shoved her into the door as he pushed her outside. Instantly, the cold slammed against her chilling her instantly without her cloak for warmth. The only good thing about the cold was that it stopped her nausea. It didn't take long for the chills to wrack her body again. And each time her teeth chattered it felt as if a metal fist was punching her cheek.

Oh, Roderick. I need you.

She quickly blinked away the tears that threatened. She had tried to tell herself to keep her distance, she had known their time together would be short, but it still didn't lessen the pain. He would come, and as much as she wanted him with her, she wished he wouldn't. She wasn't a fool. Alex had a plan, a plan that included both their deaths. Alex and his master were taking no chances.

"Here she comes now," Alex said.

Elle lifted her head to him, then shifted her gaze to where he looked. Just over the rise of the trees, she could make out Kaleno.

The harpy had returned.

Roderick stayed close to Hugh as they raced over the snow-covered ground. Thankfully, the snow had stopped falling for the time being, but it wasn't likely to last. His heart pounded in time with his stallion's hooves on the earth. He couldn't help but think that they had wasted too much time waiting instead of searching for Elle.

He lowered himself over the stallion's neck and urged him on faster. The steed responded immediately and pulled alongside Hugh. There was a rise just up ahead, and Roderick would bet his flail that was where Alex waited for them.

Suddenly, Hugh reached over and pulled back on Roderick's reins. The stallion slid to a halt and reared on his hind legs as Roderick jerked the reins out of Hugh's hand.

"What are you doing?" Roderick growled.

"Trying to save your fool hide," Hugh answered. "You will do her no good to go barreling down there."

Roderick sighed and glanced away. "I do not wish to waste any more time."

Val nudged his horse next to Roderick's. "This isn't wasting time if it saves Elle's life. Isn't that what you want, my friend?"

Of course it was what he wanted, and they knew that. He gave them a nod, more than anxious to get to Elle.

"I don't think we should go down as one group," Hugh said.

Roderick scowled. "We're better in numbers. Any other time I would agree, Hugh, but I've seen the harpy fight."

"You may be right," Hugh said. "However, Alex and the harpy only think you will come. They will think the rest of us are too scared."

Roderick smiled as it dawned on him. "I go down alone."

"Aye," Val said with a smile just as sinister. "We will come up from behind. Keep Alex and the harpy occupied so they don't notice us."

Roderick jerked his head once in agreement and started to turn his horse around when Val's hand gripped his arm. He turned back to Val.

"Stay alive," Val said.

"My life doesn't matter. Just make sure that Elle lives. Earth and the Fae need her."

Val sighed and released him.

Roderick then turned to Hugh. "I have one favor to ask."

"Anything," Hugh said.

"Once you find the answer…"

Hugh nodded. "I'll make sure Thales gets the information. Even if I have to deliver it myself."

Satisfied that everything would be taken care of, Roderick gave his friends one last look before he turned his stallion toward the glen.

Val stared after Roderick. "I should be with him."

"Nay," Hugh said. "You will be better served covering his back."

Val looked at Hugh. "While you find Elle?"

Hugh nodded. "No matter what, stay with Roderick. Once Elle is away, I will return."

Val stretched out his hand and fingered the tip of his halberd. "There won't be anything left by the time you return."

Elle's gaze scanned the snow-covered hills in an attempt to find Roderick and the others. Yet, nothing moved. The wind whistled a deadly tune as it swirled around them, the threat of more snow heavy in the air. And the threat of death nearly choked her.

"Just so you know," Alex said as he turned toward her and

pulled something out of his trench coat that looked somewhat like a gun. "My offer is rescinded."

Elle had no wish to speak to the bastard. "What offer?"

"The offer for your friends to live."

Her blood stopped in her veins. Slowly, she turned toward the devil's spawn. "Why? Because I feel nothing when you touch me?"

He only laughed and ran a finger over the gun. "It doesn't matter to me whether you like me or not. I can't stand weak women. You and Jennifer are the weakest women I've ever met. I need someone much stronger by my side."

Elle didn't think beyond hearing Jennifer's name. She launched herself at Alex, her numb hands clawing at his face as she screamed at him to die.

Roderick crested the rise the same time he heard the scream. Instantly, he knew that scream of rage and betrayal was Elle's. It wasn't hard to spot her either. He saw her small form propel itself at Alex and began to claw at his face. If the situation wasn't so dire, Roderick might have smiled to see his feisty woman unleashed.

While Alex was detained, Roderick rode closer. He thought it rather odd that Kaleno didn't aid Alex, but then again, he hadn't asked her to. The harpy eyed him as he neared but never moved. Roderick silently urged Elle on as she brought her knee up into Alex's groin. The man doubled over, and Elle gripped his hair as she brought the same knee up to smash into his face.

This time, Roderick did chuckle. He imagined no one in Elle's world would have thought the quiet museum worker had this in her. He had known otherwise from the first moment he had seen her. The fire inside her burned just below the surface. It had just needed to be shown a way out. He had done that for her. Hopefully she would look back on him favorably for it.

Alex suddenly roared and shoved Elle away from him

where she landed on her back in the snow. Blood covered the front of her gown as well as Alex's clothes from the broken nose she had given him.

"You stupid bitch," Alex screamed.

In an instant, she was on her feet and charged him again. Roderick called her name the moment he realized she didn't have a chance. He roared as Alex punched Elle in the face, sending her on her back again. Except this time, she didn't move.

Roderick seethed with rage, and the desire to exact vengeance ran deep within him. "You will pay for that."

Alex laughed and wiped at his bloody nose. "I think not."

With a flick of his wrist, Roderick had the flail in his hand. The twin spiked balls danced at the end of the chain, as if they too itched for blood.

Alex rolled his eyes. "That measly weapon against this?" he asked and pointed to the harpy.

Roderick dismounted without looking at Kaleno. "Why not fight me man to man?"

"I don't think so."

"Why?" Roderick asked as he stepped around his stallion. As if knowing what he wanted, the stallion moved a safe distance away.

"Why?" Alex repeated with a laugh. "I'm no fool."

"Oh, I disagree. You're the biggest fool of all to think we wouldn't find you."

"Puh-leeze," Alex said with a roll of his eyes. "My master is always one step ahead of you and will always be one step ahead of you."

Roderick soaked that news in and hoped that Hugh and Val had also heard it. He continued toward Alex and Elle.

"And your master would be?"

"You must think I'm some kind of idiot," Alex said, his arms crossed over his chest as if he had nothing to fear.

"I do," Roderick agreed. He stopped beside Elle and knelt next to her. There was a nasty bruise on her right cheek and another on her left eye. He raised his head to Alex. "No one touches my woman," Roderick said as he rose to his feet.

"Yours?" Alex questioned. "I find that hard to believe when she was bargaining her body."

Roderick didn't believe a word of it. He knew Elle too well to believe she would easily give her body to the man who had killed her best friend. There had to have been a reason she would have tried to use her body to tempt Alex.

"It was for me, wasn't it?" Roderick asked. "The only reason she would have thought to bargain her body was to save her friends."

The shift in Alex's eyes let Roderick know he had hit upon the truth.

"I don't know why you want her," Alex said. "She's weak. She'll only weigh you down."

"On the contrary," Roderick said as he took a step closer to Alex, "she's one of the strongest women I have ever met."

"I doubt that."

"I don't care what you think of her, but you will pay for touching her and hitting her."

Alex threw back his head and laughed. He straightened and eyed Roderick with a cocky smile. "Do your best, Thalean."

Roderick took a step toward Alex when he spotted the ray gun.

Chapter Thirty-Three

Elle came awake slowly to the feel of water on her back. It took her a moment to realize that it wasn't water but snow beneath her. She tried to sit up and nearly groaned at the pain lancing through her skull from Alex's hit.

Muffled talking reached her, and she opened her eyes to the loveliest sight in the world. Roderick.

How he had gotten there and when didn't matter. He was here. He had come for her. Maybe it wasn't because he cared about her, but because it was his duty, but that didn't matter. He was there. That was enough.

Then she realized what they were saying. Alex called her weak again, yet Roderick had called her the strongest woman he had ever met. Warmth grew inside of her that pushed away the iciness of the snow. Slowly, she climbed to her feet, careful not to draw attention to herself. She had no wish to have Alex's gaze on her again, nor did she want Roderick to worry about her. If he thought she was still unconscious, then he would fight better.

And then she saw it. The gun, and by the rigid stance of Roderick, that weapon meant something to him. She thought back over the many times he had fought, and never once had

237

he been afraid. He was immortal. Only the ray from ....

Her thought drifted away as she looked at the weapon again. A gun, but different. It had to be the kind that could kill him.

The warmth that had enfolded her secped away, leaving her as cold as death. There was no way she would allow Roderick to die. Not for her. What he did was too important for the survival of his planet as well as Earth.

Because of her love for him, she would do whatever it took to keep him alive.

Roderick halted instantly. The same weapon that had killed his brother was about to end his life. He eyed the nasty weapon, then raised his gaze to Alex.

"Where did you come by that?"

Alex shrugged and laughed. "Its amazing what my master can get hold of when he wants to."

"Are you going to play with it all day, or use it?"

Roderick waited for his taunt to spur the bastard on. The flail in his hand swung on the chain as Roderick began to move his hand. He braced his feet apart, waiting for the attack. Behind him, he heard the battle cries of Val, Hugh, and the knights as they raced towards the cottage, but Roderick never took his eyes from Alex.

"Kaleno," Alex yelled as he raised the ray gun towards Roderick.

The world seemed to slow to an unnatural crawl. Roderick could hear the drops of snow as they fell to the ground from the snow-laden limbs. At his back, he heard the whoosh of the blade as a sword cut through air.

His gaze stayed on Alex though. The bastard let out a great rush of air that slowly billowed around him just before his finger moved toward the trigger that would end Roderick's life.

To his left, the snow crunched as someone moved toward

him. He realized too late it was Elle. And he knew what she was about to do. His heart screamed for her to stay, but he didn't utter a word. Instead, he crouched and released his flail as he heard Elle approach. The rush of his blood hissed in his ears, and fear engulfed him.

With only mere moments in which to pull Elle out of the way of the laser, Roderick moved his left arm and grasped her to him. Just as Alex squeezed the trigger, Roderick turned to protect his woman.

He heard the scream of the ray as it left the gun and shot towards him. A cry tore from his throat at the raw pain that penetrated his body. He lowered his head to look at Elle. She was so beautiful, so pure and full of passion. He was going to miss her.

Her eyes widened as his weight began to fall on her. Blackness filled his eyes until only Elle was left.

"Love you," he managed to get out as he closed his eyes.

Elle toppled with Roderick, screaming his name over and over. Something warm and sticky coated her hand, and she didn't need to see it to know it was blood. Roderick's blood.

With more strength than she knew she had, she managed to turn Roderick on his back and lean over him. She didn't heed the tears that ran down her face or the battle that raged behind her. Or even Alex.

Her only thought was Roderick.

He breathed but barely. It was as if the life drained out of him with every beat of his heart. She laid her head on his chest and listened to his faint heartbeat. It wasn't supposed to be him lying there, but her. How had he known what she intended?

With her eyes closed she recalled his last words.

Love you.

He loved her. And Alex had killed him.

Rage took the place of grief as she raised her head to glare at Alex. "You'll pay for that," she said between clenched teeth.

He laughed and shrugged. "Who will make me pay? You? I doubt it."

"We'll see."

She had taken only two steps before Alex lunged at her face with his meaty fist. Somehow, she managed to duck in time. There was no way she could compete with him without a weapon, and he knew it.

Elle cursed and looked around for a weapon. She saw Roderick's flail and his sword, neither of which could do her any good since she couldn't pick them up, much less use them. How she wished she had her bow.

And then she saw it strapped to Roderick's stallion.

She glanced at Alex to see him raise the gun at her. Without another thought, she ran towards the horse, grabbed her bow and arrows, and rolled just as he let loose the first shot.

Her flesh stung where the laser skimmed her, but she shook off the pain and climbed to her feet.

"You were lucky that time," Alex taunted. "You won't be again."

Elle merely smiled as she notched an arrow.

He laughed and raised the gun. "A bow? Really, Elle. I'll fire off two shots before you even think of releasing that arrow."

"Let us see, shall we?" she asked.

She didn't wait for him to respond as she lifted her bow and took aim. Once she had him in her sights, she released the arrow the same time he fired his first shot. Having no other recourse than to dive to the side to miss the laser, Elle didn't know if she had found her mark or not. She came to her feet to see Alex still standing, and she cursed her uselessness of the bow.

Suddenly, Alex fell backwards unmoving.

Elle blinked and started towards him. She notched another arrow just in case, but when she reached him, there was no doubt he was dead. Yet there was no time to rejoice as the sounds of the fighting reached her. Elle looked up to see several of the knights dead and Val and Hugh covered in blood as they battled the harpy alone.

Several crossbow bolts protruded from Kaleno's body, but they didn't affect her at all. Another one landed in her wing, and that's when Elle spotted Mina hiding behind the stack of wood.

Val never said a word to her, but he gave Elle a look that sent her into action. She jerked as if shot and looked down at Alex. The stone still hung around his neck. She knelt and yanked the necklace off, then looked around for something to smash the stone.

Panic set in as she realized there wasn't anything. Then she spotted Roderick's sword. She pulled the massive sword out of its sheath and set the stone on the ground amidst the snow. Quickly, she jerked up her skirt and wrapped it around both hands as she reached for the sword again.

She turned the sword so that the blade faced the sky and the hilt was turned down. With a deep breath, she lifted the sword and glanced toward Kaleno. The harpy slowly turned towards Elle, saw was she was about, and lowered her arms. Kaleno gave a small nod of her head to Elle.

Elle swallowed and stared at the creature for a moment. Kaleno knew she was about to die and faced it without fear. Elle plunged the hilt toward the stone and saw Kaleno burst into flames. Light erupted as the stone shattered, throwing Elle back. She covered her eyes as the light blazed around her and then fizzled away.

"Elle," Mina shouted.

She opened her eyes to see Mina running towards her, but all Elle cared about was Roderick. She turned onto her right side to find him next to her. Her hand reached out and clasped his normally warm hand that was now nearly as cold as her own.

"Don't leave me," she whispered as the others reached her.

She let Mina help her to her knees as Val and Hugh tended to Roderick. Elle didn't feel any pain as Mina pulled away the bloody scraps of her skirt from her hands. "Is he ... gone?" she finally asked the men.

Hugh raised his gaze. "Nay, and I won't let him."

"Into the cottage," Val shouted as he hefted Roderick's weight onto his shoulders.

Elle followed them into the cottage. She refused to let Roderick out of her sight.

"Sit," Mina told her after she had closed the door and bolted it.

Elle did as commanded.

"I need some water," Val called out.

Elle jumped to do it, only to have Mina's hand on her shoulder. "How will you carry it?"

"By my hands."

Mina raised a brow, which caused Elle to look down. Her hands were covered in blood. Her blood. Despite her protection against the sword blade by her skirt, it hadn't saved her.

"Stay here," Mina said as she rushed to help the men.

Elle's hands began to shake. Not because of her injuries, she could care less about that, but because she could lose Roderick. The pain that thought brought her was too much to bear. She felt the weight of it on her shoulders and knew she couldn't withstand it. It would crush her, and she would welcome it. A life without Roderick wasn't worth living.

How much time elapsed with Val and Hugh working to save Roderick, Elle didn't know. All she knew is that she prayed every second of that time for his life to be spared. Even when Val and Hugh finished with Roderick and then came to tend her hands, she continued to pray.

"He can't die," she said.

Val turned her head until she looked at him. "Don't give up on him."

"Never," she vowed.

"This might hurt," Hugh warned as he turned her hand and picked up a bottle.

Elle shrugged. After what Roderick had done, she would endure physical pain of any kind.

Hugh poured the bottle over her wounds, and, though she fought to stay awake, she succumbed to the blackness that called to her.

Val caught Elle just as she slumped over the chair. He pushed her hair away from her face, amazed at her bravery. "She killed Alex."

Mina nodded. "And destroyed the stone."

"By herself," Hugh added.

Val held her as Hugh finished bandaging her cuts, and then he picked her up and carried her to where Roderick lay. Gently, Val laid Elle beside his friend and stepped back.

"I'll forever be thankful that Gabriel left some of his herbs. Without them, we might not have been able to save Roderick."

Hugh sighed. "There's still a chance he won't survive."

"He has to. Elle will never forgive herself otherwise."

Chapter Thirty-Four

Roderick turned toward the warmth and hissed at the jolt of pain in his side. His entire body ached, as if he had been beaten to an inch of his life.

Or shot with a laser gun.

His eyes flew open as he recalled everything that had happened. With his heart hammering in dread, he looked around at the cottage and saw Val slumped over the table by the hearth. A soft moan beside him turned his gaze, and he nearly cried out with joy.

"Elle," he whispered.

"I'm glad to see you are coming back to us."

Roderick lifted his gaze to find Aimery standing beside the bed. "Was it close?"

"Closer than I, or Elle, would have liked. I'm glad to say you are both doing fine now."

"Both?" Roderick repeated and tried to sit up so he could see where she was injured.

Aimery reached out and pushed him back down. "Not yet. You're wound is still too new. You'll be proud of your woman."

Just hearing the words from Aimery's mouth brought a

flush of delight to Roderick. "Why?"

"She not only killed Alex herself but also destroyed the stone."

"Alone?" Roderick couldn't believe it.

Aimery nodded. "Alone. She took your sword and hit the stone with the hilt."

Roderick's eyes jerked to her hands atop the covers, bandaged and unmoving. "Were the cuts deep?"

"Deep enough," Hugh said as he joined Aimery. "She used her skirt to try and shield her hands, but it only did so much. You should have seen her. It was amazing."

He smiled as he gazed at his woman. "I wish I could have." His smile faltered. He looked at Aimery and swallowed. "My father?"

"Is doing much better," he answered. "We had a nice long talk, and he wishes to see you. Very soon."

Roderick sighed. "When I'm closer to learning the answer to stopping this madness."

"I think you should go once you are healed. Your family needs you."

"The Shields need me," Roderick argued.

"What of Elle?" Hugh asked.

Roderick hadn't had time to think beyond killing the harpies. Now that the mission was over, he needed to think about what his plans were.

And he needed to talk to Elle.

Elle fought against the receding blackness. She had no desire to face the world again. Not yet. Not without Roderick. Yet, whether she wanted to or not, she was awake. She kept her eyes closed and moved her legs. She was in a bed, and by her guess it was at the cottage. That had only one bed.

Before she let herself think beyond that, she turned her head and opened her eyes. She was alone in the bed, and since there was no way Roderick could be up so soon after such a wound, that left only one answer.

He hadn't survived.

The pain that lanced through her brought a flood of tears. She turned her face into the pillow and cried at losing Roderick, at never telling him how she felt, and at not having a future with him at her side.

Hands gripped her shoulders, but she pushed them away. She needed time to grieve ... alone. And nothing Val or Hugh could say would help to lessen her pain.

"Elle."

Her heart stopped, and her eyes flew open. Slowly, she turned toward the voice and soaked up the sight of Roderick. Tears began again at the realization that she hadn't lost him.

"I thought...."

He nodded. "I know. I'm not, however."

"Thank God," she said and sat up. "How?"

"Gabriel's herbs. Hugh and Mina brought them with them just in case."

"Well, I'm glad they did," she said. "It saved your life."

"And your hands," he said as he looked down.

Elle studied her hands and shrugged. "It's a small price to pay to end the evil."

She raised her gaze to him. After all that she had been through, gained, and nearly lost, the fear she had lived with nearly all her life was gone.

It was either ask now or wonder forever. So, she took a deep breath and asked, "Did you mean what you said?"

His brows furrowed. "When?"

"Right before you passed out."

His forehead smoothed out, and he smiled. "You mean, the 'I love you' part?"

"Yes," she said and swallowed hard. She might tell herself her fear was gone, but directly asking Roderick left her feeling as though she was falling into a pit of nothingness.

"Aye," he said finally. "I do." He sat back and sighed. "I should have told you sooner."

"At least you told me."

One corner of his mouth lifted. "True."

It was then she noticed how nervous he seemed, as if he were waiting for something. When she realized what it was, she nearly laughed out loud. "Do you mean you don't realize that I love you, too?"

"You do?" he asked, his lips pulled back in a huge smile.

"Of course, you silly man."

"Thank the gods," Roderick said and pulled her into his arms.

Elle sighed and nestled her head in the crook of his neck. She felt more than heard him wince and pulled away. "You're still hurt?"

He nodded sheepishly. "I may be immortal and heal quickly, but the laser does something to my body that slows things down and can kill me if hit in the right place."

"I know," she said and lowered her eyes.

"You were willing to die for me."

She nodded, still looking at the covers. "The thought of you dying left me with too much pain." She raised her head and asked, "How did you know that was what I planned?"

He shrugged. "I just did."

Silence grew between them. Elle had used all her courage to ask him if he loved her and none remained to ask him what their future would be.

"You need to rest," Roderick suddenly said and rose to his feet. "Val, Hugh, and Mina returned to Stone Crest to retrieve some clothes and food. They thought it best if we stayed here for a bit."

Elle never got to reply. Roderick left the cottage so quickly she was left staring at the door.

Roderick paced in front of the small cottage. He had wanted to speak to Elle of their future, but he didn't know what kind of future they could have. The Shields needed him too desperately for him to leave, and in truth, he couldn't leave. He had yet to learn the answers to help defend Thales. He had to stay with the Shields.

And yet, he couldn't leave Elle.

"I suppose you would like to talk now," Aimery said as he walked toward him.

Roderick stopped asking a long time ago how Aimery always knew when something bothered them. Instead, he nodded. "I love her."

"I know," the Fae said. "And we are glad for you, Roderick. Each one of you deserves it."

"Then why do I feel so awful?" he asked and raked a hand through his hair, then grimaced at the pull in his side. "The Shields need me."

"As does Elle."

Roderick grunted. "Not nearly as much as I need her. Was the decision so painful for Hugh?"

"Nay. The situation was so that it worked easily for both Hugh and us."

"And my situation?"

Aimery sighed. "Not nearly as easily."

"Let me go with him," Elle said from the doorway of the cottage.

"Nay," Roderick and Aimery said in unison.

Roderick walked to her and wrapped the blanket more securely around her. "I cannot allow you to take the chance of death."

"You mean like you do? It's all right for you but not me?" she argued.

"For me, it is different. I am immortal."

"I don't forget that," she said testily. "It still bothers me to see you wounded."

"But I heal. You won't."

Aimery stepped toward them. "Not to mention, that you are needed, Elle. Once the other three women are found, we can finish off this great evil."

"Do neither of you care what I want?" she asked.

"I do care," Roderick said. "It's the reason I want to keep you safe."

She jerked out of his arms, her face twisted in anguish. "I'm tired of being safe. I want to live again."

"I cannot lose another person I love," Roderick roared and walked away.

Elle blinked, stunned at his angry tone. She looked at Aimery. "What was that about?"

"I shouldn't tell you," the Fae said. "However, I know Roderick isn't intentionally keeping it from you. 'Tis that reason alone that I am sharing the story with you."

She shifted in the cold, anxious to hear the tale.

"Come inside," Aimery said and opened the door for her.

Elle quickly stepped inside and sat by the fire. She knew better than to refuse the Fae, but her nerves were wearing thin.

"Roderick is a prince on Thales. His family is very powerful, and yet his father is a fair ruler. The people of Thales love him."

That glimpse alone told her so much about Roderick and why he had such knowledge of what was right and wrong.

"He was the middle child."

"Was?"

Aimery nodded. "A second son. He and his older brother were very close, and like most brothers, they competed at everything. Roderick knew he wasn't meant to be king and never resented his brother for that."

"And the younger child?"

"A sister."

Elle licked her lips. "What happened?"

"There was a raid on Thales. Roderick and his brother defied their father's orders and followed the troops. They joked back and forth that one was better than the other until his brother said he could touch one of the enemy troops and return without a scratch."

"And because he was immortal, he thought he could," Elle

said.

"Aye. Roderick dared him to do it. His brother raced away, and it was only then that both realized the enemy carried the lasers."

"Oh, God," Elle said, feeling sick to her stomach.

"He was hit almost instantly. Roderick picked his way through the troops and carried his brother's body back to the palace where he took full blame for his brother's death."

"Didn't he tell his family what had happened?"

Aimery shook his head. "That didn't matter to Roderick. All that mattered was that his brother was dead because of a dare he issued. He took responsibility for it and left Thales that night."

Elle could only imagine how his parents felt. "They lost two sons in one day."

"We found Roderick soon after that, and he became a Shield. Since that day, I have tried to convince him to return to Thales and explain to his parents what happened."

"Why won't he?"

"Because I swore to myself that I wouldn't return until I knew how to eliminate the evil that plagues Thales," Roderick said from the doorway.

Chapter Thirty-Five

Elle jerked around to find Roderick behind her. "I understand that, but your parents need to know what happened."

"I haven't earned their forgiveness yet," he argued. "When I save Thales, then maybe I can ask for that forgiveness."

She knew better than to argue with him when he got something in his mind like this, and, in a way, she understood. He had to redeem himself. By the look on his face, she knew he had something to tell her, so she waited for him to take the chair opposite her.

"I promised you I would never leave."

She nodded. "Yet, you did."

"Only because my father was dying. I thought I had enough time to go to him, explain what had happened between my brother and I, and then return to you before the harpies attacked."

"I don't need an explanation," she said. And she didn't. He had come back, and that's all that mattered to her.

"But I need to explain," he said, and the sadness in his eyes tore at her heart.

"All right."

"I shouldn't have left."

"It was your father. A father you haven't seen or talked to in years. That's understandable. I just wish you had told me." But something in the way he held his head let her know something was up. "You didn't see him, did you?"

Roderick shook his head. "I saw the harpies as Aimery took me to Thales. I demanded that he return me immediately."

"But you went to your father first. Right?" she asked. When he wouldn't answer, Elle turned to Aimery. "Right?"

"Nay," Aimery answered. "I promised him I would tell his father what had occurred so he could return to you and his duty."

Elle stared open mouthed at Roderick. "You missed talking to your dying father for me?"

His eyes shifted to her. "Aye."

She swallowed back the tears. "Is he...?"

"Nay," Aimery said. "He is better now."

Elle turned back to Roderick with a smile. "So, there is still time for you to go to him."

Roderick moved off the chair to kneel in front of her. "Please understand that I can't. Not yet."

"All right," she answered, though she wished he would change his mind.

"About the future," Aimery said.

Elle rolled her eyes. She wasn't ready to get back to that since she knew neither man would change their minds. And she wasn't willing to let Roderick go so easily. It wasn't every day that a girl found the kind of magic that had made her heart beat again. "I don't want to leave you," Elle said.

Aimery smiled at them. "Maybe you don't have to, Elle."

"What?" Roderick asked. "You must be jesting."

Aimery shook his head. "Indeed, I am not. Elle has shown remarkable fighting skills, and with you and Val with her, she will be well guarded."

Elle squealed and leaned over to kiss Roderick. For a moment, Roderick just sat there, then he returned her kiss, leaving her breathless and wanting more.

"Only," he said as he kissed her neck. "If you promise to stay away while we are fighting the creatures."

She laughed. "I promise."

Roderick sat back and looked at the woman that had completed his life. "Are you sure?"

She nodded, a giddy smile on her face. "I've never been more sure of anything."

"Then it's settled," Aimery said happily.

"How did she do it?" Theron, King of the Fae, asked Aimery.

"She's a woman, and Roderick loves her. I knew it would only be a matter of time before she convinced him to return to Thales."

"Amazing," Theron said. "Do you think I wouldn't notice that you interfered with Roderick's father?"

Aimery grimaced inwardly but kept his face devoid of expression. "Do what you must to punish me, sire. After everything Roderick has given the Shields, I felt it only fair to help his father's body repel the sickness so that he could live longer."

"Don't be so severe," Theron said with a smile. "If you had not used your healing abilities, I would have."

"And if he didn't, I would have."

The men turned to find Rufina coming towards them. Aimery watched as husband and wife embraced before his gaze shifted to the ornate murals on the walls of the palace. The Realm of the Fae was a most fantastic place, and he couldn't imagine living anywhere else.

"I'm rather surprised at you," Rufina said.

Aimery raised a brow. "Really, my queen? How is that?"

"You allowed a woman to join the Shields."

"I have never been against a woman joining them. 'Tis only been men that we have found willing and able to fight for us and Earth."

"True," Rufina said with a wink. The smile vanished then. "Three creatures this time. Before it has always been one. Only one."

"He is either gaining strength or 'twas a trick," Theron said.

Aimery shrugged. "Either way, we must be very vigilant. We need more spies."

"Spies, we can get," Theron said. "Consider it done. And the matter of them knowing of Elle?"

"I know not," Aimery said. "That has bothered me since I learned of it."

Rufina walked to a table against the wall and filled three glasses from the magnificent blue decanter. "If he knows of the women, then my guess is he will send the creatures to where they are."

"It will make finding the women easier," Aimery agreed.

Theron sighed as he sat and accepted the glass from his wife. "Only three left. I pray we reach them before he does."

Aimery took his glass from Rufina and drained it in one gulp. The fiery liquid scorched his throat as it slid to his stomach.

"Aye. Only three."

Elle wiped away the tears as she hugged Mina again. "I hate to leave so soon."

Mina hugged her tightly before pulling back. "I am sure that I will see you soon."

"Aye," Hugh agreed. "Once the other three are found, I'm sure Aimery will want the women moved to a safer location."

"True," Mina said as she moved Elle away from the men. "Thank you."

"For what?"

"For convincing Roderick to return to his realm before 'tis too late. It has made Hugh happy and in turn has made me happy."

Elle laughed and glanced at her new husband. She still couldn't believe the ceremony had taken place only that morning. He had surprised her last night when he had asked her to marry him.

"I was astonished that I wore him down so soon. It just tells me that he was as anxious to return as I am for us to go."

"We'll have much to talk about when we see each other next," Mina said as she choked on her tears.

"No more," Hugh said as he took her in his arms. "Roderick, get your wife gone before mine cries enough to flood the bailey."

Elle smiled and hugged Hugh before turning to Roderick and Val. Aimery waited for them just inside the trees. At first she hadn't understood why they couldn't say their good-byes in the bailey, but once it was explained that they didn't want the villagers to see them disappear, she understood.

"Good-bye," she called out to Mina and Hugh as they rode away. She turned to Roderick then.

"Ready?" he asked.

"Ready," she said and took his hand as the three of them stepped into the trees.

Epilogue

Roderick stared at the once magnificent city he had called home. Buildings were burnt, most toppled nearly to the ground. Even the palace hadn't been spared. The granite stones were crushed as if they were sand pebbles.

He felt Elle's presence before she touched him.

"Are you all right?"

He shook his head. "This saddens me. This is what would happen to your world if the Shields weren't there to defend it."

"Why isn't anyone here to defend Thales?" she asked.

"Thales is alone. Earth was blessed to have the Fae so involved, but even the Fae have limited resources. They cannot help every planet in the universe. Some are left to defend themselves."

"That is sad."

He nodded. "The sooner we find the answer on Earth, the sooner I can return and end it here as well. Then, the city can be rebuilt."

She turned towards him and rose up on her toes to kiss him. "Do you feel better now that you have talked to your family?"

"Nothing will make the pain of being responsible for my brother's death go away."

"Time. Only time, my love."

He pulled her against him and spotted Val walking by himself among the ruins below.

"Son."

Roderick jerked at hearing his father's voice. He turned around to find his mother, sister, and Aimery with his father. He moved away from Elle and embraced his sister first. She had grown into a woman since he had left. "Find a good man. A man that will cherish you and love you like you deserve," he whispered.

"I will," she said as she stepped out of his arms and dabbed at her eyes with a piece of cloth.

Roderick then turned to his mother. Where once her hair had been a glorious golden hue, it was now a tad less bright, and he knew it was because of the war waged on Thales.

He took his mother in his arms and kissed her forehead. "I'm sorry I didn't return sooner."

"You've done what you thought you had to do," she said.

He then turned to his father. He held out his arm for his father to take, but his father pulled him against him and wrapped his arms around Roderick. Roderick closed his eyes and returned his father's embrace.

"You should never have stayed away," his father said as he stepped back. "We needed you."

Roderick shook his head. "You need me with the Shields. It's the only chance we have to win against this evil."

His father sighed and gave him a sad smile. "We're very proud of you, of what you've done with the Shields. I won't lie and say I wish you hadn't returned sooner, but I'm just glad you're here. Now, we have a bit of a surprise."

"Surprise," Roderick repeated and looked over at Elle who stood with his mother and sister.

Aimery moved to stand beside him. "Come. We've a little time before you must leave."

Roderick slowly followed Elle and his family as they walked toward the ruins of the once grand palace. Little of the palace still stood other than columns and a few walls that hadn't tumbled down. Happy memories of his childhood raced through his mind as he walked among the remains.

Then, he stepped into what used to be his favorite room in the palace. Not much of the library remained other than a few shelves and columns that had braced either side of the many windows, but there stood a table in the middle of the library laden down with food. In a corner stood a group of musicians and all around him Thaleans cheered as he stood before them. No roof graced the tall walls of the library, but the bright sun raining down upon them was better than anything he could have imagined.

And what made it all the better was seeing Elle smiling at him with her love shining in her eyes.

Read on for an excerpt from
A DARK SEDUCTION

the third book in the thrilling
Shield series

Chapter One

LeBlanc village
Westmorland County, England
Summer 1244

Eyes as sharp as a falcon's scanned the crowded village as people shuffled from place to place in an effort to accomplish their chores.

All was normal in the small, sleepy village, except for two men who stood silently against the loud backdrop.

Cole, the taller of the two by mere inches, found his gaze returning again and again to the three story tavern. He straightened from the blacksmith's shop as his hand brushed the handle of his war axe.

"What is it?"

Cole glanced at his companion. Gabriel stood tense, his hands relaxed by his side, ready to grasp his bow and arrow at a moments notice.

"I don't know," Cole finally answered. "There's something in the tavern that draws my attention."

In response, Gabriel reached behind his head and drew his hair away from his face and tied it off at the nape of his neck with a string of leather.

Cole grinned at his friend. "Ready for some action?"

"I was born ready," Gabriel said and flexed his shoulders.

Just as Cole lifted his foot to step into the street, a flash of yellow caught his attention. He stared, transfixed, as a shapely leg peeked out of an upstairs window.

"Is that...?"

"Aye," Cole answered, unable to look away. To his glee, more leg was exposed, and then a slender arm joined it. It was only moments later a shapely backside also moved through the narrow window.

Gabriel leaned forward for a better look. "What do you suppose she is doing?"

Cole chuckled and crossed his arms over his chest. "I have no idea, but I'm enjoying the show."

During that time, the girl had managed to extract the rest of her body from the window and hung perilously by her fingers and toes to the side of the building, her faded yellow gown blowing in the slight breeze.

"She's going to plunge to her death."

Cole agreed with Gabriel. Yet, by the way the woman hung on, as if she didn't have a care in the world, he had a feeling she knew exactly what she was doing.

"She's not in a hurry," Cole said as he glanced at the open window to see if anyone followed her.

Gabriel snorted. "Then why in the name of the Fae is she climbing down the tavern."

Cole shrugged and involuntarily took a step toward the woman when her foot slipped.

"We need to do something," Gabriel stated.

Cole was surprised that they were the only ones who noticed the woman. She hung above the villagers and any moment could come crashing down atop one of them. A smile pulled at his lips as the woman slowly worked her way to the corner of the building and then climbed down. He heard Gabriel mumble something beneath his breath when the woman's feet touched the ground and she untucked her skirts from betwixt her legs.

All Cole managed to see through the throng of people was strands of brunette hair that had escaped the cap atop her head. She had caught his attention as any women who would brave such dangers would. He couldn't wait to have her in his arms.

Before he could go to her, Gabriel's hand on his arm stopped him. "There's no time."

Cole looked back toward the woman. She was just making her escape from the town when two men caught her and roughly dragged her back into the tavern.

It was just as well, Cole thought. His rod would have to wait while he and Gabriel gathered what information they could. With his mind set to forget the woman, anger sliced through him when one of the men backhanded her so hard she fell to her side in the dirt. It took every ounce of will for Cole to turn away. He couldn't make a scene.

Not yet.

Not until they knew what evil lurked in the small village.

As they walked down the dirt road toward the castle high up on the hill, he spotted Gabriel fingering his dagger. Gabriel had a keen sense that the Shields always listened to. Cole wasn't about to ignore it now.

"What is it?"

"The castle," Gabriel murmured. "There is something about it, something that doesn't seem quite...normal."

Cole's eyes immediately went to the imposing stone towers that reached toward the clouds. "You think the evil resides there?"

Gabriel slowed his pace. "In the past, anytime the Fae has moved us through time, we always arrive once the creature has begun to plague the village."

"Yet no one acts as though their lives are in danger. Do you suppose the creature hasn't yet arrived?"

"Nay, it's here. Aimery said as much."

Aimery. Cole wished the Fae commander was with them to shed more light on their quest. Being a Shield was something Cole prided himself on, but a little more information could be as valuable as gold.

Gabriel punched him on the arm. "Don't tell me you still dislike being thrown into a time and place that you know nothing about."

Cole shook his head at the grin on Gabriel's face. It was a rare occurrence when Gabriel smiled, not to mention jested, and after all they had been through with being separated from Val and Roderick, then losing Darrick to death and Hugh to his heartmate, Cole could barely muster a grin, much less jesting.

"Knowing what we were up against could give us an added edge, at least."

This time Gabriel chuckled. "As if you need it. An immortal that can use a war axe like others use a sword."

It was true, but Cole didn't like to advertise it. He'd been trained by the Fae themselves, and with his unnatural ability to use his war axes more effectively than most, he was deadly.

Cole lengthened his strides. "With time running out on us, why don't we tackle the obvious first? Let's see what the lord of the castle has to say."

Author Bio

Bestselling, award-winning author Donna Grant has been praised for her "totally addictive" and "unique and sensual" stories. She's the author of more than thirty novels spanning multiple genres of romance. Her latest acclaimed series, Dark Warriors, features a thrilling combination of Druids, primeval gods, and immortal Highlanders who are dark, dangerous, and irresistible. She lives with her husband, two children, a dog, and three cats in Texas.

Visit Donna at www.DonnaGrant.com

Made in the USA
Lexington, KY
25 October 2012